The Green Children Help Out

Gillian Polack

Aggadah Try It, an Imprint of Madness Heart Press
2006 Idlewilde Run Dr.
Austin, Texas 78744

Copyright © 2020 Gillian Polack
Edited by Lisa Tone
Cover by John Baltisberger

First Edition
www.madnessheart.press

Dedication:

This novel was made so much richer through my fannish friendships, so of course it is dedicated to all my friends in fandom. I have carefully placed Easter eggs in entirely inappropriate places, just for them. I like naming one person to represent the many and that person here is Milena Benini. I miss her so much.

Acknowledgements

The people at Madness Heart are amazing. They took on this book during the pandemic and have brought it to the world despite so much the pandemic threw at them. John Baltisberger and Lisa Tone in particular have gone above and beyond to get this novel to its audience.

The last four years have been difficult, and those who support my work have meant I could continue as a writer. In some of my novels I hide my research self a bit, but not in this one. Using my research self so directly gives me an excuse to thank everyone who enables me to research culture and history even when the world is decidedly unobliging. Without ArtsACT, Deakin University (especially Helen Young) and my supporters on Patreon I would have had to leave this very important part of my life behind.

The Green Children Help Out has deep roots and most of my friends in European fandom have played a part in helping me develop the concepts and explore the locations. So many cups of coffee, glasses of wine...

Science fiction fandom is generous and supportive and this novel is my thank you to fandom for all it has given me. I can't explain the whole, or name everyone unless I write thirty pages of explanation and names, but I can give some examples. Where I don't use surnames, it's because those friends don't share them publicly.

In the novel itself, I've named just one friend (Fia Karlsson) because she was part of these conversations and she also helped me with a critical aspect of Data's life. She represents so many friends and so many fascinating conversations.

British friends helped me get at least a little bit past presenting yet another Tourist Britain novel: where I've fallen into Tourist Britain, it's entirely my own fault. Without Jean and Roger and Chaz Brenchley the Newcastle scene could not have existed, for example. Kari Sperring gave me Cambridge. Catherine Butler grounded me over lunch in Exeter when I was about to go very much in the wrong direction.

I did the core research for the whole French and Tsarfat strands when I visited Amiens to attend the European science fiction convention there. My fannish friends, the tourist office and a surprising number of local residents helped me sort out so much so quickly.

Devin Jeyathurai and Joyce Chng and friends who I haven't seen for years (and miss!) helped me understand how to create an expat Singaporean. Dev then read a draft and helped me further. I will always worry that I have sidestepped or been offensive, but without my friends then there would be no David and my world would have been significantly poorer.

Swedish and British and Irish friends gave me insights into how different types of communities might try to change the world. A chair in the foyer of one particular Dublin convention was the best place a writer could ever be.

Johann and Linnéa Anglemark helped me sort out some critical language issues. I'm pretty sure I didn't tell them why I was renewing my interest in linguistics in such a precise way. I'm also pretty sure they knew there was a novel involved.

Multiply these stories twentyfold, and that is how my friends supported this novel. Most didn't even know why I was suddenly obsessed with this or that. They knew I was looking for answers and understanding to write something I found challenging and they helped me find these things.

Chapter One

It's a pity that the first incident happened when it was wet. It's bad luck to begin a novel with rain falling over London. This novel is probably doomed for other reasons as well. Superheroes are snares to bring stories of darkness and despair. London in the rain … less so.

The Embankment was wet. The Embankment often is wet, for London is a city that enjoys its rain. The chill fell straight from the sky that day, and the few people walking the Embankment hurried to get where they were going. They looked at the gentle ripples in the wetness of the surface beneath their feet and kept an eye on it rather than checking the buildings or the sky, for the rain rendered the grey surroundings bleak. If their intention had been to stand near the edge and lean on the sturdy stone and admire the London Eye, this intention was washed away with the first cold drop, and tourists went back to the station or straight to another tourist hotspot to find comfort.

The wetness grew colder and damper, then even more cold and yet more damp, and thirty metres of the Embankment rumbled softly into nothing, stone by stone. All that was left was half the road. The remaining rubble separated from solid land and dropped down into mud and crumbled rock and the ever-changing border between Thames and land. The infrastructure the granite had hidden was replaced by an old verge. The old verge was littered with scraps of everyday life.

Although five people died, the comment the media ran with was from the moment when a politician stood on a half block of rock too close to the shoreline and, looking down to the river, exclaimed for the media, "Bloody hell, we've lost eight hundred years."

He then fell the half metre off that rock and, clutching his phone for safety, was doused by the new mud at the base of the new slope. The politician staggered to his feet, still clutching his phone in his right hand but holding a small (but muddy) white pipe in his left. He bent down to rinse the pipe, then walked back up the slope and stopped before he reached the bustle of journalists.

"I was wrong," he said, being somewhat of an amateur historian. "Make that four hundred years."

It may have been this comment, or it may have been that the politician was right, or it may have been the urgency of the loss of infrastructure at that particular corner of London, for everyone involved instantly handed the problem upstream to the Permanent Secretary for the Non-Natural Environment. The Non-Natural Environment offices were sent the pipe for analysis, along with a goodly measure of mud and rubble. The pipe came to the Permanent Secretary after its time in a laboratory. The mud and rubble remained in the laboratory.

Near the Thames, the Embankment and its hidden infrastructure was rebuilt as quickly as possible.

The second incident took place in Milk Street, where the rain was much lighter. It was a Saturday morning, and the regular folk were headed to their regular event down the road. One of the people was a new visitor to London. She said to her recently-acquired best friend, who had to lean over a bit to hear her (since one was short and bright and the other was tall and slender and frighteningly elegant), "You realise that if we were walking in this very place in our own universe, the synagogue would not exist?"

"Why do I bring you places?" her friend asked rhetorically. "You're not even Jewish. Let's go to the pub and have a drink. I need a glass of wine more than I need a group of devout people doing the proper thing in the proper way."

"What about the person who wanted to meet us here? I mean, isn't there a meeting?"

"As long as we're back by the end of the service, we'll be fine. We can catch her on the way out. We're not really supposed to meet today anyhow. She works, and we work, but we're quiet about it because otherwise it would be offensive. And we should whisper some things. No-one knows where we come from. Remember?"

"I don't want to remember. I refuse to be a hero when I can be a sodding alcoholic. I need that drink."

As they turned into Poultry, a big bang echoed around them and rattled the windows.

The younger woman turned and darted straight into the mess. Her friend sighed and followed the blazing purple spiked hair. She was able to remain sedate because her friend carried that banner to her presence everywhere she went. Her own hair was politely tinged to match the colour in her favourite scarf.

There was a silence. Injured people. Dead people. Broken building. Tattered …

"Hey, Green, look," said the younger.

"Don't pick it up," said Ari Green. "Take pictures and then

let's get out. We have to report this."

The explosion had torn down the front of the building. The stones at that precise place were different to the building that remained.

Not stones. Bricks. Old building had been replaced by new. It looked like the buildings on the other side of the street, except the new, torn building had posters, and those posters were government ones featuring a swastika.

The ambulance came, and the police came, and they helped the wounded and packaged the dead and sealed off the whole of that second tiny corner of central London.

No-one would be doing any work in that street or attending synagogue nearby until the government had investigated. More for the Non-Naturals, although this time it was delivered first through those photographs and only later from the slow official investigation.

The younger woman had already sent the pictures home, as well as to their contact. It had taken her mere instants, and her hair had attracted more attention than her work. That hair was indeed a very bright purple.

The Permanent Secretary wrote a small note in reply to those pictures. It arrived at Ari Green's postal address the next day. Then she went to a funeral, for one of the dead from the second incident was a civil servant.

✡

The Letter

Ms Green,
Further to the discussion concerning recent events, we believe our people could usefully work together. We have reached the realisation

10

that the source of both our difficulties might rest at least partly within the United Kingdom and that it now demonstrates clear evidence of dangerous intent for both our countries.

We look forward to working with you again, however disappointing the reason. We will arrange for the tourist visas you and your new associate hold to be modified accordingly. We will also arrange accommodation.

You will work directly to me. I will expect you in the office on Monday morning.

Yours,

Benedicta Beja, Permanent Secretary for the Non-Natural Environment (on behalf of both her own Office and of the Office of the Merlin)

PS. On a personal note, when you next send us material through your associate, we would rather they did not address it to 'Magic Inc'. Our formal name will suffice.

Chapter Two

David was having a good day. No-one had asked him for his Chinese name or said he spoke English surprisingly well for ... anyhow, no-one had asked. He didn't have to handle it. He could put it right out of his mind.

The highlight of his day so far had been when two women had walked past his desk and towards Her Maj's permanent staff. They had been given temporary desks near his and were working their way through stacks of paper, with occasional pauses for chat. This ought to have been a sarcastic highlight, he amended his thought, for in this office, he was the aberration.

If it hadn't been for the vitality of the younger woman, he would entirely have remained his normal sarcastic self. In her late twenties, same as him. Possibly another PhD student. Possibly someone Her Maj knew politically. Very cute, with that hair and that skimpy top and a scarf that clashed with both so enthusiastically.

The moment he heard her voice, he fell entirely in love with her, for her accent was a kind of French-Australian he'd never heard before. The bonus was that she wore the best earpieces he had ever seen. Wired for sound, with coloured inlays that changed according to who-knew-what, but he'd find out. His dream girl.

"David." Her Maj interrupted his reverie of true love. "I need you to tell me what you found out about those legends."

This was the sort of thing he'd been brought in for, so he was ready. Even though Her Maj's intensity made him feel small, he was ready.

"I've got a few," he stated. "Three, in fact."

"Tell us." She walked him into her office personally, and the remainder of 'us' were already drinking tea. Not tea, he noted, coffee. Her Maj must really respect them if they had coffee in hand without the great fuss of sending out for it.

'Us' was dreamgirl and her companion, who he noted now was a few years older and two decades more sophisticated. David played in his mind with the three women being the crone and her two younger … then he remembered he had been brought in to answer a question.

"Sorry," he said. "A bit vague today. Middle Ages—there are three accounts of the Green Children of Woolpit. One by Ralph of Coggeshall, one by William of Newburgh, and the third by Gervase of Tilbury."

"Does the green fade after they emerge from underground?" The older visitor was charming in her curiosity, and David thought to himself, *I can do this. I belong here. I'm sure I belong here.*

"Do they even emerge from underground?" This was the French-Australian.

The older woman spoke pure Frenchish English. Maybe from the Somme region, but maybe not. He needed to hear a bit more to find out. The gutturals weren't quite Paris or upper-class French, anyhow. Almost, but not. Also, the vowels suggested that she was definitely not from Poitou or Normandy. Maybe he could get her to speak French. That would sort it instantly. David loved placing accents. In his mind, he was Henry Higgins from

Pygmalion. In his reality, he spent too much time in his mind.

He called that mind to order. "Yes, they came from underground. The boy died, but the girl faded to normal human skin colour. They could only eat beans, or something."

"The food isn't important," the French accent said dismissively.

Her height made her dismissiveness sound imperious. Not like Her Maj's tones. Her Maj was so actually important that he knew he had to listen, regardless of how she spoke. Also, she was intense. She never needed to sound imperious, despite her real nickname. He politely tried to not think of her real nickname.

"It's a bit rude to assume that green people don't look human," the girl said.

Her Maj laughed. "Let me introduce you all, and you can argue about humanity and the colour of skin. David is a PhD student I've borrowed; he's taking time out from his degree. Ms Green is one of my older friends, and, despite this, and despite her name, I don't know what she feels about skin colour. Ms Data is a brand-new friend of mine, and she has very strong feelings about the greenness of skin."

"Data?" asked David.

"The colour of my skin amuses me," Ms Data informed her. "I call myself 'Data' because of that precise level of amusement."

"Star Trek! TNG!" exclaimed David, charmed. "Although he was gold, rather than green."

"Green in some lights, seen on some TVs, none of which exist in this world at this time as far as I know."

"That's very precise," said David, almost enviously. "So, you're referring to a green that's only visible to select people."

Two women looked at him blankly.

"That's it," Ms Data said. "You can see a tinge still, if you look."

"You're assuming David has clearance," Her Maj said.

"I'm assuming he's intelligent, to be honest, since you asked about green children."

David was fascinated. "You're descended from the green girl? She actually existed?"

"It's a bit more complicated than that," Ari said. "When you get clearance, we'll tell you if your guesses are right. How does that sound?"

"It sounds as if you've accepted him as deskboy for this particular job," Her Maj said.

"Totally," Ms Data said. "If he'll call me Data and know why it's the right name for me. I don't understand at all why you put Ms in front of our names anyhow. They're completely invented."

"Ms is completely invented," David essayed. "But I think you're referring to your proper names?"

"I'd better get you that clearance," Her Maj said to David. "You're beyond the limit of what you should know already. To be frank, these friends either accept at once or they never accept, so you just passed." She reached for the phone.

David looked across at Data and decided at that moment that he needed to find a better nickname for Her Maj. Her title was impossible in any language, and she wasn't a first name person. "Big Ben" was not somewhere he wanted to go, even in thought, and even if it was England's nickname for her. He wondered if an old-fashioned "Auntie" would do. Maybe. Maybe not. Direct speech was a mumbling "ma'am," and he really terribly much wanted to never ever introduce her to anyone.

He'd done it. Once. "My temporary boss," he'd stumbled to get out. Worst introduction ever. His supervisor hadn't minded and had instantly admitted he knew her well.

"Ben!" the professor had said and shook one of her hands with both of his, "I hear you want to steal my best student."

David had been entirely flustered by those thirty seconds.

That introduction was branded deep inside his skull, never to be forgiven.

Benedicta Beja wasn't scary. Except when she was.

How could anyone call her "Ben" or even "Benedicta"? She was the opposite of a first name person. It was less that she intimidated all the time; more that when she did so, she could be genuinely frightening.

Her Maj was scary a mere half hour later when the next report came in.

David was in Moneypenny mode at the time, which was just as well, considering. Tea for everyone (no coffee this time, David noted) before the news hit. Tea and scones rather than tea and biscuits.

The taller of the two visitors looked at the scones dubiously. Data, on the other hand, exclaimed "Scones!" and dove in.

"How can you possibly know scones?" Her Maj asked.

"She's been here a bit," said Ari.

"My mum makes them. I didn't know you could get them here."

"I didn't know you could get them where you come from." Her Maj sounded bitter. She hated missing facts.

David felt he should start counting facts she missed, but decided on the safety of not reacting to her bitterness.

"Your mother's Australian? That explains your accent," David interpolated quickly.

Everyone looked at him.

"He's very good with accents," Her Maj said. "But how can your mother be Australian? That's impossible."

At that moment, a junior staff member came in with a message, and the message turned sarcasm to scary instantly.

Policemen had attacked people attending a perfectly legitimate meeting. They had broken down a door, rounded the attendees up, and four of the people at the meeting were now in hospital.

That meeting had been a group of rabbis, whose sole aim had been to find a way around issues Judaism currently faced.

"Including all humankind doesn't exclude Adam and Eve," the Chief Rabbi had said. "Go and see if Talmud and anything related to it can demonstrate ways of understanding humanity that present more than a simple binary in gender terms. If it's one of the commentaries, I want it backed by substance; we need strong results."

The Rabbinate had set up five committees to examine the current state of humankind, but the one the policemen had violated was the best known. It met in York. To hurt the rabbis of York was to recall Clifford's Tower and the mass murder.

Her Maj couldn't say that. She couldn't explain the history of mass murder as if it were nothing. Instead, she called on that other stalwart moment of York Jewish history.

"Don't they respect the Bridge-Builders?" she fumed.

"Bridge-builders?" Ari asked.

Her Maj, stopped in her storm, turned to David. This was not because of his earlier answer on the subject of Australia; it was because anything historical was the reason he was here. It was the pipe that had brought him, and the fact that he had done a paper on popular literature concerning the ground under the Embankment. He was versatile in his knowledge.

He responded almost on automatic. "It's a pivotal moment of British history. It was part of my secondary school history, because it was one of the rare occasions where European and Asian traditions overlap. The bridges in York were cursed by a spirit, and Jewish women were the only ones who could build bridges there or maintain them."

Her Maj blinked. "Things look different in China."

"China? How do you speak English with that accent?" Data

was curious.

David began to explain, "Chinese majority doesn't make my homeland part of China—"

Data's earpieces flashed different colours for a few seconds while her Maj called out, "Enough!" and brought things back to order. "Christians say the Devil, and you say spirits, and we say it doesn't matter. What matters is that there is a monastic order specially trained to protect Jews in York, and it did not do this simple thing."

"Specially trained?"

"It's complicated."

Ari said, "But this monastic order didn't stop the police."

"No."

"And police don't normally do this kind of thing."

"Not here, no. Maybe in other countries."

Ari asked, "Were they your police?"

"Good question," Benedicta replied. "Could they have come from round your way?"

"No, but there are others. There was the incident that you called us in over, the one with swastikas."

"Your way?" David was entirely confused.

"Hong Kong?" Data was rather amused.

"You're saying Hong Kong on purpose, aren't you? You do know I'm Singaporean?" David thought he was getting the hang of this. Maybe. Data was more Australian than she was French, and he knew Australians. He knew Australia. He ... was missing the conversation again.

"Data, stop laughing and explain to all of us the relationships between worlds. You know them better than most."

"Since I was a child," Data admitted, her voice full of regret but her face still amused.

David noted that her earpieces reflected mood. Possibly also connected her to the internet, since she obviously knew where he was from. Maybe body temperatures? Maybe just larking about. He sighed.

"Don't you want to know?" Data turned to him.

"I do, but I was trying to work out how you've colour-coded your earpieces. They're remarkable."

"Everything language and culture and history, that's David. It's why I borrowed him for this little exercise. Now stop wandering off. Universes."

"We come from France, in our way," said Ari. "The Somme region."

David nodded. He didn't have to wait for one of them to speak French.

Ari continued. "This universe is occasionally wobbly in its relationships with parallel universes. Not unstable enough to cause the incidents this week without provocation, but nevertheless, not entirely perfect in its relationship with its neighbours. There are pocket universes with links to this one. We come from one of those. Our ancestors escaped the Nazis, for the most part, and we made a new life."

"You didn't want to go home after the war?" David was curious. To him, World War II in Europe was odd. He wanted to know why people made life decisions from it and what decisions they made.

Data said, a trifle bitterly, "I wish it was that simple. We could've simply flooded back and changed France."

"Be fair," Ari admonished, "most Tsarfati were never going to go home. Too difficult."

"Remember," Data spoke directly into Ari's face. "Remember why I'm here now and not in Tsarfat with my mother? I needed extra time to adjust to the two realities because I went home too soon the first time I went through that door. Remember why?"

Her face was hard. This was a big emotional issue for her. David wanted to know the story so badly it hurt him, and he didn't want to know it at all because it hurt her.

"I remember," said Ari, everything softening.

"Tell us," Her Maj commanded.

"The first time I ever saw Data," Ari said, "she was carrying her dead brother on her shoulders. They'd just come through the door, and she wouldn't give him up to anyone. 'We're *both* going home,' she told us over and over. 'We're both going home.'"

Something inside David froze and remained frozen for the whole account. Maybe longer. His mind played himself as Data's brother and his sister (a dentist) as Data.

He'd visited the Somme fields as part of a World War I memory trip with friends two years ago. His mind had no problem placing Data in those gentle hills.

"Bob didn't survive the transition," Data said firmly, as if she were trying to remain grounded. David couldn't see how she could not be shouting and weeping. Losing his sister was the worst thing he could think of. No, he was wrong. The worst thing he could think of was losing his parents or his remaining grandmother. "It's why I care so damned *much* about making things right. I don't have your religious need to give myself up for the betterment of the universe. I care because of how my brother died."

The subject had stopped the blockage that was holding back the flood, and Data's story poured out in a stream that was slowed only by her voice refusing to go as fast as her memory.

So much passion and so much sorrow, was David's thought. He had enough trouble in his own life, but he couldn't imagine carrying a dead sibling home to his parents. It was inconceivable.

That thought coloured everything Data said. Her words felt like a flood, but even as he listened, he realised she was still damming her emotions. Not many words. Her mood contradicted her language, and they were both arguing with her mourning.

"Families are forbidden from sending more than one child through the door. My mother didn't want either of us to go. Both of us were encouraged to go. That was racism, and I will fight so that no-one has to walk through doors like that, then find out that it was planned by someone to destroy their mother's soul."

"You carried your brother back home?" David was fascinated and horrified and everything in him wanted to hug this woman. All he could do was ask questions for which he'd already been told the answer.

"That's right. I carried him across fields, down tunnels, through mud. I carried him home."

"How can you be Australian?" Her Maj asked, as derailed as everyone else but derailed in her own way.

"My mother was lost when her family visited France. She was stuck in Tsarfat because no-one would let a child leave, and she didn't speak Tsarfati back then and couldn't argue her way out of a paper bag."

"And now you're here and she's …"

"Really, this is not a good thing to talk about," Data said. "I can't help my mother right now. I *can* help other people." She was adamant in a way that suggested she was arguing with herself. "I can."

"And we need to," admitted Her Maj. "Most of these events appear to be from shifts of universes, which is why I brought you in."

"Data has the links to our people and the science that might help." Ari turned brusque. "But we need more information."

"We need to know exactly when and where, and to do that, we need to find out who." Data's speech had lost those strong emotions, but David saw that she had a tinge of the pallid green she claimed came from her putative namesake. He couldn't imagine what she'd been through.

"We need to find out why," said Her Maj. "Rubble and personal hurt are unlikely to be the endgame."

"If we're lucky, it'll be something personal," Data said. "What destroyed a part of my mother's life was mostly personal. What destroyed the other part was the same thing that happened to those rabbis."

"I don't like to ask, but ..." Her Maj left the sentence unfinished, and Data dutifully filled the silence.

"Someone attacked her? Not her. My father. He was kicked to death in a shop. No-one helped. That's what worries me about the York incident. The naked lack of detail in the report says that it was like my father's murder, but maybe the fault is in the reporting? Did anyone come to help? How are those rabbis now?"

"What worries me is whether they were beaten because they're Jewish or because of the politics."

"This is England; Jews aren't beaten here," said David, his voice ringing with confidence. He knew this not from his recent years in London but because one of his childhood friends had been from an oddly Hokkien Shanghai family who'd been in Singapore for business. They'd moved from Malaysia to Shanghai, which is why he always added "oddly" when he thought of her. It was the movement of the culture that stuck in his mind. It was thanks to Beng Beng that he'd found the courage to come to this land.

Her Maj nodded. "Except in the normal run of thuggery. We fight racism and have done for hundreds of years."

"Good to hear that," Ari said acerbically. "It's not necessarily relevant, however. Most of Tsarfat is Jewish, but it wasn't the Jewish majority that killed Data's father. We can't assume anything."

"Most of Tsarfat is Jewish ..." David's eyes took on a dream.

"Stay with us, young man," Her Maj instructed.

"Yes, ma'am," he said dutifully, then lost his mind to invention almost instantly when his boss said, "Are you the only superheroes from Tsarfat in town? How many resources do we have?"

"I wish you wouldn't joke about it. We're not superheroes." Ari's tone was warm. Her face expressed the sorrow of one who has suffered a very mild betrayal from someone they love.

Superheroes, David thought and let his mind wander without losing the conversation. Maybe today was special for more than the colour of Data's hair and those wonderful ear pieces.

"Just us, I'm afraid," said Ari. "We're spread a bit thin. The UK has different problems but is not the only country in turmoil."

"I'll work with you directly, then. David, can you postpone that doctorate a bit longer and work with us for as long as we need you? I'll have my staff make the arrangements."

"Ari," Data's voice kept bringing David back from his dreams, "can I have those names? Of the people who died today?"

"Names?" Her Maj sounded sharp and aware. She was used to being in control.

David knew these two superheroes would drag her with them rather than being her loyal followers. This was another good reason to be part of this work.

"It's another Star Trek thing," Ari said dismissively.

"My term for it is Star Trek," Data said passionately. "I do not believe that Red Shirts should die in vain. Nor scanners. Nor anyone. I am collecting the names of everyone who is killed in these incidents. Every death is a murder, and I am going to make a list of their names and share it, when we come to an end, with all our offices. They're not roadkill. They're human beings."

"David, would you help her?" Her Maj's voice was much softer, even though her face looked grim. "If you'll join us."

Repetition means it's going to happen. David smiled to himself. His supervisor was turd incarnate, and this place was like a vision of his perfect world. "I'd be delighted. I'd better talk to my supervisor myself," David said quietly and firmly and somewhat boldly, while his brain still echoed, *Superheroes!*

✡

Benedicta was at the funeral as part of her job. She was the most senior dignitary the government could call on. The dead man was part of an important New Jewish family. They had arrived in Britain in the twentieth century and had done well. They deserved the official imprimatur of her presence for a parent of three lost to terrorism.

The funeral itself was pretty standard Orthodox. Prayers down by the open grave, said privately. Spades of earth upon the body once it was lowered. More prayers, this time in unison. That kind of thing.

It was the easiest type of funeral to attend in one way, because when she was there to give support, she knew how. Her normal suit-with-pants had been swapped for a skirt. Because it was a Continental-origin Orthodox family, she stood back and let the men do the main work. She knew exactly what to look for in order to give the most respect. Lines of people hugging or shaking hands with the mourners. Rending of cloth. Washing of hands. Cohenim staying outside the gate, forever isolated because of their duties. After she'd washed her hands again, she stopped to hug a cousin who was caught outside.

"This is one of yours?" she asked her.

"My daughter married his brother. It's a terrible thing."

"It is."

"Why are you here? I can't think how you'd know the family,

unless through me?"

"I didn't know him." Benedicta admitted. "He did some very good community service, and his loss was so tragic that I've been asked to represent the government."

"I'll let the family know it was you."

"I think they might work it out for themselves," Benedicta said drily.

"I'll tell them. It will mean a lot."

One of Benedicta's hands was in a fist at her side. "We should've stopped it. Dammit, but it makes me cry when the good people are hurt." She made her farewell and got back to her car as quickly as she could. Despite her emotions, she thought when she was in the back seat how regular the funeral had been. How reassuring.

She wanted to go to the post-funeral part of it. She could, given her cousin had been there. It would not have been reassuring, however, and she had no time.

That side of the family was so very frum. They lived religion. Her cousin would have to deal with shiva for the week and the minyan in the evenings. And the food. All the food! Benedicta found this depressing. She rang her cousin's sister and asked if someone from the family could represent her. "Someone warm and supportive," she suggested. She looked up when her driver repressed a laugh.

✡

Earlier in the year, Ariette reached to knock on the door. Home. This was still home, despite all the changes and the life she was now living. It was the same knocker it had always been.

Her grandfather had ordered the knocker because he had always dreamed of a door knocker like that. It reflected everything he and her grandmother had done when they'd built the house. *Refugee stuff* was how she thought of it now, but it was perfectly normal for her family at that time and in that place. Starting again.

Except that her grandfather had said, "We can do better." Instead of repeating the past and copying everything they had once had, as some did, he had cast his memory over every part of the house he had grown up in and said, "I liked the way the reception room caught the sun," and replicated that, and "The children's bedrooms were too small and dark," and changed it.

The changes were not big, for the most part. The family home was still familiar. Some of them were small but significant, like the use of a fleur de lys as a doorknocker so that everyone who entered the house always knew that France was still in them and they were still of France. There was a mezuzah in the usual place, so close to the fleur de lys that the door announced, "This is Jewish France. Respect it." That door was the strong, well-kept wood that he knew and loved from his childhood. It was not just any Jewish France he remembered, it was the Jewish France connected by the Somme.

Ari didn't knock, in the end. She slipped round the back, took the spare back door key from where it was hidden, and came in through the wet room. That wet room was big enough to make wine in, to dry clothes in during the rain, and was the place she and her sister and brother and their friends had spent half their childhoods. It was one of her grandfather's changes.

Outdoors wasn't as exciting as the games they played indoors, for Maman liked to test the games she made, and the children treated the wet room as their test centre. They never knew what they would find there when their friends visited. Maman left games set up, ready to play, and it was always a discovery. There were never any rules. Maman would use their reports and interactions to create the rules, she said, though, Ari always wondered how true that was.

The wet room floor was crowded with memories, but the actual tiles were void of anything except equipment for making things or for washing things. Maman had sold the business when Papa became ill. Even here, extra money was essential for life-changing treatment.

Home was what it always had been, even though she had been away for a while.

The smells of Passover drew Ari further into her old home. The lights, the noise, and the warmth all announced that the family had already begun.

There was a place at the table for her. Ari sat down. Her mother smiled at her; her grandfather nodded but kept talking. Her brother said, "Hey, that's for Elijah," and no-one reprimanded him. Her sister said nothing. Ari hadn't seen any of them since Rosh Hashanah. She'd sent presents ahead in case she was detained.

Family life as usual for her. Even to the shambolic greetings. Nothing changed.

When had it become family life as usual, she wondered as the family worked its way through the seder? Ariette was allowed to do her share of helping with the meal and making sure the elderly friends and relatives had access to everything and were respected. But she was across the table from her sister, who talked brightly the whole time without sparing a single word for Ariette. And she had been given the chair right next to the stove, which was on, for it was a cold day in spring. Ari layered all the clothes she could take off on the back to her chair, and it wasn't too bad.

The comfort of home finally reached her, and Ariette smiled and was bright. Not as bright as her sister, but in her own way, she was bright. Her uncle made all the usual comments about her not yet being married.

No-one asked her about her work, but then, they never did. Ariette left two-thirds of herself at the door when she came home to visit.

The gossip was about what someone had found out from the computer link to Earth1. It was still the world they cared about, it would always be the world they belonged to, and now that it could be observed from afar, political events were like a television show.

"I'm glad we don't have Donald Trump here," was the consensus. Everyone had an opinion about how the Americans had taken that path. Everyone made the right comparisons to the 1930s. They were worried the US might take people to a place of no return, but without a Tsarfat to hide in. Ariette didn't argue. Her politics were different. Her reality was different.

When a cousin realised she was silent on the subject, Ari gave her usual excuse: "I don't really have time to follow Earth1 news. They don't know about it in Earth2."

The uncle who usually said, "They have the links. They just don't talk about it," and who was part of an increasing number of Tsarfati who wondered why they supported the Green Children and their work, was kindly silent.

When she'd returned the first time, everyone wanted to talk. Now everyone wanted to tell her things. She was so glad when they didn't. Ari made a mental cheer to match the actual one in the seder. If the family had done this, it would have been enough. Dayenu!

The family lets me share the seder. Dayenu!

The family welcomed me (after its way). Dayenu!

Even as I sit here, saying Dayenu and wishing someone would smile at me, I love my family, Dayenu!

She stopped there, because it was becoming depressing. Ari excused herself from the table and joined the children, who sat on a rag rug and were playing some of Maman's old games. They welcomed her, and she spent a lovely hour while the adults argued at the table. That was most certainly a Dayenu.

Eventually, the family rejoined at the table and finished the seder and finished with "L'shanah habah." Every year, Ari refrained from her usual irony, but she thought it. Every year, she looked around the table. Every year Ari hid her sarcasm behind a nice smile while the sarcasm echoed her thought that next year in Jerusalem was safe to think about but none of them would actually dare the door.

It used to not be sarcastic. It also used to not be Ariette. Her brother had said that one, regularly. He stopped making the joke the year Ari dared the door. It had been like the doorknocker, a regular part of family life.

Ari had waited for him to change the joke and include the fact that she could, in fact, have chosen Jerusalem, when she came back after being outside. She said it for him. He had glared back, as if she'd done something quite wrong.

Later, her brother and sister had pulled her aside and said, "Don't make that comment anymore. You've probably even been to Jerusalem and not told us. But it's the wrong Jerusalem. Cousin Albert has always wanted to go to the real Jerusalem and never can. You hurt him by saying that."

"Just don't talk about life outside Tsarfat," her sister had added.

That was the way it was these days. Those two family members were the only ones who didn't want her to talk, but they'd silenced her in such a way that the rest of the family didn't even know that Ariette had been silenced.

Ariette dealt with the silence the way she always did. She used the time to watch and treasure and learn. She needed her family with her when she travelled. Her life wasn't even close to being safe, and she needed something to love, and so she was alert every single moment she was in the house.

"Are you coming to shul tomorrow?" her mother asked as she put her layers back on, ready to go.

"In London," Ari said. "I'm catching the late train tonight."

"Safe journey," Maman said and gave her a warm hug.

Her sister gave her a look that said 'London. You're just saying that.'

It was going to be a strange Passover this year, with work looming and the time she always took off being eroded.

Benedicta had found her a seat for synagogue and invited her to second seder and all would be well. Strange and full of work at a time when work should not be done, but well. This was the thought Ariette took with her onto that late journey that crossed worlds and the Channel both.

Chapter Three

Another loud noise and shaking of window panes. Then another. And another again.

The rain in Newcastle was needle-fine, but not too cold. Not as iconic as the rain of London, but still, rain.

These rumbles added up to an incident on a Friday afternoon, heading into the evening. That it was Friday meant that Big Ben's Office was sent information almost before the incident was over. It also meant Big Ben herself couldn't go. These were Benedicta Beja's own fuming words. Big Ben was known and feared for her implacable calmness, but David had seen her nearly lose that calm three times in a week.

Maybe not 'in a week' ... *maybe only in this week,* he thought as the mental image of the explosions rattled his own brain. He watched and learned that her temper was directly related to her sense of her own helplessness. Benedicta stalked the office, fuming about the fact that if she didn't turn up to synagogue at the right time, everyone would judge her. Ari received a polite tongue lashing for being just as Jewish but not hampered by anyone missing her at synagogue. David noted that Ari did not accept that tongue lashing well. She herself admitted she was as secular as a Jew from Tsarfat could be, so why did it worry her that no-one would miss her if she didn't turn up on a Friday night or Saturday morning?

The area hit was in Newcastle, just outside the central zone, Benedicta said, her finger pointing to a location about three kilometres from the castle and its trainline. The bridge still curved and was not broken or bent, although the moment the pictures of explosions went up on world news, jokes about coals in Newcastle occurred, and notes about Newcastle having Sydney's bridge and questions about whether the stolen coat hanger had been damaged also arose. This was inevitable. It was also a lot better than the Office being labelled as unsympathetic to thirty per cent of Britain, which had happened when the rabbis were hurt.

The upshot was that Ariette Green packed her portable office even while Big Ben lost her temper.

"It may not be for us," Benedicta warned her. Her tone implied that it had better be paranormal or supernatural in some way because if those explosions were purely chemical, electrical, or firearms, whoever set those explosions would have to answer to her, personally.

"It needs checking anyhow," said Ari, "I can get there within three hours if I leave now."

"Take David," Benedicta ordered. There was no time to argue. There really hadn't been time for Benedicta to get upset either, but she managed anger and activity at the same time, and her response times for both would make Olympic record if they had been official Olympic events.

At the back of David's mind danced a little refrain, *I would not like her to lose her temper at me. I pity whoever's doing this. I wouldn't like to be them.*

32

David was on the next actual train with Ari, busy being ignored by her. He had his overnight pack with him (since he carried it to work every day, just in case; this was the kind of person he was), so he didn't mind being ignored. He could dream or work or worry as he wanted. What he wanted was the time to do a bit of research and chat with Data online. He needed to find out why it was so important to get there that evening and why they were catching a train and not something faster.

"Coal explosions," was Data's explanation. "They're what cause our pocket universe to rattle and even to jump between universes. No-one knows if it's the explosions or something related to them or if it's even just coincidence that there are explosions, so anything that has a hint of other worlds and an explosion is a must-do. Newcastle has coal. Newcastle gets instant Green."

"I hope 'instant green' isn't a pun on anyone's name … I don't know what you mean by it if it isn't. Can I check the details of the Tsarfat explosions?"

"Green light for one of the Green family to attend. Needing a Tsarfati on the job. Speaking of which, I'm already on the earliest explosions. Find something else to check."

David decided that a neat timeline of what had happened earlier and what was happening right now would be useful. Better than dreaming of doors between worlds anyhow. He could follow the latest on social media and beat the news if he were clever. Although, if there were a door between worlds in the city they were going to, where would it be?

This led to the thought that should have been his first thought. Why did the Tsarfatis think that someone might be trying to create a door to another world? It was as if he had walked into a conversation halfway and everyone knew more about what was going on than he did.

David decided on that first, after checking tourism reports

and taking a look at blogposts by science fiction and fantasy writers. One of the writers had visited a building in Newcastle some years ago and had commented that it looked like doorways into other worlds.

Given his background contained magic history but no actual magic, that blogpost could work. There was a building that looked as if it could extend into other worlds. There was nothing magic about it. Just a feel to the architecture.

It was a stupid thing to put onto the list, from that angle. From another, it was ineffably wise. It wasn't the place's special properties he was looking for. It was the things someone would look for if they wanted to find a place that linked to different worlds. This one was in Newcastle and was one of only two buildings in that city discussed in the science fiction world. Either of those, then, would have the right cultural properties to have attributed magic whether or not they were special in any way.

David had talked with Data earlier about this, about science fictional realities. They both wanted a way into problems that did not take them through the establishment. If Benedicta Beja's people had come up with anything, she would not have recruited so very imaginatively in the early stages of this particular set of crises.

"I got lots of SF friends," Data had said confidently. "I'll set up an app to check online stuff from the places they talk about. Online haunts for those who don't fit into the establishment."

"Your friends do not surprise me," David had replied. "I'll read the people I already follow, then, and check the links they share."

"How do you know that'll be useful at all?" Data sounded doubtful, but he looked at her face, and she appeared genuinely curious. He liked this woman. Possibly a bit too much, but David liked her.

"I'm not looking for new information; that's what you're hunting for. I'm looking for approaches. How people describe the world."

This conversation was why he had done a search for Newcastle and come up with two places. One was described as haunted and was part of a ghostly or faint horror reality in David's mind. It was also linked to a Newcastle sculpture that reminded him of a scene in Monty Python. The Lit and Phil was worth checking for that. If the doors were seen as leading into death rather than into other worlds, then the Lit and Phil might be the place targeted.

If it were portals, then this other place was the bomb. *Bad pun. I should not be making bad puns right now.*

David looked over Ariette's shoulder and at the countryside passing too quickly. He could check (and if possible, exclude) most folklore components of this event using the reasoning he'd applied to that list of well-known buildings. His dream last night was of his grandmother, and she had told him not to go to Newcastle. Since he had no choice about this, he needed to distract himself from the fact that being on this train was not a good thing.

David managed to exclude most possibilities using his earlier reasoning. Newcastle was full of glorious folklore and had no doubt been intensely studied as a well of traditional culture. Britain and Russia competed as the most studied world folklores. Singapore was sadly down the list. Or maybe not sadly. Singapore was much more comfortable about its 'non-natural' inheritance. Comfortable was not the right word. In tune? Less obsessed with writing it down rather than living with it? Ghosts were not artefacts of decayed superstition, they were simply ghosts.

None of the stories matched each other the way the descriptions of those two buildings had, and even the ones that were caught in the thread of science fiction and fantasy influence were not useful at all. The closest he came was a local fascination with Alice, Lewis Carroll's Alice. That could be important, given the stories of tunnels and underground that he'd heard from his new Tsarfati friends, but those depended very heavily on Tsarfat being known outside one particular government office. It wasn't. He knew it wasn't because he'd checked the moment he'd discovered its existence.

The folk stories were easier to analyse. Witnesses were not reliable, or tales were told with too much inventiveness, or people hadn't done even basic research. He noted there were at least three libraries that might contain useful books if they needed references. One of them was the Lit and Phil. That building must be his special place in Newcastle, for it appeared over and over again in his research. On this side of things, it had pictures that suggested hauntings and portals to other universes. This was the problem with Newcastle. The architecture opened it up to arcane suggestions.

David wrote this up with a list of buildings and that list of libraries and had just two starred items on both lists. He passed them to Ari, then turned to his account of what was happening as they sped north. Between the first and the second was what passed for dinner.

Neither he nor Ari had thought about food in the hurry of their departure, and Ari refused to explore train food beyond a trolley. So, trolley food it was. Cups of tea and cheese and onion crisps and a sandwich. Very English and actually the kind of train food he liked—just as the kind of street food he liked was the one the hawker near his parents' place sold him for breakfast and that didn't exist anywhere in England ('leftover curry sauce on pancakes' he'd described it to a friend once, 'random mutton-flavoured or more likely fish' totally failing to communicate the level of his need for it)—but not precisely the best dinner in the world.

The best dinner in the world was chicken rice, which was his comfort food. He missed chicken rice. So much he missed chicken rice. Trolley food was enough to fuel the next step, which was to unravel what had actually happened in Newcastle. It wasn't enough to assuage his homesickness.

He wanted to write that it had begun with a big explosion. It really hadn't. The press reports had begun with a big explosion, claiming that there was a big explosion. To be precise, as he tracked it, there were six explosions. Several buildings damaged. No loss of life. The no loss of life was interesting because it meant these explosions were carefully planned, especially given that the explosions thus far had occurred in a city and during working hours.

Six explosions within three hours. If he tracked them on a map, would a pattern emerge? It would if this were a magic police mystery, and it might anyway since police mysteries with magic were so very popular right now. People copying stories, that was his specialty, and so he had to test it before he wandered elsewhere. David hauled out a map of Newcastle and marked the events on his screen. He coded them as paler for older and darker for newer.

"Look," he told Ari. "They're moving."

"Good," she said. "I didn't understand your links between folk stories and buildings. Movement of explosions … that's more practical. Underground?"

"I suspect overground because earth tremors aren't a major feature, but I'll check for earth tremors in more depth, and I'll check for tunnels and things. I've only got a half an hour before we get there." Another pun. This was a good day.

"Check quickly then," Ari said, smiling to take the edge off the pressure. "Because if we can find out where the next one will be, we can surprise someone in the act and catch them and all go home early."

"Huh," was all David could think of saying. He wanted to argue for the likelihood of anyone doing explosions following cultural patterns and being predictable, but he'd given the information about that to Ari, and it didn't matter how sore he was that she'd dismissed it. Soreness was beyond him, quite suddenly. Too much was beyond him. Including words. He kept forgetting how junior he was. He'd not seen evidence of superheroicism, and he dismissed seniority when it was attached to magic talents. His mistake. Huh.

"I'll get Data to check the underground and earth tremors and add them to your map, if you could set it up so that she can get in?"

"OK," David said, not OK with this at all. This added to his mental angst. He was an academic. A very new one, but still an academic. Shared documents meant version control was impossible, and if someone did something stupid, everyone paid. He was the junior person here, and Data was the computer expert, and they were already talking about things on the actual documents they were creating as they talked, and really, he had not a leg to stand on.

International English was not up to this job. He needed to be more colourful than it permitted. Standard English used bad language for very small things (and really, this was not the biggest annoyance he was likely to face this week, given the company he was keeping) when all he needed was a heartfelt, "Aiyah." His sole vocal option was to say 'OK' tersely, as if that would communicate all his concerns.

For a brief unhappy moment, he wanted to be back at university, doing his doctorate like a normal person. Not caught up with paper politics on a train.

Maybe, he thought, *I'm scared.* In an acknowledgement of the fear, he let his mind return to the dream of his grandmother sitting in a comfortable chair at home, saying, "Do not go to Newcastle."

Ten minutes later, Data had upgraded the map and included everything. She had added her own version control, and when he hovered the cursor over one of his contributions, a merlion roared at him. Now that she'd made a Singapore joke, she had no excuse for claiming he was from Hong Kong. None. He felt a lot better. Grumbly in a good way.

While he mentally grumbled, David added the folklore element (such as it was, and whether Ari accepted it or not) to the map. Nothing fitted where the explosions had hit. He amended that to 'so far' as Data sent him a note about a new one. This wasn't one incident, it was a long series. It must have a goal of some sort.

There must be a pattern to the damage. Newcastle folklore wasn't well documented in public places. He had to dig deep to obtain enough to see what kind of stories it told about itself. Newcastle didn't talk about earth moving or explosions or monsters dwelling deep. Unless there were legends specific to the coal mines? He couldn't find any online or in his databases. They would take a library visit.

There were dragons and strange beings, some of which were well-known in the everyday. Those quiet ones that helped householders, those angry ones that did the opposite: he put these on the map. Then he noted that these beings had been validated as real but that dragons and wyrms had not. Britain being the land of civil service magical validation had saved him so much work. Normally, it created paperwork, and this time the paperwork created … David scolded himself and got on with things. The countryside was still passing, after all, and soon they'd be officially in the north, and it would help if he had results by then.

Having added the notes about other beings in the Newcastle area (with their little lions roaring angrily for being disturbed by his evil cursor), however, meant that he could demonstrate that the folklore he hadn't recommended to Ari was a waste of time in this case and include his successful research into cultural odd places.

What he wanted the map to say was that he wasn't arguing that magic wasn't involved, but that if there were magic, it was unlikely to be locative magic. Everything he'd researched said the magic that came from Newcastle locations themselves had nothing to do with the explosions.

Magic can be in a place and not of that place, he thought as he stared into the racing countryside and pulled his thoughts together.

He wondered what Her Maj would think. She was one of the best magicians in the country, but her magic was magic of a culture, not of a place or person. The woman sitting next to him and the one on the other end of the computer were practitioners of magic of a person, magic unique to them.

He wondered when anyone would admit what their particular magics were. That was why they were superheroes, after all, because they were unique and strange and fighting for the good of humanity.

Me, I'm not magic at all. I merely study culture and magic works within culture, so I get to meet magic beings unexpectedly and have to handle their reality, which is far too different to mine for comfort.

It was easier to dismiss incidents as newspaper headlines and interesting stories and belonging to someone else's world than it was to sit alongside a magic user on a train, heading into who knows what.

And now I'm losing it again, he thought and turned back to that map.

As more and more explanations crowded the map, it became very obvious that whether the explosions were chemical or magic or simple coal ... they were explosions. Explosions needed a reason for existing. They didn't just happen. The map might have the answer, even without the folk element.

He texted this to Data when she gave him news of yet another explosion in Newcastle.

"Let's switch off the folklore and take a look at what's left," she texted.

David and Data played the map until fifteen minutes before the train was due to arrive.

"Look." He showed Ari. "I thought it was just explosions, but see where those explosions go. We've got an idea of the purpose from that, I think."

Ari pointed to a building.

"Here?" She pointed to the Black Gate.

"Yes. I annotated a nearby building as something my science fiction friends talked about once as ideal for portals to other worlds, but this is more likely to actually become a door somewhere exotic if pushed between realities. Data agrees. It's part of the castle from Newcastle. Sort of. Even though the castle itself is nearby. I don't understand medieval architecture."

"Everything ends there?"

"More that it will end very close to it sometime later tonight, if the explosions follow the same paths they have been. I was hoping they'd end at the Lit and Phil because it has a much stronger reputation for magic. It's the place where local scholar-magicians hang out. But the Lit and Phil is off to the side, and I'm bereft."

"That's where we'll set up base, then, or as near to it as I can get. Let me look at the map." She played with the map and exaggerated the streets until everything was named. "Milburn House," she said. "I know someone we can rent a room from. Ben's office has a link to the university. It's too late on Friday to ring Ben. I'll ring her cousin and make it happen." A few minutes later, Ari was speaking—to David's great astonishment—to the Merlin himself.

"He'll meet us at Milburn," she said. "He doesn't want us to be without someone senior simply because it's Friday."

"If all of this is intentional, these bombings could be on Friday to keep Her Maj away. Like the Saturday stuff being in the street of a synagogue."

"I thought that," said Ari. "In theory, to keep me away too, but I'm not religious. We'll get a taxi and have time to check it out, then settle into the office and play a waiting game for the actual event."

"You agree with the timing, then?"

"Very much so," Ari said. "It's going to be a long night. The Merlin says he'll bring a proper meal, since he's coming by the back way and he wasn't impressed with our choice of sandwiches."

"The back way?"

"No-one knows what the back way is. He gets around quickly when he has to, he says, and he calls it 'the back way'. Someone told me once that it's surfing using the wind. People will say anything about the Merlin. I'm not sure we should trust any of it. He's so different to Benedicta that it's hard to believe they're related."

An hour later, David found himself in a seminar room, pizza on the table before him, lecturing to the most senior magician in the British Isles, whose 'back way' was a car from Durham. The pizza came from Durham, for he had a favourite place there, he explained. David liked pizza, but dumplings would've been better tonight. Dumplings were almost always better.

42

The Merlin explained all the small things and none of the big.

The Merlin was researching the same problem as they were and had been looking for exactly what Data and David himself had found, but the Merlin's measurements (done by magical arithmetic, he explained vaguely) had not brought him close enough.

Learned, scholarly magic isn't quite as magic as it appears from the outside, David joked to himself in order to ground himself as he prepared the computer to display on the wall.

"Tell me what's happening here," said the Merlin, "and I'll tell you what I was checking up."

The Merlin was his cousin's opposite. One of the most comfortable looking men David had ever encountered, with a friendly style to his chatter. *He ought to be a counsellor or maybe a used car salesman.* His tie was awry, not in the sharp way that a great magician's tie ought to be awry, but in the charming way of someone who was only wearing a tie because someone had asked politely if he would mind putting one on.

The Merlin didn't look like someone who scared as many people as Her Maj. Maybe he wasn't. Maybe it was all a beat up. And maybe Her Maj was a softie.

One can believe all kinds of untruths when one is beyond nervousness and into panic, David thought. *This may be an impossible situation, but I'm here, and I can handle it. Also, there's pizza. Pizza will help.*

Ari introduced the Merlin to David (avoiding the Merlin's proper name, as was correct), introduced David's map, then handed over to David. David would have been happy to hide behind the computer, or even behind the pizza, and not be seen. Really, he would have been.

"It won't be the same as the explosions that have happened so far. From the press and from the data, they're all build-up. Look." David's pointer highlighted bits of his map as he explained.

"There were six when we started, but now there are twenty-five, and they're making a spiral."

"Is the spiral significant?" Ari asked.

"Aren't you the magic expert?" Merlin asked back.

Why, David wondered, did he do that, when Ari wasn't even local?

"Yes, but not the expert on English folk material. How relevant is the spiral here, David?"

"In Newcastle, it's not. If we were at Newgrange, that would be different, maybe. Newgrange is internationally famous for its spirals."

The Merlin gave a lazy smile and, turning into a friendly university lecturer, said, "Not quite, but close. The spiral has relevance in English magic. In this case, you've interpreted that relevance correctly. Whatever they're aiming for, the spiral is part of the attempt to bring unattached magic in for whatever result they're after. By the way, before I forget. From here on, not just for this piece of work but whenever we're in public, call me Uncle. It means you won't disrupt any do-not-notice-me spell I might have operating. Speaking of spells, any idea of what might be the goal here?"

"I was thinking portals," David said. "But that's because of this building." Both faces looked at him. "I don't mean that this portal has a building, I mean this building has ... Let me start again. I'll use the map." He flicked it onto the wall from his portable projector.

"You're not going back to that list again?" Ari asked, not quite warningly.

"Only to give an explanation. You're right, and there's no reason for it to be this place specifically."

"Here?" Ari was surprised.

"This seminar room, the one we're in right now, is in one of the buildings I starred on the list," David explained.

"Why did you star buildings? And why did Ms Green dismiss them?"

"She dismissed them for a perfectly good reason. I wasn't looking at places that might contain or influence magic at that point. I was looking for culturally significant locations. There were several paths into determining culturally significant places, and Newcastle is so full of them that I was trying to find means to differentiate one from the other. The castle and the Black Door, for example, are places that inherit our dreams and thoughts. The general public uses them when they want to re-create something magic they've read about or seen in a fictional narrative. A lot of culturally significant places were places that are known as magic or thought to be magic or used for magic because they already have meaning. Some are historical, like the Black Door, and others are ones that had attracted the attention of writers and artists. In Newcastle, the writerly one is the Lit and Phil, which is so very full of magicians and books and ghosts that it fits into the otherworldly places already. There was a fan film of *Ghostbusters* done there, and then tourists visited the building expecting to find the ghosts. It's not anywhere close to where the spiral will end, though, so the fact that it ticks both boxes is irrelevant."

"Go on."

"Did you notice that the outside of the building follows the shape of the street in a very ordinary fashion, and inside of this building is a very pretty Art Deco design, and that the doors radiate out from the centre?"

"How could we not notice that," said Ari ironically, "given we walked across it and down the hall?"

"There was a science fiction convention in Newcastle a few years ago. This building was used as a not-quite-legal shortcut, and the building itself became a running gag. Each of these doors, they said, led into different worlds. I thought that this was the kind of cultural construct that non-magicians who've discovered they have magical abilities late in life would love. They wouldn't know they're going against tradition because they've never learned tradition."

"This is why Ben brought you in," said the Merlin. "You see things from outside."

"I have no magic, and I come from the other side of the world."

"Why is your English so good?" Ari asked. "I've been meaning to ask you, and Data has always laughed it off."

"Data knows more history than you, my dear," said the Merlin, turning into a favourite uncle mildly correcting his erring niece. What was this man's real personality, anyhow? "Singapore is part of the Commonwealth. English is its working language, even though it has its own mother tongue and its own English dialect and culture and magic systems. Your accent is more British than most, however." He turned to David.

"Partly my family, partly it's not a TV accent," he said. "Also, I was an undergraduate at Sydney University and then came here. I've been in the UK three years now." He was very proud of not asking, 'Are people incapable of speaking their own languages where you come from? We code switch, what's so extraordinary about that? We speak the right type of language for the occasion.' David was a bit embarrassed that he'd dwelt on it.

"Useful," was the Merlin's comment. "What about regular magic?"

"No religious magic documented within the couple of hundred metres that this event will target. No sightings either. This is odd, considering how close to the heart of Newcastle we are. It must be a factor in choosing this city for this event." The word 'factor' was echoed by an explosion in the far background. *Coming closer*, David thought. Both Ari and the Merlin took it without so much as blinking an eye. In fact, Ari reached out and highlighted the aspects of Data and David's map she had been talking about.

Somehow, she'd absorbed the work he and Data had done and caught up on the implications of it. She was quick, this woman. Scary-bright. David felt as if he were constantly running to keep up. It was a good kind of race. His brain loved it. His brain would have loved it more if Ariette had realised he was a native English speaker, however, and that she herself had excellent English for a non-native speaker. It wasn't colonial patronisation because Singapore had never been a French colony, but it came pretty close.

He had to stop dwelling on it. He had to focus on the fact that bombs were coming closer and that he didn't want to be hit by them. They needed to find solutions.

"That means I can exclude the numinous for the moment. It's probably craft magic. Let's look at that map and see what else we can add, then we'll go for a bit of a walk and see what's happening on the ground."

"Check the Black Gate?"

"I sincerely hope it's not the Black Gate they're targeting. But if it is, we need to know."

"Can you protect it? You said something a moment ago …"

The Merlin looked up at Ari (who was a bare two centimetres taller than him, but it showed). "Thanks for the reminder. Let's do that first, then come back to the map. Bring a slice of pizza with you," he said to David. "I know Bennie and food; I bet you haven't had a proper meal in two days."

"Pizza is not a proper meal," said Ariette mildly.

"Do you even have pizza in Tsarfat?" As he spoke, the Merlin closed the door behind them, and they all wended their way outside.

"If I tell you, you'll write another paper about it."

"I won't publish the paper. Not until our agreement lapses and I don't have to keep you a secret anymore."

"On that, I trust your cousin. You don't want us to be secret."

"I want France to have the problem of dealing with you."

"Excuse me," interrupted David, who had decided against pizza, despite his new uncle's advice.

"Yes?' the Merlin said.

"If Tsarfat has a largely French culture and the portal is somewhere in France, why is its main relationship with the British Government? And why are Commonwealth countries so excluded that Tsarfati don't trust Australians?"

"Good questions," Ari said.

"A two-word answer," said the Merlin. "Jewish magic," he continued flippantly.

"If even a hint of that got out, it would make antisemitism worse," David answered seriously. Both his seniors stopped dead in their tracks and stared. "The bit of the stereotype that says Jews are taking over the world? The one Hitler pushed so hard that it reached Southeast Asia?"

"Why had I not thought of that?" the Merlin asked rhetorically.

"Why did *you* think of it, is what I want to know," Ariette said to David.

"The incidents in London were failed doorways. That's why I included doorway potential in the map. All the incidents everywhere look like failed doorways in one way or another, but the London ones actually crossed universes. One of the doorways was to a time when the Jewish population of England was at one of its modern lows and there was a lot of persecution, and the other was to an Earth where swastikas decorated public announcements."

"Obvious, now you say it," said the Merlin, not quite ironically.

"Sometimes we need an outsider."

"That's what the boss said when she recruited me. She hates the professor but likes my work. Ms Beja told me that a Singaporean was going to produce someone who was both insider and outside, and that without that, we were all in danger. I thought ..."

"Keep going," said the Merlin, "Even if it's something you don't want to say. I need to hear it."

"I thought she was playing politics. But the more I get to know her, the more I see that her intellectual view of life has integrated with her magic. She has insights. They're like the map Data and I made: her insights bring everything together. That's why I trust her. I've lied to my supervisor about what I do because I trust her more than I trust him, given the way they each work. I see her think in that way that all the great Jewish magicians have thought, bringing numbers and language together, and I see how it influences the way she leads her everyday life and how ethical she is and ... she's my gold standard for magic in politics. That's why I accepted the job, even though it is not my thing and might ruin my academic career. I don't know why I was put forward for this position in the first place, but me doing well here is a nail on my coffin in my supervisor's books."

David stopped speaking very suddenly, realising that the Merlin had done precisely what his gentle manner had suggested he would and persuaded David to say more than he ever intended. David knew then that no matter what happened, he would trust Benedicta Beja with his life and only trust her cousin with whatever Her Maj said he should. The Merlin's manner was certainly comfortable, but no-one should be the recipient of confidences on a night like this, when an incident was in the process of coming down. Not just any incident. One he had been warned about.

"Interesting," the Merlin said as they turned the last bit of turning and reached the Black Gate.

That was the last word for a little bit and, David thought, the most appropriate summary of the previous ten minutes. Unless he went with 'Idiotic.' Idiotic was better, really.

The Black Gate was lit, so the stone shone in the dark and the steps to the gate itself looked as if they led to magic lands forlorn. Not a very bright shining, but enough of one so the Merlin had to flicker his hands and persuade the light to dim a little. He climbed the steps to it and murmured Latin to himself.

"It's still strange seeing magic committed," said Ari. "But magic done in Latin is comfortingly foreign."

"Tsarfat?"

"Is not magic. Has never been magic, if one discounts green skin," Ari said strongly. It hurt her that the assumption was even made. "We're techo. Our technology is the stuff your society craves. When we come through the door to here, we become magic. A bit magic. In our own way."

"So, you learned Hebrew and Data learned Latin to do magic in our world? No, that doesn't work."

"Your theory doesn't match our magic. That man," she gestured up the stairs, "is worried by me because he was the person who demonstrated that we don't belong at all on Earth2. He proved that we came from Earth1, which we could have explained if anyone had asked. We're the product of another Earth, and we come here from that rare thing, a stable pocket universe. This is what he proved. It was going to mess up thirty years of sound work between my lot and the British government. Benedicta ran with the superhero tag to shut him up, pretty much. It fitted the rumours that we were odd, and it worked. He's not happy about it. Or about my people."

"He doesn't dislike you, I don't think?"

"No, he enjoys my company. He doesn't like the fact that I represent much strangeness. That's why what you said about the racism makes so much sense. He's scared of our techo in the same way that anti-Semites are scared of a non-existent world takeover by Jews."

"If I said 'Interesting' at this point, would you look down at me and sneer?" David asked.

"Probably," said Ari, a smile lighting her face for the first time that evening. "If you're going to call him Uncle, call me Ari or Ariette. It's my actual real-life name. Green is a stupid joke someone made when we first came out from underground."

"Green Children. I am so slow."

"It's a quirk of our pocket universe. Our ancestors had perfectly European and North African skin before they entered Tsarfat. Also, neither Data nor I have very green skin now. My two best friends are much bolder but quite different shades. One is a bright perky green that makes her look as if she's walked straight out of a children's novel or as if the sun is always shining on her. The other is the best green of all, soft and dark, like the last sun on a fir tree in the evening. I used to be a morning version of that, much less attractive to men than my friend, which was just as well, considering. It fades with the changes that happen when we leave Tsarfat. Data wears makeup to hide the fact that she still has green tinges in the right light, but she doesn't need as much as when she first arrived here."

"So why are you Green and she's Data? I'm missing the logic there?"

"You like everything to fit together."

"I'm afraid so. My internal scholar rules my brain."

"The first of us to be known in your universe announced themselves as Green. Pretended we were all related to hide our cultural oddities. Anyone who asked who any of us were was told 'The Greens.' When we were mistaken for the political party, we started calling ourselves 'The Green family.' That stuck. Most people know of us as the Green family or the Green Children. Data, being Data, said that she could be a cousin because she wanted her own name."

"Given her accent isn't the same and her culture is different, being a cousin makes sense."

"You do know you're the only person who notices that we don't quite speak the same as the French do, and that our culture is different?"

David shrugged his shoulders in the dark, then realised it would not be seen. "Sorry," he said.

"Sorry," was what the Merlin said immediately afterwards too, as he came back to them at that precise moment. "That took longer than I expected. There's something coming, but not to this door. I did the protection anyway because that gate is historically important. I put out a tracer after that. We need to follow the tracer."

"It'll lead us to the actual spot we need to be?" asked Ari.

The Merlin didn't answer, he simply started walking. David noticed that his head was always at a fixed height. He was following something with his eyes, and the rest of him was automatically going where the eyes went. David also noticed that he was going back the way they came.

"Is this thing on the other side of the building?' David asked. "Because if it is, then it's faster to go round, even if it's longer."

"He's focussed on the trail," said Ari. "He can't change it at this point without delay, and if he hurries, well, we might be closer to the end point of this game than we thought."

Whatever mysterious object the Merlin was following led them straight into a wall very quickly. "It's this building," he said.

"We just came from this building," said Ari. "This is Milburn

House. David's starred building."

"Maybe your friend was right in his cultural attributions."

"I didn't know culture made magic." Ari sounded defensive even as she examined the wall for a way through.

David sighed. Those two were always on the brink of an argument and never actually made it into one. "Can we go inside and see? We're running out of time." For the explosions were closer. Much closer.

"We need this part of the building." Their honorary uncle stood firmly with his nose pointed at that wall.

"I can find that from inside," Ari said and led the way back to the front door.

Where she took them was that well, that heartland where all the doors came out. Not quite a circle, not quite angular, with door after door leading off and the centre looking like the centre of …

"See, popular view of how a built portal would look. Not one universe, but many. Each door a different place. The central region, with its glyph, the place that holds the magic together."

"Whoever they are, if this is their game, then they want to do more than find a door," Ari suggested.

"They want to make doors," David said, "and bring other universes that fit their politics into play."

"If we're reading it right. But there's no-one here."

"The explosions," said David. "I know they were pushing everything here, but I don't know from what direction."

"What do you mean?"

"What's their trajectory? There's a point at which a spiral stops. Is it at the wall your lead took you to, or somewhere in the building? It's one of them, for certain. That's what your tracer was telling us. Where the end point is."

"You bright boy," said his honorary uncle. "How does the wall from outside match up with the spiral? Where does it match?"

David was lost without the map, but Ari walked around the open area and stopped at one door. "This is it."

Merlin went over and began an incantation. "Indeed it is," he said. "In the fabric of the door itself. All we have to do is wait."

"But what's happening?" David asked plaintively.

"There was portal magic behind those explosions, and they're linked to magic that collects other magic, and they're all moving to emerge here. I'll have my people come right down to test this. All the explosions will need checking. Ari, I'll send you the results, and you can tell us if they match anything in your own situation."

"I'll have to ask permission for that."

"Then ask," the Merlin said sharply. "We need to know."

"I'm not certain that anyone needs to know how to break down boundaries between universes, nor even that our case can be duplicated," said Ari mildly, "but I take your point. And certainly we can find out if there are any physical similarities between the explosions—"

At that point, the world around them shook and rattled and made a big bang. It finished Ari's sentence for her.

Their ears rang, and words were useless. David pointed at the door. The door itself had been pushed off its hinges by the explosion and lay on the tiled floor. Behind it, the doorway wasn't empty. In that doorway was a replica of the pale wood, except this door was slightly ajar. In the small gap a male body, wearing jeans and a white t-shirt, rested about a metre from the ground.

David went to pull it through.

"Leave him," Ari said. "He might still be alive, and if we move him, that could be his death."

A dull thud interrupted her. The body had fallen to the ground. There was a lot of blood.

54

"Not all the magic arrived here at the same time. Bloody amateurs. The damn body's been bifurcated. It's too late for this poor soul," the Merlin said. "David, take pictures. I'll ring for backup. We need to track this."

David whipped out his phone and took pictures while Merlin and Ari both made calls. When he looked at the door and at the body, he felt sick. The concept of bad magic was a lot sexier than the reality. He squinted while he photographed. Then he moved the phone around to get pictures on either side.

The ground rumbled again, rather faintly.

"Look," he said to his companions and pointed again.

"Oh fuck," was Ari's response.

The body now lay in sections outside each and every door, including the elevator, random components scattered generously over the floor. The art of the floor and the awfulness of the body parts left David feeling as if he was trapped in a surrealist horror painting.

"People die," David let the words out, even though he wanted to suppress them and run screaming. "People die as they leave Tsarfat."

The Merlin looked at him grimly. "Keep photographing. I'm counting the pieces," he said.

A minute later, he was back. "Not the same count as the explosions."

"More or less?" asked Ari.

"More."

"We documented the explosions that were reported and the ones we heard. There may have been more."

"David, the moment we're out of here, I want you to get that information."

"OK," David said miserably. He'd signed up to superhero central not to a horrorfest, and now he felt very sick. He would ask Data. She was following everything, and maybe she would help him feel less sick simply by existing. Maybe.

"There's our technical team. I'll hand this over. You two get out of here. No, wait. We'll go together."

Handover didn't take long, and the technical team looked just as ill as David felt. It comprised four people with very portable equipment, and David was relieved. It had come so quickly, though. The Merlin knew more than he was saying. Didn't his office talk to Her Maj's?

Dreaming about interoffice rivalry between magic in Britain meant he didn't have to look or smell or, in fact, deal. He spent the next five minutes inventing reasons for feuding and interoffice distress. He'd just reached the Office of Merlin being distressed that Her Maj refused to celebrate Christmas when the Merlin said, "Right, we can go now. I'll get my team to pick everything up from the seminar room and follow up everything we've left undone or half done. Let's get to London."

It all happened so quickly.

The shortcut to the station was that long corridor David remembered earlier. They walked into it, and four people walked into them. Three male. One female.

"I'm so sorry," said the Merlin, politely. David echoed it. Ariette had been bowled over and was trying to pick herself up, but the others were in the way.

"Can someone help me?" she asked.

"We just need to get through," said one of them. His beard and his Star Wars t-shirt made him look like a person David ought to know. A science fiction nerd.

"If you let me get up, then we can go where we're going, and you can go where you're going. It's not hard," said Ari.

That was when David noticed that one of the men was actually holding her down with weight placed in just the right spot. He moved over to help.

"None of that," said the bearded man. "You're foreigners."

"They're my guests, and you are annoying me," said the Merlin. His hands fluttered.

"Ooh, magic,' the young woman said and laughed. "You can't do that here."

"Can't?" the Merlin asked and stopped his incantation. "Is it forbidden by law? Is there a custom?"

"Nothing like that. We've stopped it. Taken all the magic and over-ridden it and used it and ..."

The three looked at each other. Ari shook her head very slightly. David reached down to help her up. At this point, he wished he had paid more attention and remembered everything from his time in National Service. He had no idea how to handle this. It was his own fault. His head was full of dreams, even now, when he was surrounded by danger.

The Merlin turned on his charm and said, "You don't need us then, you've got this covered."

"You can stay and watch," said the tallest of the group. "It's very cool."

"I need to be back in London tonight," the Merlin said. "My family is ill."

"You'll take these two with you?" asked the bearded man. "If I trusted you, which I don't, that might be OK."

"She's not so bad," said the one man who hadn't spoken yet. David heard southern English in that voice. Not very southern, but south of London for certain. "She's French, but she's not bad. We could wait for the others and let them go then."

I bet, David thought furiously, *that there is one other for each of those explosions. Or maybe two people for each.*

"My friend and I have a plane to catch," Ari said, still half recumbent. "We're running so late it's cutting it fine. We're going to miss it, I think. Under the circumstances, that is not a big problem. We can always have a longer holiday. Would you mind, Uncle?" She turned to the Merlin.

"I'll talk to both your parents. I'm sure you can stay a week longer. See the sights. Or these kind people could let you go, and you could catch that blasted plane."

This didn't work either.

David wasn't surprised. He had no idea what Ari and the Merlin were doing. Possibly verbal magic. It sounded like nonsense. Ari obviously thought it was nonsense too, for her face took on a resigned look.

More of the creators of explosions had arrived during the conversation, and the three of them were surrounded.

"I hope you don't mind," Ari explained to all and sundry. "There may be a few headaches happening shortly. I'm letting you know as a courtesy."

She looked up at the sky, and the clouds split apart briefly, showing a scrap of moon and a hint of stars. Out of the moon and stars, a rumble of thunder sounded. A flash of lightning lit the area immediately above them and descended to earth. It struck the cobbled pavement next to the man with a beard.

"That's what I thought," Ari said. "The high reaches are beyond your magic drain. Let us go or I shall call down lighting. A bolt for each of you. You've got the count of five to decide. Five." She paused for an extended moment. The sky above them lit up with thousands of tiny silver flashes.

"Four." The silver flashes extended across the whole Newcastle skyline, lighting up the gate and everything round it. The only darkness was the river. The bridge shone against the silver and black as if it were made to be in a display.

"Three." The white flashes changed their little dance and moved to just above their heads. The thunder played the music to their dance.

"Two." The group that had been around them was no longer there. When the light flashed immediately above everyone's heads, David glimpsed them running away.

"I hated doing that," Ari said conversationally. "And if you call me Storm," she said pointedly to David, "you're dead to me."

"Interesting," the Merlin said. "Your weather magecraft is like nothing I've ever seen. Not much craft and far more direct connection to weather elements."

"I was banking on that. Do either of you have headaches?"

"Yes," David admitted.

"Then let's go before I have to do this again. I would be happy if I never, never had to do this again. Jamais encore. Jamais." It was a sign of how trapped they'd been that the French slipped out. Ari's English was normally so colloquial.

This was his first superhero moment. David was certain of that.

While David's mind flickered with the lightning display he had just witnessed, his brain was fiddling the Merlin's comments about Ari's weather magic. Somewhere alongside that, it also played around to determine the common factor in those voices until that resolved as a simple every voice showed evidence of advanced education. University background. He wished he were a real linguist and could do more than the Henry Higgins act he sometimes pulled, but he knew he was right about the education.

The three walked as quickly as they could straight to the station, silently updated their tickets, and were on a train in no time flat.

The moment they were sitting on that train, the Merlin rang his people and said, "It's bad. Somewhere between ten and thirty people. Mostly male. Some carrying weapons. We encountered four face-to-face."

David noted that he himself had not noticed the weapons. He hadn't even thought to look. He was not a good person to have round in a terrorist crisis, he decided thankfully.

"There aren't enough of us, and we were in the centre of it," the Merlin continued, "so we've had to pull out. Get our things from the seminar room and bring them to London when you've got the culprits and cleaned up the mess. There's a victim to identify. I'm sending a map as soon as my people here have updated it to show the latest."

David pulled out his netbook from his messenger bag and started doing precisely that, listing everything talked about so that there was a record. He quietly copied Data in and saw that she copied Her Maj in to everything. Good.

"Couldn't you have told them earlier?" Ariette asked when the Merlin hung up.

"Didn't you see that we were being watched the whole way to the station?"

"I was trying not to react to those bodies."

"One body," said the Merlin.

"Three arms," said Ari. "And an extra foot. One mutated body. Or more than one person."

David was listening from the seat behind, and this made him look up. "You counted?" Another piece of evidence to demonstrate that he was not hero material and that Ariette Green was a real live superhero with a proper superhero power.

"It was either that or be very sick," Ari stated bitterly.

"You could use your abilities and feel changes in the atmosphere to find out where those bodies came from," said the Merlin.

"I could. I don't see why I should, however, given the price I pay for them. Also given I had no idea how you intended me to have used them in that place and at that time until you explained it now."

David wasn't certain he should be listening to this, so he stepped in with, "I've updated all the information we collected before we went downstairs, and with what we saw downstairs, and with what's been on the news since then. Sir, if you have an email address I can send it to, the people you sent to replace us can have all the data."

"You're offering me all this without checking with your employer?" The Merlin was amused.

David almost enjoyed saying what should have been obvious. "We've already copied her everything. As soon as Data and I finished it, she checked with Ms Beja about your people getting a copy."

"How can you be communicating with Bennie's office from here?"

"Through Data." David felt as if he was explaining laboriously. Not just through the seat, but through a veil of poor knowledge. He didn't know if he could say what Data could do.

Ari said it for him.

"You can stop blocking our airways, you know. Benedicta said you did that when things got tight. Things are not tight anymore."

"True, and I would have raised the blocks when we reached London in any case. What I want to know is why the blocks didn't work. Your computer is perfectly ordinary, isn't it? Let me check." He reached his hand back for it.

"Don't give it to him, David," said Ari. "It's yours, and you're not his. Besides, he gets briefed on every Tsarfati cleared for work here, so if Uncle doesn't know what's happening here, it's because he doesn't read his own briefings and he wasn't watching what I did out there with the sky. You don't have to explain a thing."

"I liked the sarcasm in that 'Uncle'," the Merlin said

approvingly. "Give me the short version of your new companion's special abilities."

"Electronic magic," was all Ari said, but it was enough.

Maybe not enough for the Merlin, but enough for David to see how the colours in her earpieces worked and why she was hard of hearing but never missed a word and why she never had a computer and yet had checked Singapore and chatted happily away with him online at the drop of a hat. *If I had a magic talent,* David thought, *a single superhero one, I'd like one like Data's rather than Ari's. I need to ask her about viruses, though. If she's open to them now that people know about her, I need to introduce her to that group from school.*

He didn't trust anyone magic, really, except Data and Ari. Superheroes were different. Not trusting was new, though. It was those horrid limbs strewn over the floor like a bad zombie movie. It was also the Merlin, Her Maj's own cousin, playing politics with Her Maj's people at a time of crisis.

This job sucked in some very unexpected ways.

It also had its good points.

Well before they reached London, David and Ari were told that the results were in. Fifteen people had been arrested but weren't giving useful information. They claimed it was an instamob thing and that messages had appeared on their phones after they'd joined in the game online. They didn't know each other. They claimed they were carrying weapons because they were creating explosions in the city on a Friday night and wanted to protect themselves.

That was the sum of it. Poor excuses made over and over until everyone was tired of hearing them. The formal statements would be there when everyone appeared in the morning.

London was investigating the communications. The Merlin's people would handle the charges and making those charges stick.

Legislating magic was his office's jurisdiction. Legislating and reinforcing and codifying, and this made David wonder what the Merlin himself thought about a type of magic that couldn't be codified or legislated. At least in this case, almost everything was over for Beja's team, which was good considering the hour.

The deaths meant that Benedicta could skip synagogue. Or rather, the fact that the deaths were reported in all the press meant that she could skip synagogue. The Merlin's people had only arrested half the perpetrators and hadn't cleared the random body parts from sight before journalists had found the building.

David wasn't certain he'd be able to sleep at all with all this on his mind. What kept floating through his brain as he eventually lay in bed was the pizza they'd left in the seminar room and the information Data had snuck through to both himself and Ari on their phones.

"We intercepted a message from the most senior person involved. None of the people involved with this incident know the person who told them what to do, not even the organiser himself. Everything was done online. No-one knows anyone, they say. That's the bad news. The worse news is that they knew that an explosion shoved Tsarfat into our world and were trying to mimic it. They used magic to fill in the gaps of their knowledge. Our door kills four out of five people who pass. This one kills everyone."

Chapter Four

David and Data dubiously examined a brief. It covered all the basics but said nothing they couldn't have worked out for themselves. They had three days of briefing and paperwork ahead. There was not enough coffee in the universe to get them through that amount of dullness.

Data was more affected than David. Ari Green had taken her to see *The Mikado* the night before. Ari had a crush on one of the singers and had pointed her out: a body curved beyond all logic with energy to power a city and with a voice that carried the whole production. Data would rather have more operetta than so much paper. She had downloaded the tunes: her brief had its own music attached. The surname of the grandest voice from the night before tickled her. 'Beja' wasn't what she'd expected to see as a common English name.

"Is it all going to be this glamorous?" David asked Data.

"Your guess is as good as mine." She wasn't going to tell David about having a little list, nor about the tree by the river where a little tom tit sang willow-tit-willow-tit-willow. She liked David a great deal, but she found her sudden addiction to nineteenth century England just a little bit embarrassing.

The briefing certainly brought them up to date. It also confirmed all of David's guesses. The current theory was that a group of still-to-be-determined terrorists wanted pocket universes to run world-conquering dreams. There was a secondary theory that a government might want to establish pocket universes as dumpholes for refugees, but this didn't work because not a single briefing arguing this could explain why the attempts at developing pocket universes radiated out from the UK.

Work by other members of the Green family established clearly that these odd explosions and shifts in reality were not happening elsewhere. It was a year of crises, and this was the real world. In movies, crises were all linked; in reality, they were simply impossible to manage. The extensive Green family could not be called upon, not without sacrifices.

Too many crises, everyone agreed. Whatever the reason for the UK problems, the brief said, Tsarfat was involved. The research that proved Tsarfat was involved was, unfortunately, above Data and David's clearance, but the statement that Tsarfat was involved was very firm.

David pointed to it and said, "I'd interpret this as someone thinking that someone else needs to be convinced."

"Is that someone else us, though?" Data's voice was slightly querulous.

David understood how this paperwork could be vexing, especially when it was not given to Data electronically. She had to read it the slow way, as he did. This made her think of home, she said, and so it turned her miserable.

"I don't know. I'll tell you something I do know, however."

"What?" Data was less interested, David suspected, than she was tired of reading papers describing situations they knew most of already. Or maybe it was the printed paper that tired her. It would be interesting to get electronic material straight to the brain, he felt. One could do so much more work that way.

"Your home is affected by all of this. Whether or not anything from Tsarfat comes here, Tsarfat is changed by the things that are happening. I can see why Ariette went straight to Newcastle. She knew this."

"Let's get out of here," Data said. "I've copied all the papers, and they don't have anything we haven't talked about, and I am sick to death of this office."

"I didn't mean to make you uncomfortable." Admitting this made David himself uncomfortable. He suspected he might be developing feelings for Data.

"You gave me words for what I knew, that's all."

David felt far too relieved when she said that, as if he had confirmed an inner truth. He was right about his feelings.

Data continued, regardless of the thoughts she was overriding, and David couldn't drift off as was his wont. "I needed to know. We must move forward quickly because these people have been planning forever and we've only just started looking for them, and those damn papers go round in circles. Let's get out."

The two went to a pub, and Ari joined them for an hour.

The only one of their team who didn't drink too much beer was Benedicta, and this might have been, David thought, because Benedicta wasn't there. She expected them to work non-stop on all those stupid papers because that's what she would do. Here they were. Data and Ari made notes on napkins because only David had brought paper and refused to share (because why should he? Data didn't need notes) and explored English beer.

Once Ari was gone again, the two of them became very drunk. They also had some success in outlining what needed doing. All those people exploding Newcastle meant that there had to be a trail. This was not a lone gunman scenario.

It was so simple to fuel thought with beer.

David and Data tried to set up the trail from those involved in the Newcastle incident, but with no success. They needed someone who, because of who they were and who they knew, could lead them into the heart of things. Or at least let the team know what sort of people might be involved so that they could find that heart themselves. What was needed, then, was an expert. They kicked their idea and their reasoning upstairs and then called it a night. David felt rather smug.

Then Data said, "It's a nuisance that we can't talk unless you've got your computer on. Can I do something to your phone? I want to be in touch."

David wondered if that made their drinks a date. Or if Data was all work and very misleading. He handed her the phone without saying a word, then watched the earpieces play the light that would tell him what she was doing if only he could read light.

An hour later, when he was almost asleep, his phone beeped. "Drink some water so you won't have a hangover. Data's orders." David laughed and did just that.

✡

A few weeks earlier, in Tsarfat, a perfectly ordinary dinner took place. The table was perfectly arranged and there were no empty seats. Four people was the perfect number for the table size. Those sitting were about to start the cheese, having nicely demolished a very fine main course, when there was a knock at the door.

"I'm so sorry," Ariette apologised as her aunt walked her in. "I know it's very late and it's the end of the week, but I wanted to see you all before I went out again."

"I'm glad you came. I thought we'd missed you this visit." Ari's aunt brought her into the dining room and pulled over a chair.

It was a plush dining room. It belonged in Paris, Ariette thought, and her aunt must've designed it from pictures. Plush and a bit elegant and not really comfortable. So often she had visited but was just noticing home now that she didn't get to see it often.

"Before I sit down," Ari said, "I'd better give you this. Since I'm to blame for your addiction." She took off a small backpack and unloaded coffee and chocolate. "I had tea, but ..."

This gave her aunt a moment to find a fifth chair.

"I'm glad you gave it to her," said Ari's cousin, her own age, but with skin pine-needle dark. Ari had always been envious of her cousin, but now that her eyes were used to skins all the shades of pink, white, and brown, she realised she looked for different qualities these days. Sadly, her cousin was still beautiful. "She needs something to take her mind off what happened to her husband and her children. My boyfriend's brother brings other things in for her, but he always forgets tea."

"He doesn't forget it," said Ari's Aunt Colette. "He drinks it himself. I dropped in to pick up those jams you made for me and caught him, red-handed."

Everyone laughed.

"Who are you talking about? And won't you introduce me to your new guest?"

Ari placed herself on the wooden chair, sitting upright and trying not to knock over the stack of gifts she had brought.

"Oh! I'd better take those." Colette stowed them safely in the cupboard for which only she had the lock and key. She came back looking guilty. "I ought to make your coffee tonight, but it will keep everyone up, and I've already made the real thing and ..."

She drifted off, embarrassed.

Ariette laughed. "I didn't bring the coffee for tonight. Everything I brought is for you. Just don't let that friend of yours at the package this time."

"CD was distraught that night." Her uncle excused his best friend. "He had just been sent home from work."

"For bad behaviour, if I recall correctly," said their guest.

Ariette spoke with great care. "This isn't something I can talk about, I'm afraid. I don't get to drink our coffee nearly often enough, so I shall enjoy this cup."

"Except that I don't know you!" The guest was enthusiastic. Men often were around Ari. Tonight, it didn't annoy her. "I've never met anyone so fair. Your skin colour is quite random."

"Our Ari is an Envoy," Colette said with gentle pride.

"Ah," said the guest, who was still entirely unnamed. Since they'd been through all the regular chatter that should have preceded an introduction, this meant that he was yet another person her aunt and uncle didn't want her to know. They were very careful about which of their friends she was to meet. "You live in the Residency Banlieu. I don't often meet people from there."

"I live mostly in England right now," she said, taking the clear and obvious path to safety. "I'm our permanent representative to France and the United Kingdom. That's what I came to tell you," she said to her relatives. "It's been confirmed. Also, that I can't stay long. I'm expected back in London tomorrow morning."

"You can stay a few hours, surely? I can walk up the street and get more family."

Ariette laughed. "I'm driving in France and catching the ferry and then driving again in England. I don't want to be up all night. The road's not so safe there if I'm too tired to drive straight. Without techo, you know."

"Two hours and you'll be there," said the guest.

"By plane, maybe, but I've got to get to the airport and be checked in and … You really have no idea. Earth2 is the same size as Earth1. You know the Earth1 sizes."

"I can't say I do," said the guest.

"Do you remember the map we all were shown way back in our school days? The one with Tsarfat drawn to fit inside another map?"

"Tsarfat in France." Her aunt nodded. "I know that."

"Well, that map showed that we are a bit bigger than a certain area."

"Yes, France," said her uncle.

"Not quite France." Ari valiantly held back a sigh. "Two regions of France. Normandy and Picardy. I have to drive through both of those, catch a ferry, then drive again. Timewise, it adds up to crossing Tsarfat five times. It's not just the distance. They don't have our guidance systems or our velos. Their cars don't even get off the ground. Earth2 is as backwards in terms of techo as our Earth was."

"Uncouth, that's what it is," Colette sniffed. "Not at all civilised." This was the woman who had tried to create Paris in her dining room.

"Quite probably. Again, I'm sorry," Ari said, standing up. "I have to get moving."

"You only just got here!" Colette protested. "You haven't even had time to drink that coffee."

"I finished it, and it was delicious. It took me back to my childhood and visiting you after school."

"Your mother was too busy with work."

"So was my father," laughed Ari. "You can see where my driving need to get back to work came from."

She said her farewells, and her aunt saw her out, and Ari felt relief and puzzlement. Relief at not having to endure it any longer. When did that happen? Puzzlement at the guest. It was quite improper for him to sit there not introduced. He must be someone they thought she knew, or someone they were embarrassed about. Either way, that bore checking out. Everything in her life was political these days.

She rang her mother (interrupting work, apologetically) and asked if she could find out. "My new offsider is the one to send the information to. She's got something working so that she can communicate between zones. I don't know how, but it means you can send messages."

"I'll find out who he is if you do something for me."

"There's something you want me to bring back?"

"No. I told you I didn't need anything from outside. Not ever. I want more messages from you."

"I can do that. As long as I am in this team, I can send you a message a day."

"Every few days is fine. I need to know if you're alive, that's all."

"What aren't you saying?"

"Every time someone comes back, they're hurt or someone else has died. Every time. The death rate is increasing."

"I didn't know. If you could send me news and statistics about them when you tell me about the guest at auntie's, I'd be grateful."

"Why can't you do it through official channels? Either of them, in fact."

"Like you, I don't feel so safe. I'm investigating problems that might be related to this in England, but what if the things you've noticed are linked to Tsarfat?"

Her mother's voice softened. "I'll send you anything I can find, then." That was the thing about her mother. She would do all the work if she agreed deeply with the aim. She would do nothing at all if she didn't.

The fact that her mother was perturbed enough to be an unofficial research assistant dragged at Ari's footsteps until she had emerged to her car, parked on a country road not too far from the Somme. Every footstep plodded and her whole life felt slow.

I am going to have a life outside Tsarfati. I'm not going to ignore my feelings about people, and I'm going to start going to theatre again. Also sport. I shall find a sport.

These resolves didn't stop Ari's footsteps from plodding, but they helped her keep walking.

✡

David's supervisor had a secret life.

His special gift was to merge culturally with the environment of his choice. He had used that special talent to build a life for himself that had nothing to do with his origins. For many years, his existence had been governed by building up a life of his own, one that had no links to his past.

Then his cousin asked him for help. Today was one of those days when the help proved itself.

"I know why you hide yourself," the letter had said. "I do not want to bring you to the attention of those you would rather not know that you were still alive. However, we need you."

Exeter was a far better place to live than anywhere back home. It had history, for one thing, and that history felt solid. It was not as Jewish as most of the rest of England, and that felt even more solid. Here, he was not held back by his ancestry. His accent changed to give him every advantage, his name changed to hone that advantage. So much about him changed.

Rupert had transformed himself into everyone's English lecturer of choice. A little bit charming, a little bit forgetful, a little bit fuddy-duddy. The sort of scholar who would dream of other worlds but could not possibly have known them.

That was how he presented himself today. He walked uphill to work, for it wasn't far. Other people lived out of town or in town or in a newer part of town, but he chose to live close enough to the university that he could walk to work every day. The city centre was a longer walk away but still not that far. No-one knew he couldn't drive, only that he didn't have to.

The walk had become a ritual—up a hill to work and enjoying the splendid views as he walked down the same hill to reach home. This was his England.

His change had helped him fit into it. He thought of it rarely, but today was one of those times. People would forget his name, but not his reputation. He used his special gift to enhance his reputation.

When he had moved to Devon, he had used his change and his wish for power to become senior in his own department and in his own academic circles. For the longest time, he didn't move outside any of those. The few kilometres of the university and of central Exeter had given him most of what he needed.

He would walk down to the Custom House and feel the puffery of living so close to a building hundreds of years older than Tsarfat. He would eat food that had been imported from halfway across the world. He would visit Oxford and Cambridge (but never Paris) for conferences and to give guest lectures.

Rupert relished feeling wanted and essential and being the person his youth had denied him.

His cousin, however, had written.

That letter was why today would be a new test of his talent. He should be able to be accepted by his new men, even if they had no idea who he really was. Even if they forgot his name and relied on the internet to contact him. This was the time when he would pull strings in towards himself and play his marionettes.

When the letter arrived, Rupert had to make some important choices. He would have to adapt his life, for he knew that there was no complete escape from his past now that he had been found. The question was what choices would he make?

Rupert didn't go home, for going home would announce to everyone he was still alive. He had no idea how his idiot cousin had found out about him, but the same idiot cousin was possibly the only person in Tsarfat he still cared for. Everyone else from his childhood was … disposable.

Rupert answered the letter. He sent his answer to a post office box in London.

That letter reminded him of all the things he had been as a child, about what he had buried deeply and forgotten. His own magic changed him from that professor to someone merely acting as a professor. His needs demanded it.

His needs were what his cousin had reminded him of: how their futures back home had been contained and how they had been hurt.

That letter had reached him ten years ago.

He had written back immediately, "I will work with you. I will lead all matters outside Tsarfat; you can have dominion within."

Rupert knew his cousin would never leave. Most people were too scared to go through the door and would always be so. He also knew that most of the work would have to take place in this wider world that his cousin knew far too little about. There was potential power in this situation.

He and his cousin decided to work initially with those outside Tsarfat. He didn't care about the hurt his cousin had suffered, nor the woe of being treated as less important by those who ruled the land of their grandparents. Rupert was quite happy to change the way the Envoy system operated, which was all that was needed to give his cousin the space and the respect he asked for. That would work for him.

Rupert wanted to live in his small safe place and yet to grasp the wider world within his tendrils. Eating food from the other side of the world was no longer sufficient for him. He wanted the world to listen.

He reached this stage in his recollections as he turned off the main road and walked through to the part of campus that hid his office. One of the things Rupert loved about this campus was that his office was sheltered from the gaze of passers-by and the building it was in was clean and modern. He liked to feel the age of his wider surroundings, but his everyday needed to be the familiar of the new. Nothing in Tsarfat was as old as Exeter, and he preferred not to think of that unless he chose.

When he reached his office, Rupert spent the minimum time necessary on university paperwork. He efficiently demolished his teaching preparation and set up notes for his next three papers. That took him past morning tea time. He had an hour left to handle the other side of his life, that side that had climbed the hill to work with him that day. The sun shone directly onto his desk, creating an omen.

Today was a good day to change the world.

While he and his cousin worked to reform the Envoy scheme, Rupert alone began to work for the good of a far greater number of people.

He wanted to take the ideal of Tsarfat in healing the world, but do it his way. He wasn't Jewish; he didn't need that philosophy. Rupert had learned so much in the many years he had been subsumed underneath a very safe exterior. He didn't leave Exeter. He didn't leave university. He even wore tweed jackets and pottered around in his garden. He rode a bike.

Rupert's life was a screen. It was no longer a reflection of who he was. It was physical comfort and would only be given up when more than comfort was there waiting for him.

He told no-one his plan. Not even his cousin.

Today was the day he took off the tweed jacket, metaphorically. From this day, he would live fully as himself. He might wear the jacket to go home, but it no longer illustrated the inner man. Losing it was like losing the French accent he had when he first came to England.

There were those who would sacrifice their lives to achieve his goals, and he would honour them, beginning today. There were those who would be sacrificed and who deserved no honour. Change as big as he planned took destruction. Destruction and the work of thousands of the willing, tens of thousands of the unwilling.

Fortunately, he had known exactly how to recruit everyone he needed. Tsarfat had taught him. Tsarfat recruited youths to train for certain death in the hopes those youths might help others. Rupert recruited along similar lines without anyone knowing they were being recruited. He had tested the system, and it functioned. The results had even been promising. Today, ten of his people would receive their next set of instructions. Today, they would all take a giant step forward.

This day would be written in history as equal to the day when man first walked on the moon. Rupert knew this in his heart of hearts.

Rupert had recruited men, mainly, to help him with this new path. Each and all of his men were well-intended. Each and all of them were from the cultural majority of their home place, and each thought that they were lacking in any of the good things in life. When they didn't get a job, for example, one of them would blame someone for the special opportunities given to someone else, normally not from their own background. When they failed to achieve their big goals, they would blame everyone except themselves. He made them feel as if they were special and their goals and dreams were deserving and he could help them achieve everything. He told his men they were all climbing a hill together. He didn't tell them his hill was in Exeter.

Rupert recruited slowly and carefully, and not a man among them knew who he was. Not a one of them knew even his pretend persona. He recruited Christians and atheists and those who weren't certain they knew what religious belief was.

He did not recruit from cultural minorities, for their wishes, he felt, could not be made to conform with his bigger goals. He certainly did not recruit from the Jewish population. They had caused his initial disadvantage in Tsarfat by standing in the way of all he could be and all he could do, and now that he was past Tsarfat and in the free world, he didn't want anything Jewish in his life at all.

This had not been his view when he first came to England, but that was a long time ago. He had grown. He was no longer greedy for power in the Jewish establishment.

He smiled and unlocked his filing cabinet. He drew out an album from the second drawer. He had time to enjoy this before he went about his special work.

This album was his most recent acquisition. It came from the moment he had changed his mind. He wanted something Jewish, after all, because he had once owned something very precious and Jewish.

He had begun to collect war memorabilia. He had a collection of World War II material he would show visitors, but hidden behind every army badge and every Food Ministry education pamphlet were three items that were as closely linked to the

Third Reich as he could manage. He didn't much like the Third Reich, but he saw that Hitler's people also changed the world to meet their needs.

This album had a nice collection of World War II ration books from several countries. Behind them were hidden papers from various camps. Each one of them celebrated a dead person. That was not what the papers said literally, of course, But it was how Rupert saw them. Old paper full of the memory of murders.

Rupert didn't let Nazi ideals govern his behaviour. Not his everyday behaviour and not his recruitment to change the world. He found people who supported his dream, but he also found people who had dreams of their own.

One of his goals required political and social destabilisation, so he helped those who sought to change the universe. Some people wanted to change the universe to find help for those who were being hurt in their own society. These people he applauded and made sure they had help.

If the walls of the universe could be broken down to bring refugees in or the doors could be open to allow undesirable refugees out, as Earth1 had achieved with Tsarfat, he would not be unhappy. He would close doors again once those refugees were gone. Then, finally, he would close the door to Tsarfat.

One of his students had complained when they had been told they had no excuse but to write about the topic "That Hitler was successful." That student would never know that Rupert had suggested it in the early tests of what worked to change the culture.

His public research project, the one all his work led towards, was to make people question what they were given as truth. "Get students thinking outside the box" had been his official excuse. His reason was to begin here, where he belonged, and to get the ball rolling on that cultural change. His secret project had been that he wanted to question anything that didn't give him the position he craved. He was honest with himself about it. He wanted students to think that Hitler had done well, for Hitler being seen as a hero suited him.

Today. Everything would start its spiral into its delightful and inevitable conclusion today. And the world would find out too late.

Today his flash mob approach to scientific experiment would finally add to the calls he had put out for educated people to join him. Normally, people from his background were described as superheroes because of their skills. Rupert saw himself more as the founder of Hydra.

He was going to achieve his goals by playing on the emotional needs of the sad and the lonely. He had made them doubt their own privilege. For five years now, they had told themselves that the world was hurting them.

Initially, his targeted supporters hadn't been interested. Only one of the people he'd approached on the internet for his first big project, using his alias, wanted to join him. The others were all, "Not today, dear." He changed his tactics. Then he changed them again. When an aspect of his work resonated, he used it. Gradually, he found his path and brought his people in to walk it.

He had recruited gradually. When someone's life was damaged, he approached them, recruited them, trained them. When a country's economy went bust, he looked for more recruits. He didn't have many followers, and they were almost all white male. They would do the job.

One group had defected, but no-one believed its members when they talked about it. His disloyal followers had faded into a quiet rumble, like one of the many failed portal attempts. He had successfully turned all the Jewish conspiracy theories out to play, so the actual conspiracy wasn't taken so seriously.

Rupert smiled. *I am very good at my work*, he told himself. *Also. It's time.*

Chapter Five

"I wish they'd turn the lights off so I can cry in peace." Data's voice filled the room.

Some people lost their voices under stress, Data's voice grew to fill a room. Ariette thought this often, then reflected that 'often' only meant recently.

I need to know more, she thought. *I can't put it off any longer.*

It had been easy not to talk about it when they first met, when Data herself needed time and space and to be busy. All those things Ari could give. Persuasive speech was harder. Not as hard as first names, but still almost impossible.

Data came from such a different background to her own. Same schooling, same training, same so many things. Same streets, same hovercars and velos, same everything public. It wasn't that hero moment when she carried her brother home that made Data different. It was her upbringing. Their private lives had been very different.

Ari had to get over treating that single difference as a major stumbling block. She had to be the mentor she had intended to be. It was time to talk.

"Telling us about your brother can't have been easy." That

was the best she could do.

"It never is." Data's voice didn't reflect the existential gloom of the words. As it so often did, it reflected the deep reality, which, in this case, included tears and an ever-open wound. "We were tricked by our mentor. He set it all up."

"You were what?" No wonder this girl was distant. Ari knew that Chevalier had not done well but never that he had achieved a personal goal in so doing.

"Monsieur Chevalier had all the right words to tell us we were doing the right thing. You know Chevalier?"

"Everyone does. But how did he convince the committees to let both of you come? I've never understood that."

"Same way he convinced us both to cross through. Only Mum saw him for what he was. He made Mum's life hell for that, starting the day they met. Now, she has no children, her life is even more hell, and it's lonely. One day, I will get even with Monsieur Chevalier."

"Getting even is something I considered once. Let me tell you about my childhood."

"I'm not sure this is going to be good listening." Data sounded flippant. That upbringing of hers was dauntingly impolite at times.

"It's something that most of our families live with every day. Yours doesn't because your mother isn't from that same background. That would be how Chevalier got through. Your mother was different."

"He kept reminding everyone of that."

"You know everything, but I'm not sure you've put it together."

"What do you mean?"

"What is our religion in Tsarfat?"

"Judaism—except for odd families like me and the Chevaliers."

"Correct. Why are so many of us Jewish?" Ari felt like a schoolteacher. She had to do this. She had to remind Data of the obvious, and it was going to hurt.

"I've never really thought about it. I hated history."

"Your mother knew. She told us when she taught us English that she was allowed to make Christian jokes if she wanted. She was defiant about it."

"That's Mum. She argues everything. Except I always thought of us as atheist."

"She told us that your father was …" This was not going in the right direction. Ari needed a better approach. "Wait … I know how to explain this. Tell me about your father's parents. Where were they born?"

"Germany, before World War II. They had been working in France, so when they tried to rebel against Occupation, they were put into a camp in France, and they fled with all kinds of other people and found Tsarfat, and I can't believe I'm so damn stupid."

"You've got it?" Ari felt relieved. All she had needed was the right approach to take this first step.

"My family was discriminated against because of Mum. No Hitler in her background."

"That's right. Not even the amount of Hitler your father had."

"How much did Dad have, do you know? Half Hitler? A quarter Hitler?"

"That's your mother again." Ari couldn't stop her voice from sounding disapproving. "Halves and quarters are like half Jewish and quarter Jewish. Eugenics. They put us Jews in our place as not quite human. Potential humans, but we can be divided into halves and quarters and even eighths. 'Mischling' was one of the names for what you call halves and quarters."

"Leading to discrimination if you're lucky and death if you're not. Those classes all come back to me. I didn't realise I knew this stuff." Data's voice sounded as if she was torn between wonder and self-hate.

"We were never supposed to be born." Ari tried to keep this conversational, but she had a lot of trouble even saying it. Stuff she knew and stuff everyone knew was sometimes stuff that didn't bear talking about. "None of the Jews in Tsarfat are supposed to be alive. Our grandparents and great-grandparents were scheduled to be sent to death camps. When they ran from Drancy and the other transit camps, they fled death. That would have been the end of it. Our parents and grandparents escaped, and we live with that."

"I thought the whole thing we do to heal the world was because of the Jewish bit. The religion."

"That's what we're taught at school. At home, we're taught, 'Don't let this happen again. Don't let people hurt the way we were hurt. Ici-nous. We are here; we have survived.'"

"Then how did everyone fail my parents? Come on," Data's voice was rough, "My father was murdered!"

"We're still working on that. Like we're working on the attitudes of those whose families teach them 'We still hide' about the outside world. The children in primary school, you know, the ones who say that."

"I know them. They won't learn about any outside. They want to be safe."

"I love Tsarfat so much it hurts, but it is wounded. Ici-nous is not a gentle comfort. It is defiance of the world and challenges the past, and it hides a history of hurt."

Data's voice settled. "I want to find my father's killers. And I want to find out how Chevalier persuaded the committees to allow both of us to be in the trials and why no-one investigated my brother's death."

"What?" The sudden jump in topics disconcerted Ari.

"No-one did the standard medical tests on his body. No-one. They said that we didn't really need them and that it would help Mum if she didn't have to deal with more tests because of the ones she had when she arrived. But what if it wasn't?"

"What if someone hates your family that much?"

"Precisely. And my mother is alone. At home. With no-one looking out for her."

"You can't go back yet. I mean, physically. I'm sorry about this, but I can't let you."

Data's voice was wounded. "I know. That's why I got systems upgrades from the Paris office. I asked for help because of my situation, and so they gave me much better equipment than I was scheduled to have. That's why you can send messages to your mother. Why I can actually talk to mine. And you can help me if she's in danger. Please."

"I thought you were crying for your brother." Ari was gentle but puzzled.

"I always do. I cry for all of them. My father and my brother and my mother. I love Tsarfat too, but it hurt my family. It's still hurting my family."

"Yet you are giving our causes your life."

"I'm not Jewish, but I'm from Tsarfat. It's not Mum's home, but it's mine. Ici-nous is mine too. Chevalier had one thing impossibly right when he talked us into standing for these jobs: we care. My brother and I wanted to heal Tsarfat."

"The way my parents taught me to want to heal the world." Ari's voice was so soft, she thought Data would never hear.

"Too damn right," said Data.

"Tell me," Ari said. "What happened. Make it personal. I need to understand."

"Why?" There were many questions layered into that single word.

"Because I'm going to help you."

Ari could hear the big breath Data took.

"Can we get more coffee first?"

They did this. Giant cups of milky morning coffee. Un English. Un Australian. Very much the stuff of Tsarfat. Except the Tsarfat coffee was chicory and was earth. The brand name exploited this taste; "Fruit of the Earth", the label said, "Coffee, Ha Adamah." Data was so nostalgic in that moment. She started her story in Tsarfat itself, with the dream of that drink replacing the real coffee in front of her.

"That last day, I walked with Bob up rue Canal. It was the long way from our place to the door, but we wanted to do the thing properly. Mum joined us halfway. She'd done all her official duties except for being there while her students went through and graduated and became … whatever. So there were the three of us, and we all talked in English. Everyone who passed us gave us looks because of that. English! They never said anything, but they looked at us just so, then they recognised Mum and shrugged their shoulders."

"She's special, your mother."

It was Data's turn to shrug her shoulders in a certain way. Ari reflected that Data was truly of Tsarfat, no matter how odd her ancestry. That shrug said it all. "Yeah, all her students say that. For everyone else, it's special in all the wrong ways. They let her be herself because they're not going to let her be part of everyday society."

"Because she speaks English."

"I thought it was that, when I was little. I'd speak English whenever I could as a defence of my mother. I don't think it was that, though. I think it's because of what happened to Papa."

"We failed him." This was one thing Ari was certain about.

"Those boys murdered him, and everyone knows it, and no-one stopped it."

"It triggered so many memories."

"That trigger means that everyone's hung up on it never happening again, and when it does … they're frozen. Caught in their own nightmare. That's what we were talking about by the canal. Mum made sure we understood that we didn't have to make up for what other people couldn't do. That it wasn't our responsibility."

"Your mother gave you a reminder?"

"You mean one of those teaching things she does? Of course she did. That's why I remember every damn inch of rue Canal."

"Can you explain it? I think … I think I also need what she taught you."

The explanation Data gave was slow and soft. Her distress no longer filled a room. To an outsider listening in, it would have been almost monotonous, but Ariette Green was transfixed. There was no outside world. There was only Tsarfat and its leaving.

✡

I had a thought as we strolled slowly. There's no canal there. You know it and I know it, and the whole of Tsarfat knows it. There's that little stream that's so deep no-one ever goes in it unless they're pushed, but it's a natural waterway, and yet the street is rue Canal. I turned to Mum and asked her, and she laughed.

"Bob can tell you," she said. "He had to know when he was ten. He has special friends on this street."

"I wish Madame Cohen were still alive," he said wistfully.

I racked my brains. We knew three Cohen families, but I didn't think any of them lived near here. One was from that big mining family that is so dominant down south. Another was at school with me and married a mohel. They were both too young, but the families got together, and

*they finished their degrees and had children at the same time. The third?
I can't remember the third. I thought maybe the house we were standing
outside was hers?*

Bob said, *"The family doesn't live here anymore. Old Madame
Cohen wanted everything sold and then divided equally. She couldn't
stand quarrels. She was with the big wave of arrivals here, and when
everyone argued over the name of the stream, apparently, in the early
nineteen forties, she put down her foot and said, 'My house is here. I
used to live next to a canal.' And that was that."*

"This is one of the old streets," I said.

*All the houses were built in the 1920s and 30s. After the first humans
came but before your families. They were Art Deco and very upmarket.
Bob's friend's heir had a decent inheritance. I love that red brick and
white pointing in the old streets. If ever I get enough money, I'd like
one of those houses. I know they don't take flying cars well because they
were built nearly a hundred years ago, but I can manage without that
upstairs door if I have those little busts holding my shutters closed.*

Ari didn't mean to interrupt, but she did anyway. "I saw
them in Amiens. Not like ours, but busts of soldiers or women
or something small holding the doors closed and sitting upside
down when the doors were open."

*"I went through Amiens too quickly," Data said with remorse.
"Next time. I'll see them next time. Anyhow ..."*

*We ambled. There was always the possibility of us not having time
together, so we ambled. Mum had to go early because she was part of the
official group sending everyone on their way, but we two had the usual
appointed time and had been told that we should relax. That's why Bob
and I stopped at a café on the way and had a last drink together. I miss
our coffee. The drink here may be more correctly coffee, but it's not our
coffee. Nothing like it.*

*The last cup of our coffee I had was with Bob. My mouth still
remembers that rich milk and the flavour of the earth. That drink is*

home to me.

For Bob, it's the buildings. He could tell you every single brick and where they were made and what they meant to the building. Papa wanted him to become an architect, or maybe an historian. Bob knew that, and he thought one day, he could follow his talents, but we had obligations first.

That's what we talked about in the café. That we had to be there. Not because it was unsafe and we were full of daring. I act that way. Inside, I'm not that.

Bob was better than me. He was better than everyone. He told me, when we were in that café near the Mairie, that there was something wrong. That Mum wasn't the suspicious and worried and lonely person we thought. That she was mistreated.

"I researched it," he said. "I left a letter. If I don't come back, make sure the letter is read. Please?"

"Of course," I said.

"Promise me!" Passion whirled out. I thought just then that his magic was going to be about his eyes and about that whirlpool of emotion and about his capacity to attract promises.

"I promise," I said, and the whirlpool subsided.

There's nothing to tell you about the ceremonials. Well, our mentor was shunned. Not by us. We were very polite to Monsieur Chevalier. It was everyone else. Maybe they finally found out what he had done to Mum? I don't know. I can't ask. Anyhow, we were polite, but the moment we'd finished doing the polite, we joined Mum. On our way between the two of them, Bob dug me with his elbow and said, "The letter. There are two."

"Two?"

"Two letters. Don't forget." He himself forgot, and he expected me not to forget. Brothers!

We stayed with Mum as long as we could. We talked about this and that. Mostly her garden. Whenever we need a safe topic to talk about with Mum, we talk to her about the vegetables she's going to grow and about the fruit trees. She's so proud of her fruit trees. She promised a roast dinner when we came back and said that the potatoes might even be ready for us. We all knew they wouldn't be because it was not at all the right time of year, but we said, 'We're hungry already.'

Her roast dinners are nothing like yours. Some of the food is the same here as at Mum's, but not her roast dinner. I'm so hungry for the lamb and the rosemary and the potatoes and the vegies and the salad and … Sorry. I lost myself in memory. Have you noticed that David does that all the time? I think it's infectious.

I remember when you went through the door. Everyone lined up, watching. You saluted terribly jauntily and then walked through the door alone.

Once you'd walked into that blackness, we had to wait. I thought of all those exits when I went up to that door. I should know if I went through before Bob or after him, but I don't. I don't remember saluting. I remember thinking, "I need to ask Bob about that damned second letter." Then I was through, into the tunnel.

Bob and I took the route together. Neither of us felt anything odd. That was strange in itself. It was odd to be experiencing and even more odd to be talking about it.

All our training was exactly like yours, and it emphasised how alone we would be from the moment we walked through the door until the moment we completed our task. Then we could go to one of the offices on this Earth and be tested and find out what we'd become. Then, when we were physically ready, we'd come home, be feted, and be tested fully. So much of that didn't happen. I was tested in the Amiens office both times. Not at home. Never at home. I didn't even get a graduation ceremony.

Bob was chatty. I asked him about symptoms, and he said nothing. Not a skerrick. I didn't feel anything either. An hour later, still nothing.

We were negotiating the maze that protects the door, and we were suddenly both happy and sharing those little grins. We were going to get through the test just fine and could go on our little quest and then report in and then come back and be assigned to the rest of our lives.

Still, I had to be thorough. "The letter," I said.

"I wrote one accusing Chevalier," he said calmly.

We passed the skull and crossbones. That's why I remembered that letter when I came back the other way. I saw the skull and crossbones, and I thought about what Bob had said. I nearly asked him then and there, but he'd stopped talking, so I kept walking.

"The other letter is for the scientists. I did the tests they asked after they'd done my DNA study but couldn't get some of the material back in time. I also did some of the ones that we normally do after. I wasn't happy with the tests Chevalier listed and decided to take the time and do the rest. Better science. It's not an important letter, but it will help them document all this."

"Not important? Then why write it?"

"There were so many things wrong with our door prep. Why didn't they start tests a year before and do follow-up the way they did for other candidates? Why were we both pushed into the programme? I wanted to make sure all the paperwork was done."

I don't know what his face looked like. That bugged me. We had torches, but we had to watch the ground because it was a very dark tunnel. We needed to catch the signs and go right, left, up, down, sideways, and not to walk into a mine. I know those signs stop strangers from finding us, but they're very hard to watch for with just torches when, really, one wants to talk deeply to one's brother. The stuff he said was dreadfully worrying.

Alone would've been freakier. I was very glad I wasn't there alone. I tripped four times. Four! Each time, Bob caught me and laughed. Bob never tripped. Bob was born a superhero.

Eventually, we made it into sunlight. We walked to the station as if it was where one caught a real train, almost like back home. Except the train ran on rails and everything was foreign and not foreign, both at once.

Once we were at the station in Amiens, our quests diverged. I didn't feel alone at all. I'd stolen Bob's phone the night before, during that drinks party, and I'd put a tracer on it. I knew he'd get lost looking at architecture and I wanted to be able to find him.

My job was in Arras. At that point, I thought, "More caves." Then I was distracted, because ...

"Because?" Ari prompted.

"I could hear my technology. That was the moment I knew how my world had changed. It was nothing like what I'd expected. Hearing isn't something I've ever found easy, and now the tools I used to make it possible were ... more than hearing aids. I loved this so much. I could change the colours on my devices even though they'd only been designed to have on-off lights in one colour, and use them to ... so much. So very much. I tripped over something, and then there was this glow. It took me too long to find out that the glow came from me, that it was my hearing aids. My magic moment."

Her voice was soft and breathy. Ari nodded. Life changed when one went from Tsarfat to Earth.

"You can hear?"

"No more than before. I still need apparatus. I can do a lot more with the apparatus, that's all. I took those pictures with it the other day. Didn't you know?"

"I knew you sent those pictures quickly, but I didn't see the pictures. I didn't know they were different to other pictures."

"They're not that different. I'm not sharing the extent of my abilities with home until I've found out what happened to Bob. I faked a camera to my ears through my eyes and kinda edited as I went. The pictures looked like they came from a phone, is all. And that sounds so cute. I'm going to make that joke again. Should I stop the story? You know the rest."

"I'm not sure I know the rest of your story. Please, finish."

My task was in Arras. I had to go into the old tunnels and check to see if there was anything that linked them to us and our tunnels because something had happened. They didn't tell me what because they wanted new eyes. I checked the war tunnels, which are a tourist version of something a bit like our own tunnels. Terribly depressing, of course, but well-maintained and neat for the New Zealanders, the guide said. I checked the old tunnels under the town centre after that. They're from long before the war, but they were open to tourists. There were storage facilities, and they had access to the town and all kinds of good things like wine cellars. Nothing led to us. I reported back that if anything had happened there, nothing showed.

The office replied, "Good. And how unexpected to hear from you."

"Was I not supposed to call in?" I was so surprised.

"You ought to be out of reach for the duration."

"Must be my change."

"Must be. We'll take a note of it. You still need to spend three more days out there, otherwise, your body will pay for the change. We'll switch off so you can't be tempted to ring in again."

No-one had told me I was supposed to be on radio silence. Too late. Also too late for Bob, because he and I had taken our phones with us and promised to keep in touch. This was Bob's idea. He wouldn't say why he needed to keep in touch. That and letters meant I rang him that night in Arras. I didn't know I could talk to other computers directly yet. I'd done it when I phoned home, but I thought the phone was doing the work. That is why I texted Bob.

The message went, but he didn't reply. I rang him. He didn't answer. I thought, "Maybe I was wrong and he was hurt coming out through the tunnels. Maybe he's not one of those of us who live." I needed to know so very desperately; I pinged his phone.

His task was in Amiens, and his phone was in Villers Bretonneux. I caught the last train to Amiens and then a taxi to Villers Bretonneux.

No-one back home questioned the amount of money I spent when all was done, which puzzles me now, but then, I didn't care. I wanted to find Bob.

I found my brother along the side of the road, just outside the old museum to Australian soldiers. The one attached to the primary school. Mum's grandparents helped build that school in Earth1 when Australians decided to help with the rebuild after the world war. Bob was lying down on the street outside it on this Earth. He was alive, but not quite conscious. His bag was gone. He had his phone, and he had his wallet. Nothing else.

I told the taxi driver that he was drunk and took Bob back to Amiens. I didn't know what else to do. I couldn't take him to a hospital. I hadn't been told where the Amiens office was, I never asked why. I thought I'd been tagged or something and they'd find me.

I needed to get Bob home. I was almost out of money, which meant that what I wanted to do, which was to take a taxi as close to home as possible, wasn't going to work. I was told I did the right thing because that taxi would have led people to us. They're wrong when they say that. Chevalier is wrong, and the officials are wrong, and everyone's wrong. Bob needed help.

We sat all night in the station at Amiens. Bob was more conscious some of the time, and he told me things, and I wrote down every word. Someone had told him to go to the museum to find out ... but he never said what. Or who.

He couldn't eat, but I made sure he drank water. We caught the first train the next morning and took another taxi to bring him closer to home, for I wasn't sure he could walk. I had no money left after that, but I didn't care.

The taxi left me in the middle of what looked like nowhere. The driver was worried about my brother and about me and wanted to take us to a hospital. I said that someone was coming to pick us up. He argued with me, and I argued back. I was so tired.

Bob said, "You have to go," and the driver accepted that, and left us. To this day, I don't know why the driver accepted "You have to go." Bob's change never took, that's what I'm told. All my theories about him and what he'd become were irrelevant. Still, the driver still left us without a word.

Things got worse again. Bob fell in and out of consciousness, so I left my backpack where I could find it later, and I carried him.

"Across fields and down tunnels," Ari said. "Everyone talked about it. You were almost instantly legendary. No-one's ever brought someone from their own cohort home before. It's always been someone like me going out and finding them and bringing them home."

"They told you what happened when I came through the door?"

"Everyone was waiting for you."

"Bob was dead."

"P'tite, he died before you could get him home. The experts say that he would never have lived. His body didn't accept the change. You did all you could."

"I have not yet done all I can. Not even close. Bob felt no pain when we travelled together—it looked as if the change would be smooth. I want to find out why Bob was in Villers Bretonneux. I want to find that letter. There are three loose ends, and they are big ones."

"You can't. Besides, we have official paths for these things. The Bureau, for one."

Data snapped, "The people in the Bureau are lying. They told me my experience is invalid and my evidence was affected by returning too soon. They told me to leave it alone and to focus on my work. They've told everyone that Bob died from the change. What if he didn't? I was with him for all the critical moments. Neither he nor I felt pain during that time. Right up to when I left him at Amiens, neither of us felt any pain. The most he should have had was mild illness, according to our training. They trained you the same way, am I right? Mild illness? Not death? Not if he had none of the twinges and funny visions. I know this because we walked together down the dark road to France. No-one asked me about that, and no-one did the regulation autopsy. They didn't check. They ordered him to be buried straight away."

"What? No autopsy? That's not standard. You said that before, didn't you? Why? Why did the Department say such things? Why didn't they do the usual work?"

"I'm not Jewish, remember? My value is lower."

Ari understood the bitter voice and the bleak face. "I didn't think it was that bad."

"Nor did I. I thought that Mum was complaining the way Mum does. How could my father be killed? How can her career be affected? I always thought these things were her layering thoughts of evil onto sadness."

"You carried your brother all that way, and your brain was working the whole time."

"Not the whole time. Towards the end, it was all I could do to keep walking. I couldn't stop. I didn't stop. I hurt all through, and forever it felt as if all I could do was one step forward, then lift the other leg and move one step forward, then lift the other leg and … eventually I was dragging one leg, then dragging the other leg. As long as I moved forward, I told myself. One step, then one step, then one step. Get to this vaulted bit, then to the skull and crossbones. Small goals, then one step and one step and one step. I don't know how I made it to the door and through it, and I don't know how I stood there when I entered home, and I don't know how I waited for someone to take Bob from me. That last bit was beyond appalling. An eternity of pain. Earlier, though, was hard, but I could still think. As I walked from the taxi to the tunnels, I thought. And when the tunnels were straight in that first stretch, I thought. I tried to work out why Bob was kilometres from where he was expected to be and why he didn't have his backpack, and then I thought of the letters. I put him down and checked, and there were no letters in his wallet."

"None? I thought you said he had one with him?"

"He had. Then he hadn't. I don't know when it went. Maybe it just fell out when I walked with him. That letter was released when he died. Mum found a copy in her desk. I think it must've been a backup for her in case things went wrong and she was all alone. That was the one that accused Chevalier. The other … nowhere. And he said stuff when I found him. I don't want to talk about it until I know more because I don't want to jinx this. I want answers. I'll take time if I must, but I need those answers."

"I think …" Ari felt herself being carried over a cliff. "I think I agree with you. We all need answers."

"If our mission takes us out that way, you'll understand if I add it to our list of things to do."

Ari nodded. "If we're asked, then you need to find his things and bring them home for your mother."

"I've got some friends here from before. I wanted to ask them to check to see if anyone's handed something in somewhere."

"Before? What before is this?"

"Nothing to be angry about. It's perfectly legal. Ever since I was a kid, I've helped test the computer links to the rest of this world back home because I had English through Mum and German through Papa and French the way we all do, and I joined chat rooms and social media. I'm allowed to stay in contact and so forth as long as I don't tell them who I am or where I come from. It's partly so that we can test new systems and partly because the Bureau wants to know how this world works. You must've guessed that I knew more than the regular new recruit?"

"I did, but I thought it was your mother telling you about her childhood."

"Her childhood was nothing like this. She came from our original Earth, for one thing, and she's old enough so that the first computer she used was in Tsarfat. Earth1 was not techo the way we are either. They have computers now, but when she was a child, it was television and telephones and writing by hand. She grew up with corded phones and with corner shops and with friends who all lived in the same street. She told me once that her mother knew how to use a typewriter."

"So, what do you tell these strangers online? To hide where you come from?

"They all think I'm French but good with languages."

"But won't they know that you aren't from this world?"

"You do know that very few people even believe that there are alternate Earths? Really. What's everyday for us is not believable to even die-hard science fiction fans. Also, we've got something in common. We all love our science fiction. Some of my friends want our Tsarfati techo, and others want an alternate Earth where there is no magic. I've set up two other-mes, and one works for each."

"Other-mes?"

"Other me: a pretend person that is visiting from an alternate world and occasionally slips up. It's the rage. That might be partly my fault, because one group of my friends is very central in the science fiction world, and I started to say that other-me was better than other me because of ici-nous. I stopped before I got to ici-nous, but that's when the words started being run together. The phrase wasn't me at all; it was a group of friends getting drunk at a Stockholm convention and online with me. They were watching cosplayers and talking about how the best of them adopted the full character. I don't remember everyone who was there, but I remember one woman in particular. Fia. She introduced me to dillchips that night. Dillchips and other-me and comparing gadgets–enough to cement a friendship."

"Let's get away from your Swedish friends and back to the situation. If someone finds out that you're real and that you live one life that connects worlds?"

"Got that sorted too. Other-mes are handy. So are science fiction fans."

"Explain, please." Ariette was suddenly weary.

"None of them know the real me. None of them know the link with Big Ben. None of them know because there are so many of us who use false names."

"How is this even possible?"

"It's like cosplay," Data said, trying to be helpful. Ari wasn't certain that the effort achieved anything except a certain curiosity about dillchips. "While I'm pretending to be someone else, everyone accepts me as that someone else."

"They can look you up."

"They can. There are some brilliant computer people in our mob. They're not going to, though. Because they'd be hacking my pretend self. None of them know I'm hard of hearing even, except my dillchips friend because we talked devices that once. I'm in character the whole time I'm online or at a convention. They won't get that the places I talk about are real and that Mum comes from one and I come from the other. I hide behind imagined realities. It's a lot of fun."

"How can you know this works?" Ari was more worried than she thought she'd be.

"I tested it. Mum calls Tsarfat 'Jewish Wakanda,' and I dropped the name, and so many people jumped up and down about me using that term. It's wrong, they told me. It's cultural appropriation, several people said; even though, honestly, it doesn't come from anything ancient in Africa; it comes from somewhere modern in America. That's the argument I use to defend Mum's use of the term. I've decided it's wrong to use it because it hurts people, whether it's appropriative or not. I'm not going to tell Mum off, though, because she thinks she's being funny and I'm the only one who listens to her and she has dealt with quite enough. Do you realise that we don't talk about cultural appropriation in Tsarfat? Anyhow, I was called so many names because I was guilty of it. Some were rather vile. My favourite was 'milquetoast liberal.' All of them caused people to check where I came from, and I tracked each check, and every single investigation came to nothing. Not quite nothing. I've got some great files on nice people who get angry over all the wrong things. Some left wing. Some right wing. Some don't know what wings are. I should add them to our data set for this mission."

"People wanted to hurt you over that term, though."

"Not really; discipline me, rather. I'm very careful around them because a few of them are do-gooders without souls. I live in a complex online environment."

"Complex enough that you can hide in plain sight?"

"Precisely."

"Can we use this?"

"Maybe. Depends on what we need it for."

"Don't put this in any report, but stay online. Talk to your friends. Document what you see needs documenting. We may need it."

"Is this your gift showing? Or is this superhero policy?"

Ari twisted her head in slight doubt. "My gift is pure weather. You know this. And don't call it superhero policy. I hate it so much that people call us superheroes. I don't see how we can be super or heroes. It's one of those tags that sound cute but are very uncomfortable."

"Your thing is not at all like me and my thing, by the way. You want sunshine, and it comes. I didn't realise. I thought I was strange because everyone else has such obvious gifts. I thought I'd be able to fly or walk undersea. You're the first person I've met who has anything in common with me. I thought it was your gift, but it isn't. It's your reluctance to be seen as superhero-ish. We both hide in plain sight."

"When I do weather, I reach. I make the feeling of the weather part of my surroundings. I gave David such a headache in Newcastle because lighting and thunder always gives headaches. It's their properties when linked to my talent. I can't tell you if I press a mental switch to use the weather or if I'm always capable. It feels like part of me."

"Mine is the same and not the same. I don't know the difference between being online and being magically online. Paris wanted to test me and find out when they gave me my early treatment, but I refused."

"Why?"

"Super strong would be an easy gift, but this one? It's subtle. I need it to be part of me not quizzed gently away by excited researchers. We've both got unusual things, haven't we?"

"That's why there are only two of us for this particular job. Our unusual things are worth ten times the amount of someone who can punch the air and fly."

"Wouldn't mind being able to fly," Data offered wistfully. "And punching the air is so very much my kind of SF. Can we change my pretend first name to Rosie? Or maybe Rose, because Rosie Data looks funny. If I'm going to have subtle power, it will be Rosie the Riveter power."

"It's about time. I'll get the paperwork done and you can pick up your fake French passport when we get back to London."

"One thing I won't miss is cheating to get through borders."

"You won't say that when you've been through a queue or two."

"Don't bet on that. My mother's Australian, don't forget. She likes queues. She talks to people and feeds them biscuits to encourage people to queue because, she says, she still misses it. And, by the way ..."

"Yes?

"Thank you. That was good mentoring. You didn't even shut me up when I told you things you know better than I do."

"A part of it was mentoring. The rest I needed to know. We'll find out about your brother. I promise."

✡

Meanwhile, elsewhere, another quiet moment happened so gently that only one person knew about it.

There was a grave. On it, a young woman had just put a big bunch of flowers.

"It feels wrong to put flowers here," she said conversationally. "Your mother said that her family puts flowers on graves, though, so I've chosen some very pretty geraniums for you. They're from rue Canal. I stole them from the old family garden. Flowers are the proper Christian thing to do. You told me so. I know you're an atheist, but you're a Christian atheist. My Christian atheist. You were going to change the world for me and for your mother. I need to find your sister so that I can change the world for myself and so that no-one has to go through what we've been through. I don't know what I'm going to do yet. I promise, though, I'll leave your mother out of it. She's been through enough."

She nodded to herself and bent her head for a moment, then walked away, her tears quite invisible in the rain.

✡

There was movement. Finally. After much investigation and even, maybe, a little interrogation.

Questioning of the interwebs and the contacts the culprits had unwillingly provided from Newcastle had given three addresses in Amiens … and none anywhere else. They finally had a place to start: Amiens. Benedicta's people (351 of them if one counted the entire Office for the Non-Natural) had finally, maybe, pulled their weight.

Benedicta had to attend a funeral first.

This funeral was Reform. A Continental family again, arrived after the War. Most of the usual but done somehow in a more European way. Less British. More ritual, maybe. A proper shiva with sawn-down chairs.

Benedicta noted that more government had turned up to this moment of mourning. Not just her; she recognised the group of government officers. They were not from the Merlin's office but from one of the Departments that occasionally worked with him. This led to thoughts, and those thoughts left her mouth dry and sour.

This means the government (other than me) knows that these cases are linked. I find this unutterably depressing. The government knew so much and did so little. A scattering of people assigned. Just a few resources.

This event left Benedicta too much time to dwell on what she was unhappy about. Benedicta had not been happy that her cousin's office had done all the backup for Newcastle and that the data sent on to her people had already been processed. It indicated that her personal abilities and those of her Office had not been brought to bear on the matter.

Since the count of deaths was now at five, this was unforgivable.

She had no choice but to forgive the Merlin, but a small part of her remained angry. It was this part that propelled her to go on the next journey with her new sidekicks. She hadn't been this hands-on in years. Benedicta reminded herself that she hadn't been in her twenties for thirty years and she needed to be gentle with herself. She reminded herself that the data that led them to Amiens was her opposition's best guess and her people hadn't been able to check the core of the material.

It didn't matter what she reminded herself of, nor how often she reminded herself, she could not stay in London and wait for more incidents to kill more innocents. She needed to taste the air and make her own conclusions.

The Office of the Merlin didn't know Data's full story. Ari had shared an overview of it with Benedicta herself, however, so she thought about how it changed the small amount of information they had. Instead of fluttering papers in the back of the car, she planned—a lot to do and not a long time to do it in, but worth it for the results. More data on Data and maybe some understanding of how the incidents linked to Tsarfat, that was what they were headed to Amiens for. It was not merely a missing link, it was a *big* missing link.

She told her special team when she had dealt with the usual fuss at the office. Benedicta knew she should not be handling this case herself but … sometimes the only person for a job is the one who no longer does fieldwork.

"We're going to be watched," Data said. "They know we've found out stuff."

"Goes without saying." Ari nodded. "We need someone monitoring that back here and chasing up our leads. David?" Her question was sent towards Benedicta, for David was getting the team cups of hot drink. 'Hot drink' had been his terminology, for both the Green girls had asked for chicory. He was told the single café had chicory as an option, and he had sighed. 'Chicory' was not part of his lexicon.

"Boat is better, plane is faster." Benedicta was her usual short but adamant self. She was being kind, she thought, in offering options.

"Fast is not so good for my implants; rapid changes in altitude affect them. I'll need recovery time."

Benedicta nodded to show she had added that factor into her equation.

"How much?"

"Three hours, minimum."

"Not good," said Benedicta, thinking aloud. "Slows us down too much. Also, I can't Chunnel without pain." Admitting the physical restrictions brought on by age was difficult.

Ari suggested a compromise. Fast trip with change recovery time. "We can find my favourite big green chairs when we get to the airport/station changeover bit. By the time we get on the train, we'll all be fine."

Data made a mild protest, but was overruled. Benedicta's own assessment was that Data had recovered from much worse than a short plane flight and she was the youngest and fittest of the team. "You'll be right," said Benedicta, venturing a mild Australian joke that both girls missed.

Life is never as simple as it looks.

The flight to Paris was no drama. Even getting through to the French side of things was no drama. By the time they were through, however, Data was looking the wrong kind of green.

She was in considerable pain by the time they reached the station. The Charles de Gaulle/Roissy Grandes Lignes corner of the station/airport/everything complex had several groups of chairs that would indeed have offered Data the privacy she needed to recover from the flight. But not a single cluster of seats was free.

It took half an hour of looking, with Data fragmenting and fading further and further, before they found even one seat. Benedicta and Ariette put Data in that one seat and surrounded her with luggage.

"You can't turn off your hearing," Benedicta said. "There's no time."

"I need to turn off the implants. Everything's inflamed. Give me an hour," Data said. Her face was pale and the green showed. Benedicta knew she was wrong to not give the recovery time, but she wasn't certain she had a choice.

"An hour, then. Ariette, you keep watch here. I'll get us all some coffee."

"Not coffee for us today," said Ari. "The caffeine will be too much, I think. Something hot would be good, though."

"Leave it with me," Benedicta said.

There was a small queue at the café, and as she waited in it, Bennie considered her options. If the girls only drank coffee like regular Frenchwomen, there would be no choices to make and life would be easier. But then, if they weren't from Tsarfat, she'd be stuck in London. She wanted a bit of adventure, just this once. *It's not that I actually enjoy adventure,* she amended to herself. *It's that I was too senior too early, and I was forbidden it. The forbidden is attractive. Always has been.* She briefly thought of Bart and thought of Rupert, but there was no repining. She was better off without both.

At least she wasn't among the various members of her line who had intermarried. "No-one understands us as well as ourselves," had been the cartoon comment when the first engagement between a Merlin and a senior Jewish magician had taken place in the early nineteenth century. She had been persuaded out of doing the same thing herself and was surprised, retrospectively, that it had been something she had even considered. As an adult, the prospect looked just a bit stupid. She and her cousin were not suited to life together and never had been.

A friend who commented, apparently randomly, that England was becoming Pharaonic in its marriages for senior magicians had brought her to heel. Not before she and her cousin had a child together, but that child was another story. Many other stories. That child was irrepressible.

Benedicta still dreamed of finding someone who spoke her language. Her cousin didn't, but he was closer than anyone else. She was less alone when he dropped in, smiling and preparing to play political swords.

Bennie didn't trust him, for she knew him too well. He was a politician by choice and was going to be the first Merlin to become Prime Minister sometime soon. Benedicta was political only because her job required it, and the job pretty well chose her. No-one wanted her in it, but no-one had a choice.

That strong negative wherever she went and whatever work she'd done had hobbled her. Benedicta Beja was proud and would never tell anyone this. She wore her spinster's weeds with grace.

When she came back with hot drinks, Data was still a mess. They had been off the plane for forty minutes. That would have to be sufficient. Time for briefing. She beckoned to Data to turn on her hearing aids.

"Can you record what I say?" she asked, looking Data directly in the face. Her hearing aids were still turned off, but Data lip read as often as not in any case. Lip reading and partial hearing, Benedicta had noted, early on.

"Good idea," said Ari. "That way you can revisit what's been said here later."

"I still have to hear everything," Data said wearily. "I still have to turn everything on and make this damned inflammation worse."

"Can't be helped," Ben said. She was sympathetic, but sometimes things had to be endured.

Data winced visibly. Benedicta regretted saying 'Can't be helped.' She'd never seen Data be anything but bright or excited before. Stoicism replaced the wince, and Ben knew she'd made a mistake. A mistake to force the plane trip on Data and a mistake to not listen to her recovery requirements. It was too late, however, so she ploughed on. As she talked, she realised that she could have done a lot of this on paper or by text. Data was suffering for Benedicta's tendency to do things the way that suited Benedicta.

The moment Data turned her hearing aid and accessories back on, Benedicta knew the error was not a small one. Pain radiated out.

"Turn it off!" she said peremptorily.

Data did. The pain still took a few minutes to subside. This gave Bennie time to think. She faced Data directly again so Data could lip read. Ari moved closer to hear.

"I'll tell Ariette, and she can record it."

Data nodded, "When I'm recovered, she can send it to me as a sound file."

"Let's do it, then," said Ari.

Data slumped in the chair, small and frail.

Sometimes Benedicta Beja hated herself for doing this job. Add that to the hate she felt for having put this young lady through unnecessary pain, and she wished she were Catholic and could confess sins and feel some sort of absolution somewhere along the line. She added this to the list of things she would feel guilty about on Yom Kippur. It added to all the neglect she felt towards her perfectly-capable adult daughter and her staff. Feeling bad on Yom Kippur never stopped her feeling guilty in the interim.

Somehow, she would learn to pay attention when a person

like Data—afraid of nothing, strong enough to carry her dead brother home—said "I should not do this." One day she would learn that disabilities were every day and pay attention to the cost they claimed from those who had them. Today had not been that day. Data was hard of hearing, was sensitive to airplane pressures, and had Post Traumatic Stress Disorder. She was still ill from her double transit through that strange doorway. Benedicta had overruled everything. She had magnificently succeeded in hurting someone who did not deserve that hurt.

While Benedicta immolated herself, Ari took a good look round in the way one does at stations. A tourist examining her exotic location from the safety of a family circle.

"I think we're being watched," she said.

"That fits. They know a lot more about us than we do about them right now. One of those days," said Benedicta. "Move close in and we shall have a heart to heart. Look down on me as if you know me very well. Daughter paying close attention to a mother explaining everything."

Ariette leaned in and put her hand on Benedicta's shoulder and angled so that it sat comfortingly and supportively below the grey hair.

"How do men do this kind of thing?" she asked.

"One of the great mysteries," replied Benedicta. No-one could read her lips, and she found Ari's hand unexpectedly belonged on her shoulder. She was developing auntly feelings, God help her.

This thought provoked one of her lectures. It was a night following day thing. Friendly feelings always provoked lectures. Mostly, she used the opportunity to explain what she knew and how she knew it. She was going to turn these children loose, and they needed better equipment than they had. So she talked. And talked. And talked.

As she talked, she kept an eye on Data so she would know when they were ready to move on. She would fit in just as much knowledge as they had time to fill and no more.

What Ari didn't know in her leaning in a niecely pose, and what Data didn't know, scrunched up with pain in the chair, was that when she hurt physically, Benedicta talked faster. A famous ancestress had been known for this, and it was almost reassuring that Bennie wasn't the first woman from a rather well-known family to mask illness with power-talk.

"This is only for the two of you. If you share it with anyone from Tsarfat, or even with young David, I shall have your guts for garters." She began an entirely new thread, conversationally, as if it linked to her earlier explanation of how the British government worked and the role of the French government and how the various systems of magic were regulated and controlled and how this applied to the very strange management of this very strange case. "Do not let it drop to anyone unless they approach you with clear and obvious knowledge. Not even my cousin knows this."

Ari was paying more attention to her than Ari had ever paid to anyone in her life.

"I'm part of a small group of people, mainly British, that has worked together for a very long time. We're all friends. We're all female. Few of us are young. We're all very, very political. We're all from privileged backgrounds, and one day we realised that our damn privilege was hurting people. We decided to accept certain responsibilities that work alongside privilege. We believed back then that humankind needs a little help. At times like this, when there are murders on the streets, we believe that humankind needs a lot of help. This is not part of my official job, and what I do with these friends is kept out of that office environment. The British government doesn't know about us and doesn't want to know about us."

Benedicta paused for breath. She had been talking for a long time. All the briefing she'd done with Ari while Data slumped in the chair had been official briefing. This was the real stuff.

"I know my reputation as an impossible iron woman. That's intentional. We needed someone public and someone who could lead, and I was that woman. My family was the perfect family for this, and my personality is … what it is. I am not inclined to show softness publicly, and I don't mind how many names people call me, so I am the figurehead who can be taken down if the worst happens. We used to call ourselves The Forlorn, but as a name, it was pants. It cemented the wrong attitudes in us, and we started to think we were special. We may never know if we were special like you and Data. We're not particularly bereft. Most of us are very advantaged in social and financial and career terms. We still call ourselves The Forlorn, but it's now sarcastic. We are the group your Green Family was looking for when you first came to London."

"You couldn't tell us earlier?"

"I needed to set it up so that the three of us genuinely had good working relationships. Even friendships. My little group doesn't work in the open. Not ever. I am the fall guy for this case, and you are the people helping me see it through. The others will step in when they can."

"Then why do I, I mean we, need to know? And why here and not in London?"

"We need to unravel a number of problems, and my position was going to get in your way. I could let it do that, or I could make it work for all of us."

"So, the Merlin is our uncle, and you are our aunt? That's why the nickname?"

"In a way, yes. I can look after adopted nieces who are doing a valiant job far better than I can look after random strangers who come from mysterious parts of France."

"That's why you insisted on calling all our people 'superheroes'. You were setting us up for this. We're partly the public face of you and your friends."

"Potentially, yes. New people get factored into a problem, and you've been handled, I think, in a way that works for all of us. The main reason for the label was because you fit the stereotype of a superhero in so many ways. You have unique powers and sad backgrounds. If any Tsarfati come here and wreak havoc, they will be the failed heroes who could not live up to the dream. Superhero stories have those who attempt to be heroes who fail, after all. That will limit the damage. The number of ordinary people who could be hurt."

"The supervillain."

"Precisely," said Benedicta.

"This explains why you employ David. He interprets the stories."

"And so I can use him to provide explanations, which means I remain separate from those explanations. He did a very good job in Newcastle, don't you think?"

"The Merlin thought it was all him. Hell, I thought it was all him."

"It *was* all him. I choose the right people for the right job. That's my special gift, if you like." She said this bitterly. It was not the gift she had dreamed of. When she was a child, she had dreamed of being like Josepha and being on call to the monarch and to the prime minister, providing magic solutions to all the strangest problems and being reported on in the newspapers. Britain didn't work like that in the twenty first century, and Benedicta's abilities had pushed her solidly into the civil service. The magician for paperwork and precise recruiting, that was her, in her soul of souls.

"If we need you as a government official, we should continue to call you Benedicta?"

"And if you need me as one of a group of friends who work out of sight, then drop the word 'Auntie' into the conversation."

"Easier than all the nicknames you attract," said Ari.

"I think we have Data back," Benedicta said, and she was right.

"I'm full of myself," she said, more cheerfully but still subdued. "Data for everyone. Boss, you have an urgent email. Should I forward it to your phone?"

The email was from David's supervisor.

"Why is this urgent?" Benedicta asked rhetorically. "Give me a moment." Rupert was a nuisance, but one always made time for one's past.

The email was nothing special. He wanted to see her. He wanted to have dinner. He wanted … Rupert always wanted things. He carried with him a kind of toxic misogyny that only showed itself in certain situations. No dinner, for that was certain to lead to one of those situations. This opened several questions. Why dinner? Why now? Why urgent?

"How much do you know about David's supervisor?" she asked Data. "How much can you find out in a hurry?"

"The email had lots of fascinating material, and you want to know if it's useful?"

"No, the email was a private one. He could've rung or waited or sent a message through David. I've known him for years and yet … I don't know much at all about him. I think I assumed that no-one unreliable could be a professor at a known university. I feel the need for more data, Data."

"Since you have such perfect taste in jokes, I'll find out his background for you while we work. It'll stop me getting bored. Where are we going?'

"Three houses. All within walking distance. Let's get a move on."

The first house they visited was within sight of the cathedral. The cathedral loomed so big that the house looked tiny. It wasn't. It was a solid, old two storey place, and it was empty. There were three open shutters, and Ari peered in and saw no-one. Not simply devoid of people, the house was devoid of furniture and, as Ari pointed out, possibly even fleas.

Data said, "No electricity at all here. Something's wrong."

"I hope that my cousin's people haven't given us bad data." Benedicta said, then looked a bit guiltily towards the bright hair. Data was trying to peek behind another shutter.

"I'm not bad Data, but I'm entirely incapable Data. I can't see anyone."

The second house was a bit of a walk away. The team grew in confidence as they walked past photos commemorating World War I layered on brick walls as if they had grown there, past the new practical and very dull buildings that had replaced a whole section that had been bombed out in World War II, and finally to the Somme itself. When they reached the river, their confidence flew.

"We're lost," said Ari.

"Then you'll let me use a map?" Data pretended a pathetic and hopeful look.

"Go for it."

Data walked them down the Somme until they reached the strip of restaurants right next to it, then they crossed the river and settled down to eat the exotically named stuffed potatoes for lunch.

"We wouldn't have walked so much in the wrong directions if we'd eaten first," was Data's explanation. "Also, it's on our way. And potatoes make me feel very comfortable. You, less so, I think, given the amount of pork in them."

"True about the food," said Benedicta. "So, you have potatoes in Tsarfat."

"We have many, many potatoes in Tsarfat," Ari explained, her tone reflecting a false high seriousness. "Not as much pork."

"I've developed an enduring love for finding bacon and eating it on behalf of my family. Mum used to talk about it a lot. She'd complain because she could only get it maybe three times a year. Soup and spuds is what my Mum says about Tsarfati food. She's wrong, but 'soup and spuds' resonates."

"Do you know where we're going after lunch?' asked Benedicta, finding Data's mother just a touch annoying.

"The second place is right near here," Data reassured her.

Data was young and fit—now that she'd been given the time to recover from the flight—and 'near here' was still a walk away. Data took them on back streets, past shops and medieval houses and post-medieval houses that had a medieval air and modern houses built to match the houses with a medieval air. They were wood and plaster at first, then narrowed and achieved paint. The less space a two-storey house fitted into, the narrower it was. Then there were a few brick houses, and both Data and Ari stopped so quickly Benedicta nearly walked into them.

"This could be home," Data said wistfully, looking at a red brick house with shutters painted white.

"Even to the little people who hold the shutter open and the painted moulding above the window," Ari agreed. "I promised you they'd be here. You'll get home. I promise you that too."

"In two more years. When it won't kill me to drop in. Right now, that's a very long two years. And we're so close."

They were close also to the house they were looking for. The swans ignored them as they passed the canal, walking back and forth over bridges because Data had forgotten she was map person and wanted to look for more shutter clasps. Ari had no wish to remind her. It would rub salt into a wound.

The memory of home that had plagued Data all day wasn't the problem now. Nor, in fact, were the shutter people. She was distracted by an email from home. A very unexpected email. Before she could raise it with Ari, they found the second house.

The house had once held people. Right now, the second storey was held up by what looked like rough branches with the bark taken off. The roof bowed inwardly, and the inside was blackened and open to the world. Even the old stone fence was incomplete.

"Damn it all," said Benedicta. "Don't those people know a thing? I need to send a message. An angry one. Let's find somewhere to sit."

"When we do, I need to tell you about a message I just got," said Data. "It's from home."

They sat in a park near the canal, pretending to admire the statue. Benedicta dictated her angry memo to the Office of the Merlin, asking that the unprocessed information from their interrogations be sent to her office immediately. Then she sent another to her office to make sure they would chase it up with appropriate urgency. Then she sent a third to her group of friends, telling them that something in government was impeding the investigation. Then she turned to Data, "Now, tell us."

Data explained that she had received an email from someone who had been in her year at school. "She never took up the Envoy programme. I thought she was interested in it, but I was wrong. She was secretly dating my brother. She just told me that, and gave proof of it, and then she told me ..." her voice drifted off.

"Why couldn't she tell you that she was seeing your brother?" Benedicta was determined not to miss anything.

"She's Jewish, of course," said Ari. "Isn't she?"

Data nodded. "Mum and I would be fine with it, but ..." she

116

drifted again.

"Data, what did she tell you that was so important?"

"She thinks that something has happened to a friend of hers in the current wave of Envoys."

"They would tell me," Ari said. "I'm on the spot. Even if I were in England, I'd be the closest right now."

"That's part of why she's worried. Because you don't know. Bob told her to keep an eye on who knew what. She says that no-one checked up on him or on me during our missions. There was supposed to be someone watching us in case our changes went bad and we needed help."

"That's right," said Ari. "I wasn't even told there was a party going through now. I thought it was next month."

"She says it was brought forward. Five candidates. She found reports on two of them. She can't find what the reports are, but the notes she hacked into said that procedure was followed and no-one was to blame."

"Which means they both died."

"Quickly. They only came through yesterday."

"That's appalling," said Benedicta. "Murder simple, to send a young person to certain death."

Ari looked down at the older lady. "You're right," she said. "It's very wrong. We've been accepting it because we need to do our bit."

"I've thought that for a long time," said Data, "but that's not the urgent problem. It's why I want to find out what happened to my brother, but it's not the issue here."

"There were more candidates," Ari said.

"Precisely," said Data. "One of them is part of the group Bob's secret girlfriend belonged to. They want to find out what happened to Bob. Her main task took her to Villers Bretonneux, so she was going to ask about Bob there at the same time."

"And they're dead?"

"Missing. Same pattern as Bob, she says."

"What's her name?" Benedicta asked. "I can't call her Bob's girl."

"She uses a pseudonym; it's how I know she knows Bob. It's from a phrase that was one of our secrets. Cricket, she calls herself. Our phrase is 'No-one plays cricket in Tsarfat.'" Data finished the sentence by turning to Benedicta.

Benedicta answered with a question. "If those candidates are ill and need help, how long do we have to find them and do what we can?"

"Two days," Data explained. "Though we give it a week, normally."

"Huh?"

"They'll live or die in the next two days. Most of us die when we leave Tsarfat. That's why so few of us ever leave. It's a risk. I'm here for almost forever because I went back too soon originally. Acclimatisation saves lives. Or at least lets our bodies function normally."

Data saw the look on Ari's face and didn't want to explain any more. She didn't want Benedicta to know that she thought she had killed her brother because she was so tired and so sick that she forgot and had brought him home. Benedicta's attention wasn't on her, in any case.

"We can't do anything to help them," said Benedicta. "Our urgent task is to find out who is responsible for the bombings and the incidents. People are already dead from them. More people will die. We cannot take that detour."

"If you'll excuse us just for a moment," Ari said politely, rather than arguing. "I need to talk this through with Data. It's personal, and it's professional and, from our end, there are more deaths. I promise, we won't take long."

The moment they were out of earshot, Data said, "Why were you so polite? She was so … so … unsupportive."

"She knows our little universe exists," Ari replied, "but I'm not sure she believes in it. Secret guilds of magic users are her thing, but not other worlds. She can't quite see that we're helping her because there are very likely to be links between our worlds that affect these events we're all caught up in. It's personal blindness. Not stupidity."

"Well, it looks stupid," Data blurted angrily. "And …" Data's wrath poured out after that pause, for she couldn't help it. Too much grief. Ari was sorry David wasn't with them to ease the pain that strained its way through her voice. "Why are we helping this woman? She's useless. Doesn't know tech, can't protect herself, can't even tell when a bloody storm is coming. Did you see how those people walked right past her? How can she change the world? We should find someone else."

Data's voice rang because of that pain. Her voice always took on volume when she hurt. Benedicta heard it all. She took out a notepad and wrote it down. Not to use against someone, but because it hurt, and she needed to do something. She wrote down what they said, and while Ari talked Data out of her temper, Benedicta wrote herself out of something equally bad.

It wasn't easy being Benedicta Beja. She knew that a kind of aloneness was integral to getting done what needed doing, but sometimes it was like the world taking an ice-pick to her soul. She wrote to herself maybe, or to her friends. She wrote to a random 'you,' for that was the way she would handle this moment.

✡

It was twenty-five years ago. I was thirty-six and was at a moment when I had to decide if I was going to choose the life path that included

119

children. All the invitations I used to ignore were suddenly of terrific interest. I joined a darts group. Once a week, we'd meet at a pub, ritually lose a game (for only one of us was any good), and have dinner.

One week, the table next to us had a temporary member because their regular one had just had a baby. We all wanted to know how she was, and we also needed to meet the replacement. He was French, we were told, "But don't hold that against him." French and Jewish and spectacularly handsome—every single one among us who found men attractive fussed around that table all night. Except for me. I met him the once when my table walked over to ask about the missing person and her child, then I sat and I watched the march of people to that table and I laughed.

He saw me laughing and invited me for drinks the next day. I was, as I said, deciding if I wanted family at all, and he definitely added some weight to the 'family' side of things. We spent some time together.

My own family was not impressed that I had found a man in a pub. We don't do things that way. They checked him out. His history was a void. I stayed with him because a void involved no political issues. He was safe. We spent a year with each other.

He was attractive and within a decade of my age, so we had much in common. We both walk in complex worlds. But ...

There were issues. He didn't like being equal in a relationship. Twice, he didn't accept that no meant no for both of us. I tried to walk out, simply, as one does when that happens. Attractiveness is nothing if there is no safety.

Towards the end of our relationship, I found out that he talked about me. He was full of puffery about having snared me. Now that we mixed in the same community, the talk came back to me. He was no longer a void. He was certainly not safe.

I discovered that he didn't talk about the things he told me he loved in me. He boasted about my particular background and that I had the ear of Queen and Cabinet and that I was no longer married, that the Merlin is my second cousin twice removed. I escaped him and found that my life had changed when I was with him. I was more judgemental of myself and more excusing of other people. I hated myself for the changes. This is why I never married.

Now I wonder, all these years later, if he was even Jewish.

Disbelief should not be incremental. I need to reform how I express my views on Tsarfat. I know it exists. I do not need to share my hurt.

Chapter Six

Writing was the exorcism she had needed. Benedicta put the pen in its proper place in her handbag, folded the paper up very carefully, and called Ari and Data over.

"We're going to split up. Ariette, take care of that girl." A weight lifted from the air. She didn't like saying the next bit, for what Data had said still hurt, but ... "Data, you come with me. We will find that third person. If we have time before we go home, we will also go to Villers Bret." Data was not Rupert, after all.

The third house was a nothing-place. Someone had seen a space and filled it. It was a thin sliver of white and stucco in between two nineteenth century mansions.

"It has electricity and Wi-Fi," Data said.

"Good," Benedicta said, and she rang the doorbell. They were both invited in by a man in his sixties.

"You read my article." The ray of light that was his reaction to this thought didn't even come close to illuminating his glum visage. Benedicta began to feel hopeful, however, that this time they had found someone who knew something.

"I did," said Data. Benedicta noticed that in French, her accent was perfectly of the region. David's accent analysis was infectious.

"I brought my auntie to meet you because it was so important. You're not known across the Channel. My aunt is English, and I thought that she could tell people. I think I explained it badly, though, so I brought her here. I was hoping that you would tell her all about your work. It's too important to let slide."

Benedicta was very impressed with Data's swiftness. Now Benedicta's own very English massacre of French would not be a problem.

"Let me make coffee," he said.

"Thank you."

"And where are you from?"

"Me," Data said, "I'm from Albert. My aunt is from London."

"Well, I will speak slowly, then. I will try not to fall into ch'ti, for you will speak dialect, but your aunt …"

"She does very well for an English," Data defended. "But no, she learned Parisian French. Her side of the family hasn't lived here for a long time."

Data had been doing homework and was using that to skirt truth and avoid the lie direct, Benedicta noted, for her family had some links with France, but as Data had said, they weren't recent.

The man didn't want to stop talking once he had begun. He gave so much about his history that by the end of it, Data had probably read the article in question electronically, for she occasionally put in a word or two to show that she, at least, was getting everything. Benedicta got the gist.

He had written a scientific paper about the end of the world and how to stop it, and had written a popular version of the same. He assumed Benedicta had read the popular version. He assumed many things about Benedicta, and she found this amusing.

Pierre, was his name. An ecologist by trade and training. His view was that no-one should have children. That everyone who had a child was a criminal and complicit in the destruction of the universe.

"I only had my child because my wife would have been unhappy without a child," he explained. This, Benedicta suspected, was the reason for the tortured face. He was preaching something that he himself was not willing to uphold. He condemned parents in strong terms, and yet he had a child.

Benedicta decided she needed to know more about where his views came from. How far did they extend? She began with the extent. "I haven't had a child," she lied. "I am incapable." His reaction to this comment would define so many things about his personality.

She was still a bad person, it seemed. Because Data was a family member and Benedicta had not prevented Data being born. "My brother is dead," said Data, reacting to this instantly, as she did to everything.

"Every death helps the world," he said. "Every human birth damages."

"And yet you and your family ..."

"I live in shame, Madame. Every day of my life, I punish myself for having had a child. Every day, I do what I can to atone."

"Your writing," Benedicta commented, less amused the more he spoke down to her. His body language suggested that she was a pest and a nuisance and was not able to hold an opinion of her own.

This was their man. The question was, how much could they learn before his ego stepped down from its high horse long enough for him to see the two women as threats? Right now, it looked as if they would have a lifetime of listening to his hatred, but this type of person could turn in an instant.

His body language was already changing. It had begun as affable but superior. It was still superior, but now his words were spat out. He said he judged and targeted groups. He had an avenging spirit that would redeem the planet.

Benedicta listened to the subtext and realised he didn't hate women. He regarded them as objects. All women were objects. Including his wife. She was unable to feel guilt from the evil she had done in persuading him that they should have a child. She was incapable of redemption. Very Christian, thought Benedicta, but not in a way most Christians would approve.

"All women have children," he announced. "You are one of them." He believed she had chosen not to have a child, but this was not relevant. It was the child-bearing capacity of women that hurt him, not whether they expressed this capacity. This meant that women could not save the world, in his terms, by avoiding childbirth. Women were eternally guilty.

His diatribe swivelled and became quite different, just as Benedicta predicted. Not in the way she feared, though, this time. She realised Data had never taken her bag off her shoulder. Benedicta nodded to herself and prepared her handbag likewise. Without Ari, they were more vulnerable than she had realised. The new girl through the door needed help, and this was the result. Benedicta hunkered down, now equally ready to leave as to listen.

Now this gentleman was punishing himself from giving up his career. He was utterly determined to save the world from itself through his work as an environmentalist, but he'd given it up because he'd done a vile thing in having a child. He was tormented.

Benedicta needed to get out of his house, but he still had things to say, and she needed to hear them. He had an Italian pot, and the air smelled of ashes.

"Your coffee!" she exclaimed.

"It's dry and dust," he said, gloom taking over his face. He went over to the stove and, picking up the pot by the handle, dumped it in the sink. The sink was damp and the fizz of the water as it touched the overheated base was not a good thing. *Poor pot*, Bennie thought.

"Let us buy you coffee and maybe something to eat," said Data. "It would be a great honour for us."

Benedicta wondered what had called this offer forth, but it was what she had been about to propose herself, so they all went round the corner and soon were sitting on the high stools by a window, sipping coffee.

She listened to his arguments and analysed the internal contradictions and then, looking across at the way he hunched slightly over his drink, she realised that she was looking at the wrong thing. She'd been leaning on David's work at home and forgetting to analyse narrative.

This man had a framed narrative. He was twisting and turning in his argument and not accepting simple links because he was framing himself in the centre as well as himself as aggrieved.

Benedicta put her cup down, quietly but firmly. It was time to ask him questions. If this were a novel, then it would be chance that he was here, in Amiens, where Data and her brother had separated. In reality, it was always better to test events and apparent coincidences, she found. He had boasted about his memory, and now was the time to test that boast.

"There was a young Australian here a few years ago," He said. "He shared some of your views, I think. What was his name, Rose?"

"Bob," she said. "Bob Green."

"I remember him. A friend told me I had to talk to him, so we met at the station."

Benedicta noticed how quickly he'd moved from lecturing them to trusting them. This told her a lot about the circles he mixed in.

He stopped for a moment. "We thought Bob would join us. We don't have enough Australians. I told him what we were doing, and I explained how we had to go about it. He didn't see the big picture. He didn't see that we are killing this planet. Bob was wrong in not self-denying and in wanting family. Bob had a girlfriend."

And they wanted children and this was wrong, Benedicta mentally finished his sentence.

"Did you kill him?" asked Data.

No answer. No denial. No surprised recoil. Simply no answer.

"Tell us what you did, the full story," said Benedicta. She wrote the words she needed on the napkin in front of her with her fingertip, and they glowed pale red. She read them aloud, and her eyes flashed red, and the red matched the anger in his soul, and he told them.

It wasn't merely that Bob refused to be the right kind of person. It wasn't merely that Bob wanted children. In fact, there was no 'merely' about it. The answer was big.

This representative of these people admitted that he knew that Earth1 had climate change, that Earth2 was able to be destabilised politically and space made in the ranks of power for those who were more fitted to it, and that everything was a mess. Governance from Tsarfat had never been an option for Bob, nor had fleeing to Tsarfat, but was one of the ideas this man toyed with. He was passionate about everything dying and he himself having to make enormous personal sacrifices to help, but he rambled about different solutions. It sounded as if the incidents were due to his people exploring one possibility after another, with the end goal of pushing aside others' needs and asserting themselves as 'special.'

This was not technically world domination. The final outcome was not fixed. The ideas of these dreamers shining and other voices failing was fixed in his mind. As suddenly as he'd begun to rant against the injustices and let seep the underlying story, what was really happening and why the events were being forced, their source returned to the personal.

"I am a reasonable man. I don't believe that everyone should follow my exact views. I gave the young man from underground all the choices a reasonable man would. He was tied up, and he needed to drink, and I didn't give him water. I took him miles away from anywhere and left him."

"Not Villers Bretonneux?"

"On the road near there. He was rude, so I bashed him round a bit. Don't mollycoddle the Green Children, we were told. Use violence if you have to, we were told. They're dangerous and evil, and I didn't believe it, but your brother," he looked straight in Data's eyes, "your brother," he said again, to make sure she heard and understood he knew who she was, and then a third time, "Your brother didn't listen. The world is better with fewer humans. I'm not sorry he's not around."

Data's fists were clenched, her jaw wired with pain, and Bennie wanted to throttle the man. Data saw the movement and stopped her.

"We have a crisis!" she said, low and urgent. Anger rather than despair. Benedicta found herself nodding, and she let Data take the lead. This was her error. Benedicta's grip on his mind failed completely. He stood up and bolted out the door and around the corner. Within minutes, he was lost to them, for once in the little alleys around the water tracks that led into the Somme, it was easy to hide.

He had given them so much but withheld everything critical. And he knew who Data was.

"If we find him, we're going to have to start again," said Benedicta.

"Huh?"

Benedicta smiled, even though she felt grim. "If I move now, I've still got a small link with his mind. I want to erase this conversation from it. He knows who you are. It would be easy enough for him to find out who I am. I want us not to have met."

"Good idea. You do it, and I'll watch."

It took five minutes and left Benedicta feeling bruised. There were so many reasons she didn't use her skills. This capacity to hurt other people was one of the most unpleasant of them.

Data saw she was finished and then said, "Do we look for him again?"

"I don't think so. I want more, but the fact that he recognised you and knows about Tsarfat ..."

"We're going to have to find a new trail," Data said.

"Don't I know it," said Benedicta, this time grim all the way through. "Let's get back to the train. We can check with Ari from there."

They took the route by the Somme because it was the one that required the least brain, and Benedicta didn't feel up to negotiating through the shopping district. It calmed her to walk by the river. Data had a call along the way and held up her power module and pretended to talk into it.

"Tell me where we're needed, and I'll get us there as soon as I can. Did you get that information together? No? Well, while we finish here, do it. We can't help her if we don't know what's happening. Send it straight to me, and copy it to Ari."

"Have you promised us to someone?" Benedicta asked.

"Bob's girlfriend."

"You didn't even know he had the relationship, and yet you talk to her as if you've known her forever."

"We went to school together. Makes it easy."

"We need the station to get anywhere, don't we?"

"We need to be at Villers Bretonneux."

"That place keeps coming back and back and back."

"I wish it wouldn't."

Ari was waiting for them at the Villers Bretonneux station.

"Data said you'd be here," she told Benedicta. "I've left her somewhere I hope is safe."

"How is she?" Data asked. "She's my brother's secret girlfriend's best friend, and this is becoming incestuous."

"That's the missing piece I needed," said Ari. "I wanted to know why she was special."

"Why are we here?" asked Benedicta.

"First," Ari said, "the people at the Museum won't talk to anyone from Tsarfat at all. The moment I said, 'I'm from a place called Tsarfat,' they shut down on me. Same with 'I am from the Green family.' They've decided we're a group of people playing practical jokes on them. Your superhero thing is getting out, and they don't believe it at all. They think we're from Paris, even when we use chti."

"Chti?"

"Regional dialect," explained Data. "Our chti isn't quite the same as the aboveground chti because Tsarfati came from a larger region. Lots of Parisians, for instance. David would have a field day with it."

"You do realise he's not a linguist?" Benedicta asked.

"The Australian uncle I never met had cigarette cards when he was a boy," said Data. "This didn't make him an historian or even an antiques expert. He still enjoyed collecting cigarette cards and knew so much about them that the whole family used to try to come up with questions he couldn't answer."

"Enough," said Benedicta, "I'll do the talking. Data, you go to where this girl is hiding and keep her safe. We'll have a phone on if you need us."

"I can do that," said Ari.

"If the museum people won't talk to Green Children, then your earpieces need to be out of sight."

"I can turn them off and be your niece who has trouble hearing," Data suggested.

"I'd rather have you fully functional," said Benedicta.

"Besides," Ari added, "I think you might like to talk to this girl alone."

"What state is she in?" Benedicta asked.

Ari was clearly reluctant to answer. After a few steps, when the museum was in sight, she sighed and said, "She has changed. She's hurting a lot. Part of this is because she was pursued and beaten. Part of this is because it was not a good change. Not one that will kill her, but not good. We need to get her to Paris and under watch, but she won't go."

"Won't go?" Benedicta asked sharply. She stopped still and so did the others. They were on a street corner in Villers Bretonneux, in sight of anyone watching, and Benedicta didn't care.

"Someone in the Paris office is working with our enemies. There were three candidates this round who went through the portal without immediate pain."

"This is normal, I think, these days," Data said. "The data I was given shows no pain on the other side of the portal. No pain in the first hundred metres of tunnel."

"How do we have that much information when the candidates have always gone through individually?"

"You were the last group to go through alone. My brother and I went through together, and since then, everyone has."

"Since then?" Ari sounded as sharp as Benedicta. "That's one group."

"Three groups. That's why they sent us in teams without telling anyone. We were pressured into going, and everyone after my year was given six months training instead of three years."

"And the death rate?"

"Only one new Envoy since me."

"This is murder," said Benedicta.

"We need to find out how and why," Ari said. "And we need to stop it."

Two minutes later, Data was on her way to protect the new girl and the other two were in the museum. There was a queue at the museum. Ari and Benedicta were silent so Ari wouldn't be spotted as a Green Child or as a Tsarfati. This left her reflecting on what had happened since she went in search of Data's brother's secret girlfriend's best friend.

The message she had been given through Data had taken her to the town closest to the Tsarfat doorway. Because her family was mostly so cold, she had developed a pattern, years ago, of visiting them, then leaving Tsarfat and all its childhood memories and exploring this town.

Liévin had fascinated her as a child, because when she made a map in primary school and overlaid France on top of her home, Liévin was there, right on top. The portal was a kilometre away from her home, so Liévin was on top of the portal as well. It had been hit by the 1906 explosion that had connected Tsarfat to Earth1 and had been rocked by the 1974 one that had moved Tsarfat to Earth2.

In both universes, Liévin had been turned into stumbling ruins by World War I. It was in the Red Zone and should not have been resettled so soon, but people didn't want to leave their homes. They took the rubble and they rebuilt: they lived in a region that was unsafe and they made it safe.

What had puzzled Ari throughout her teens was the lack of a door between Tsarfat and the town above it. In 1918, obviously, it was unsafe to make one. There was too much happening and too few places to hide with the rebuilding, and the earth itself was poisoned from the war. When the rare people who dared danger and left departed, they came out on a farm. Back then they knew the Tsarfati and the farm became a way-station.

When Tsarfat emerged in Earth2, the travellers had to start again. There were some storage facilities near the entrance to the maze that protected Tsarfat, but, as far as Tsarfat knew, the land above them was impossible to reach.

Ariette had never accepted this. It was potential, and it was danger, and it needed unravelling. When she studied for her own portal journey, she had included maps of all the known tunnels near Liévin. She'd brought everything together and drawn a new map from them. From the coal mines. From the town and its sewerage system and cellars. When she had emerged into Earth2, she'd added to that map. She had explored Liévin often enough so that shop owners assumed she was a local.

Finally, she'd found an entrance to an old tunnel in a park next to a school. The park was one of those places that had been allowed to grow since World War I, one of those zones that might still harbour poison. It probably didn't. All the bombs and mines had been cleaned out, so it was considered a park, and there was a school next door. It wasn't advertised to tourists, and it wasn't easy to get into. It was a public park that took effort to use.

Step by step, she'd explored the tunnel she had found and added to her map and found a point where this tunnel should link to another, just over a hundred metres from the skull and cross-bones. She had dug herself a pathway from the rubble, then made herself a door and camouflaged it.

She should have handed it over to the authorities, but that was the week Data's father was murdered. Ari wanted a path out.

So many families had a legacy of hurt from the wars, but Ari's family handled it badly. No facing it and no sorting it. They were left with cold and distance and unhappiness. That door out of the Liévin park was as much for Ari as it was for anyone who might need it to escape Tsarfat. The park was dense and green and had an aura of danger from the First World War, and both its nature and its aura made it as safe as anywhere to be alone.

The day of the rescue, she took a train to Lens, then a taxi to the school, waited for the taxi to go, headed into the Bois de Beaumont, and, watching for watchers, slipped quietly into the tunnel beneath it and through her hidden door. It all happened very quickly.

There's a first time for everything, she'd thought as she walked into the maze. *Including getting places in northern France when one is in a hurry.*

Soon, she had found the three people she was looking for. Two were on the ground and the third was leaning over another.

"Can I help?" she'd asked gently. The girl jumped. "I'm Ari. I was told you were all in trouble. I didn't expect you to be together."

"Are you with Chevalier?"

"Hardly. I'm not supposed to be here. I'm working with the British."

"Oh! That Ari. I was told you were coming, but I don't recognise anyone when they've lost their colour. Why don't you use a fake name? Is it because we're from home?"

"I am Ariette Green up top. The friend who sent me to you is Rose Data. Let's stick to those names. Now, explain to me what happened."

"Jeannette had a bad reaction to the door. She was in pain just after we told someone we were fine. We only got as far as here when she collapsed. I think the universe hates us." This last was said conversationally. Ari wondered what had been happening back home that had set up this reaction.

While the candidate talked, Ari felt Jeannette's pulse. "She's dead, I'm afraid."

"I thought so, and I reported it, but I don't think I can carry her back."

Data's heroic act, however stupid, was being copied. She was somewhat relieved that this girl couldn't do such an idiot thing. "After what happened to Rose, you shouldn't," she said, as mildly as she knew how.

"Rose is fine; I talked to her."

"She's fine, but she hurt herself badly, and she still has to handle high pain. She's banned from home until they're sure she's recovered."

"She said, but …"

"I know. It's hard to accept. That she brought her brother home and it cost her that career we all expect. Now, your other friend? He's still alive, but weak. What happened?"

"He had one of those midlevel changes where everything slows down. It was at the same point, so I don't know if it was real or if they were both poisoned or something."

"He should get through it if it's a normal reaction of that level. I shall take your first friend home for proper burial. You stay here with him and do what you can to help. Do you need water or medicine?"

"I have everything. We equip ourselves."

"Why are you doing this? Why come through when you know it's likely to be fatal?"

"You did it?"

"But now it's worse. We don't know if anyone is interfering with the process but … this is important … if someone comes looking, stay out of sight."

"You've answered your own question. We're here because we want to find out who's killing our friends. It's no use saving the world if we can't save ourselves."

"That's so true." Ari bent down to lift the body. "Damn, I'm sorry she's dead. I thought all the science was to find out who could go through safely. She should never have been allowed."

"Chevalier recommended her, and what he says people listen to."

"That man is a pile of steaming ordure."

"Can I do anything while I watch here?"

"You can do something very important. Let Data know what's happening. Why you came through. Who Chevalier recommends. Anything you know about their background and tests. If something is corrupt at home, we need to work together and not let anyone know we are. Data's gift can help."

"I don't understand."

"Because you've never seen her gift in operation. Wait and she'll show you herself when we see her. In the meantime, take care of your friend. I want two of you to live, please."

While she spoke, Ari had lifted the body as considerately as she could, and then she said her farewell and took the girl home for burial. The tunnel was dark, and she'd walked slowly because of the weight on her shoulders. This had led to her mood becoming darker than she could ever remember.

No-one should have to be carried home like this No-one should die. I'm going to change this.

If anyone had been documenting Ari's life, that would be the moment she became a superhero.

Chapter Seven

Ari stopped at the door. She didn't want to open it this time. She didn't want to go home.

When her family stopped wanting to see her and now with someone intentionally sending young people out to die and with the plots they were investigating having an obvious link to Tsarfat, her world had fallen to pieces. Tsarfat wasn't the safe place she grew up in. "Well," she said aloud, "I'd better pick it all up and put it back together." Ari opened the door and walked through.

There was always someone on alert after graduation. The person on duty this time was Cesar-Denis Chevalier. Ari schooled her features so that he could not possibly realise how much this worried her.

She wanted to hand the dead boy over to his parents, but she couldn't. Her role was to give the body to its temporary guardian. Chevalier would arrange the medical tests and would watch it until the burial society came in.

The boy would never be alone, for he was Jewish. Not being alone was good. Having Chevalier for company was bad. There was nothing Ari could do but be serious and sorrowful   and exceptionally polite. She hardly knew Chevalier, so maybe, if she was serious and sorrowful and exceptionally polite, he would not realise how much she distrusted him from his bright blue eyes down to his oversized feet.

"Do you want to go with me on this?" he asked. "You brought him in. It's entirely appropriate."

Ari wondered why Chevalier was telling her the rules when she had been an Envoy for years. She opted for polite obfuscation.

"I wish I could, but I'm on duty back out there. I was the closest when we got the message, but I can't stay."

"How did you get the message?" The question was accompanied by a penetrating look. "Where was the body?"

Ari shrugged. "I heard someone was down. Grapevine. I went to see. That's all." She changed the subject. "Are you able to take it from here, or should I inform someone?"

"I can take it from here. You get back to your important work." He definitely sneered at that.

"Thank you," she said, looked down at the body, and made a series of internal resolutions. The first was the hardest to accomplish. She reached out her hand. "I'm so relieved to hand him over to you. Thank you."

Chevalier's whole body moved out of defensive mode to superior important-person mode. "It's my duty. Thank you for doing yours."

Ari hoped Chevalier would not realise in a hurry just how big a lie she'd told. She left home quickly, for Earth2 felt less unclean than home.

She found Lisette alone in the tunnel. In fact, Lisette found her. She stepped out of a black corner and threw herself on Ari, saying, "Thank goodness you're here. Thank goodness."

"What's gone wrong?"

"A man and a woman came and took my friend."

"He's still alive?"

"I don't know. I don't know! They hit him hard, and I couldn't do anything. I couldn't move. I was screaming with pain inside and was paralysed."

"Which direction did they go? Towards home?"

"They took the path out to France. I followed them until I was certain, but every step hurt."

"How does it feel now?"

"It comes and goes. Right now, I'm so very tired, but it doesn't hurt."

"That's good, then. That's your change happening. It's very like mine. That means we can get you through this," said Ari. "We've got to get you to safety. Are we in mobile range here?"

"No," Lisette said. "They tried ringing someone on the outside and were very angry they couldn't."

"You first. The moment we're in range, I'll put someone onto finding your friend."

"Can't you just go back home again and ask the gatekeeper?"

"It's Chevalier. This has been very carefully planned. We need to get you out before someone comes looking."

"We'll have to go carefully because the people who took Bernier might come back, or their friends."

"Can you keep a secret from everyone?"

"If it will save my life, I most certainly can."

"It means we can avoid the people who took Bernier. Is that life-saving?"

"They hit him on the head, hard. Then they kicked him." She sounded sick. "I can keep a secret."

"Then let's go."

They shared the work of covering all of Lisette's visible skin in the cream that would hide the green while it faded, then Ari led Lisette back through her secret route, through the wood in Liévin, to the station at Lens (for there were more trains that stopped at Lens than Liévin), and to Arras and then to Amiens. At every stage, Lisette was crippled with cramps and torment. It didn't pass as quickly as Ari's had, and Ari was worried.

She had been expecting to meet Data and Benedicta at Amiens, but she realised that a big station was not a good place for Lisette to escape attention. "We need to go somewhere," Ari said.

"Bob's letter. We can get Bob's letter." Lisette was pathetically enthusiastic.

"This was your mission?"

"No, but I know where it is."

"Where?"

"He said he left it at the museum in Villers Bretonneux."

"That's where we're going, then. I'll find you a café, and you can rest out of sight until the pain passes, just in case someone is looking there. I don't trust any of these people one square centimetre."

"Neither do I," said Lisette. "How long will it take us to get there? I don't hurt so much now. Can we do it before the pain comes back?"

"We shall take a taxi. It's only seventeen kilometres. It's becoming quite a Tsarfati thing to do, catching the taxi between this station and Villers Bret."

When they were in the cab, Ari checked her phone for messages and laughed with relief. "My friends are coming here," she told Lisette. "We have cavalry."

Ari got Lisette ensconced in a dark corner of the café on the main street and went to look for Data and Benedicta.

Ari updated Benedicta and Data had explained what had happened at their end. Ari summed it up, "Bad news all round, then."

Data said, "I have worse. The second graduate has been returned home. Bob's girlfriend sent me an update just now."

"Dead?"

Data nodded.

"That's confirmation of murder if we need it."

"I'm not certain it was needed at all," Benedicta said grimly. "Shall we talk to the people at this museum? What do we need to find out?

"If my brother has been here and left a letter," said Data. "I already have the information on how many deaths and whether they were standard."

"Standard?" asked Benedicta.

"Whether people died due to the change or if there was another cause."

"And?"

"The deaths that are clearly from the change are half what they used to be. Of the remainder, half are clearly murder. The other half could be the change or could be murder. That's why there are so few Envoys compared with two decades ago, when there are so many candidates. Chevalier is responsible for the high numbers. He's given three talks at schools recently, for example, and apparently visits families one by one to persuade them to do their civic duty and send someone through the door."

"I wish that man would go straight to Azazel."

"He might already know demons," Ari said. "He has that look. Whatever he's doing, it's taken him past his comfort point."

"What was it like, seeing him and knowing what he did to my family?"

"Why your family only?" Bennie asked.

"Because I wasn't sure about the rest."

"He's somewhere bad," said Ari. Benedicta noticed that every time Ari thought of that man, her voice sounded as if it was walking over knives. "And he knows it's out of control. That's all we can say. Let's get a move on. We have a twenty year old to get to safety, and I worry when we just stand here."

"We needed to update," said Data.

"Well, we've done that."

"We'll do the museum and catch up with you shortly. Go protect that child," Bennie said.

As Data left to join Lisette, Benedicta and Ari entered the museum. It was a shrine to fallen soldiers, all Australian. Everything was very white.

Ari was glad they had not let Data come inside. She would have looked and yearned for what she could never know about her Australian grandparents. Why had they come to France to remember World War I? Even if there were records of a family with a similar name here, in this museum, they were not her family. Her universe was not this universe. This shrine was not her shrine.

The queue stopped with Ari and Benedicta, so they had a chance to ask about Bob. "My cousin," Ari called him. "My nephew," Benedicta said Britishly. This was enough, for Bob had been there and had admitted that his mother was Australian. Australians have British relatives, and Bob obviously had a French father. This latter the attendant actually said. "His French is so very good that it could not be otherwise."

"We can't find him," Ari said. "He's gone somewhere and said to a friend that he left a letter telling the family all about it, but we can't find the letter."

"His mother is very worried," said Benedicta.

"I can understand that," the attendant said. "He left something here. That's why I remember him. He had been in a car accident, he said, and was in pain. I said he should see a doctor, but he laughed, the way Australians do, and explained that he wasn't in France to see doctors. He was excited to see our museum. He said that his grandparents raised pennies to build it, so I told him which window to look from to see the reminder of that. Every day the schoolchildren are reminded of what Australians did for us. He looked at "Do Not Forget Australia" see, here, above the shelter? He told me that it was moving. He was looking at the enamel poppies we have for sale and said 'My mother needs one of these,' but he changed his mind. After he left, I found a letter. Wait and I shall check."

"You remember so much!" Ari said, picking up an enamel poppy. "I might buy this for the family." She handed the poppy over.

"Your cousin is very good looking," the attendant admitted while processing the sale. "And very kind. He let three elderly people go in ahead of him so they would not have to stand and wait. He was in pain, and yet he let the old people through."

"He's much younger than me," Ari said. "I always think of him as a child."

"I can imagine that he was a good child," the young lady behind the counter said wistfully.

"Mischievous," Ari recalled. "But kind. His sister was cheekier."

"He didn't tell me about his sister."

"She and I are closer. Bob was a nice child."

"Let me go check." The assistant came back with a letter. Four pages of print, fluttering in her right hand. "I took it out of the envelope," she admitted, "and copied it for you. I haven't read it. I know I shouldn't copy it. I should wait until Bob collects it himself. But Australia is so very far. The original is safe, and you have a copy, so he can have his letter from you or when he collects it himself."

"Thank you," said Benedicta. "Wherever he's gone, he's unlikely to have time to get back here. That's why we came looking when we were nearby, but I'd rather you had a copy for him in case he comes back. I'll let the family know."

"If someone else asks for it?"

"Only give it to Bob," Ari said. "Anyone else who asks wants his letter. They're not looking for him, and, as you said, the letter is private. Bob will have it directly from us, or, if he wants the original, he can come himself."

"The original is just a computer printout in any case," said the attendant.

✿

Back with Lisette, Data couldn't do much. Pain killers, something to drink, that was the most she could give. Or the most Lisette was willing to accept. They both sat silent in a corner, Data watching for threats and Lisette's eyes, half-closed, pacing inwardly through the events since she walked through the door.

"I did what you're doing now," Data said. "Not when I found Bob, but when I got him home."

Lisette opened her eyes properly. "What did you do?"

"Do?"

"How did you get over the shame and the horror?"

"I'm still doing it," Data said. "I'm finding out who murdered my brother and why. I'm being a Green Child at the same time, but I've never let go."

"What can I do? I can't go home for days." She made the 'days' sound as if they were months or years, and Data guessed it would feel like that to Lisette right now, as much of a burden as Data's own years of exile.

"You can check something for me. And maybe answer a question."

"How will that help?"

"Cricket gave me data from home about who gets chosen for

144

what and by whom. It's coded in the usual way, with nicknames, but all the nicks have been updated since I left. I haven't even been gone that long, and they're all different."

"I can help with that," said Lisette. "I didn't know they'd been updated."

"There's no logical reason for them to change. It's all the people we both know. They've run stuff forever. And not every name is different."

"Tell me, then, what have you found?"

"I took all the data I was sent, and I followed the trail they made."

"Trail?" Lisette was obviously fighting to focus. This was not easy for her, but it was still better than sitting with those eyes half closed and agony in her soul.

"I brought every skerrick of information together and then tried to find the path they came through to get to me. I used myself as the point outside so that I had a place to start travelling backwards."

"What if you weren't the target point for everything you have found trails for?"

"I wasn't the target point for any of it. Nothing was sent to me, initially. I had to ask for it. It could have been sent to any of a half dozen places at that time, however, and I had to establish their relationship to me to find out why I didn't get any of it. My other fixed point was the initiating party at home, or at the Paris office, wherever."

"You liked mathematics and statistics at school, didn't you?" Lisette asked accusingly.

"Loved them," said Data, feeling the grin spread across her face. "Wait, you've rubbed some of your makeup off." Data reached into her handbag for cover-up, but Lisette was faster.

"Thanks, but your cover won't work on me. Ari took my

cream by mistake, I think. I've not faded yet. Is it going to hurt to fade?"

"It feels odd rather than hurting. Like something creeping just under the skin. Ants crawling. I still get it a bit, and I hate it. I've got some cream you can use. Not as good as the one you brought in terms of cover, but it'll help with the ants. Here, take it."

"You still need it. That's why you're carrying it. I can buy it at a pharmacist here?"

"Not a good idea. Here, they ask so many questions when you want something. In the UK, you just take it off the shelf. I only buy it every few weeks these days; you're about to get the creepy feeling all the time. Take the cream, and I'll get us both more when I'm back in London."

When this was accomplished, they went back to the critical subject.

"So, you were the base-line," Lisette said. "What did you find?"

"It wasn't very complicated, in the end. Hidden, but not complicated. Every critical bit of information was delayed by the same 'classified' person every time."

"Do you have a nick for this person?"

"Talleyrand."

"That's Chevalier. He gave a lecture to us and told us that he was the inheritor of Charles-Maurice de Talleyrand-Perigord. Talleyrand took France out of monarchy, through revolution and Empire and back to civilisation. He did it by talking and helping, and Chevalier said that not everyone could be Talleyrand but that we could all work with him to get Tsarfat through the difficult times and into a better place."

"Why don't you call him 'Monsieur Chevalier'?"

"Same reason his nick is Talleyrand. He doesn't deserve our respect. My friends and I stopped caring how old he was and started wondering how wise he was. We found out what he did to your family and ..."

"You're polite to his face so that he doesn't do the same to yours?"

"Behind his back, we hate him. We hide the hate at home so that no-one knows we're trying to stop him, but we hate him. What's he responsible for this time?"

"Let me go through everything again now that I know who the nick belongs to. Won't take long."

"You're doing this in your brain?"

"No, sorry. My change and my techo are linked. I've got access to computer files."

Lisette sighed. "That's about the best change I've ever seen. I hope mine's half as good."

"I hate this," Data announced after a moment's reconfiguration. "And I hate the Disease."

"The Disease?"

"He calls himself Talleyrand, and I call him the Disease. He didn't just delay information, he re-routed it. I think the Paris office is compromised. He has someone there. Maybe at other offices too, but Paris is compromised. If we took you there, then his people would get to you. Give me another moment and I'll get some advice."

Data texted furiously with Benedicta for a few minutes, using the word 'auntie' in every sentence. It was all she could think of. She couldn't let Tsarfat rely on the British government for this. It would lead to untold complications. "Our British contact can't stay with us for more than the trip to the UK, but she has a friend in Dover, and that friend will take care of you if we're not sure about our own folk. Ari and I will help you get there and be your contacts afterwards. It'll be a bit different to usual, but you'll be taken care of. Ari and Benedicta will be a few minutes, but they've called for a taxi. We all need to get on that train to Paris as soon as we can."

"And I don't need attention," Lisette said. "That skin creep you told me about is beginning. I don't want anyone to see me."

It would have taken far too long to get to Paris. There were simply not enough trains in the day. There was, however, a direct train to the coast. The four took that train to Calais and reached England by sea. The first thing they did when they reached Dover was to buy more cream, for the original tube had been used up entirely in the toilet at the station.

"We have an office here," Ari said, not knowing what Data had already explained, "but I don't know if it's also been compromised."

"Can you manage without it?" Benedicta asked. "Is my friend enough?"

"Lisette needs specialist help."

"That's what I wanted to know. Would magical intervention work?"

"Not your kind of magic, I'm afraid," said Ari. "I've not seen anything in gematria that would help."

"The Merlin?"

"Possibly. It's to do with connections, and there are ley lines here, and his magic comes from that base, but we can't let his whole office know all the secrets," said Ari.

"Just him. He has dual qualifications, in magic and medicine. We don't talk about it, but this time, just this once ..."

"It might save a life. How far away is he?"

"Doesn't matter. He can get here. Let me ring him."

During that difficult journey, Ari pulled Data aside for a quiet confab. She shared Ben's letter. Data added that to the information she already had. It expanded their knowledge of the genetics behind crossing the Tsarfat portal safely. Most importantly, there was a hand-written note on the bottom of the last page. He had gone to Villers Bretonneux to meet with someone who could help him find somewhere safe.

The same reason as Lisette.

"Who told you that Villers Bretonneux was a safe place?" Data asked Lisette as they went back to their seats.

"Chevalier. He has a friend in the museum, he said. If anything was wrong, she could help."

"Do you remember her name?"

"Agathe."

"Not the woman who gave us the letter, then," said Benedicta. "She was Jeanne."

"There's something else," Lisette said. "He told me that Bob wasn't sent there. He was taken there. In the Museum, one of the staff takes care of us, he said. It was a secret."

"Did Chevalier have any suspicion you were part of the group working against him?"

It was Data who said the obvious. "No. Can't have. If Chevalier had known, then Lisette would be dead. Did you get as far as the Museum today?"

"No."

"This is just great," said Benedicta. "Now everyone has no idea what's happening. Not just us."

Our travel just gets harder and harder, Data thought many times on the way to Dover. She hoped the Merlin would be there to meet them. She hoped things would simplify soon. *I never thought I'd be so happy to reach England,* was her final thought as they saw the Merlin waiting for them.

He didn't bother with greetings. He whisked them all into a car and took them to Benedicta's friend. While her friend was full of politeness and brought them all a meal, the Merlin took Lisette into a bedroom, with Ari to advise on matters Tsarfatian and to keep things proper.

"She'll be fine," he said when he emerged fifteen minutes later. "She needs to sleep. Don't wake her up until tomorrow morning," he told their host. "I'll write you out instructions."

Their host said to the room as a whole, "His rudeness is like the Tower ravens. While he doesn't change, we know that England is safe."

Benedicta laughed. "Will you be fine here, taking care of Lisette?"

"My wife ran out on me," he replied, "not my three daughters."

"We'll take that as a 'yes,'" said the Merlin, looking up from the scrap of paper he was scribbling on.

"I can computerise it, if you prefer," Data offered.

"You can read his writing?" their host asked.

"Someone has to be able to," said Data.

The Merlin gave a grunt and handed her the first page.

"I can send it to your phone, if you like," Data said.

Ten minutes later, the visitors were all on their way to London in the car. The car went oddly quickly. It was as if traffic faded in its vicinity. Data noticed while she talked. She wanted to understand what was going on. It was bigger than she had realised.

"It's not just my brother," said Data. "No. This has been going on for a while, but we thought … we thought that it was the door."

"Some deaths are still due to the door. One this time. Goodness knows how many others earlier. It won't ever be safe. But not so many. Then there are the Green Children who get through safely and are murdered, like your brother. So the question is who lives? You're an anomaly. They thought you weren't important ..."

"Weren't they wrong," Ari said with a wicked smile.

"And they were spending all their attention on your brother. This is how I read it. Chevalier made a mistake in his vindictive revenge on your mother, and so you got through."

Data was obviously thinking it through and added, "The information I have, when I break it down and put it back together and analyse it, is a bit odd. Our new allies on the other side found that those people linked to the Chevalier family are more likely to live. Since then, they've done more work, and Chevalier was using genetic studies and only let his family and friends go through if they had certain gene sequences. Add in my family, and it changes. Chevalier got ahead of himself again. My family has a different background. I just looked at the genetic outcomes of the tests, and on my father's side, there are the 'good' sequences Chevalier discovered, just as Ari, you have them on one side of the family. My mother comes from an entirely different place."

"Maybe," Benedicta said, "how Chevalier got both of you into the program was not what I thought. Nor why he demanded both of you be in it. Your family was not a test case for living or dying, it was a test to see if Chevalier was right in there being a mutation that allowed one to live. Your family was the test. You should have both lived."

"My brother wrote that letter, and he talked about it," said Data. "I bet he came too close to the truth."

"A letter? You've told us this. It contained a summary of his thoughts on genes. I just referred to it." Sometimes Benedicta sounded brusque for no apparent reason.

"Not that. Another. He had a copy of that at home, and Mum found it and sent it everywhere. Monsieur Chevalier must hate Mum for that. Anyhow, it's what made Lisette and her friends say that they had to change things. It denounced our mentor. Bob told the whole of Tsarfat that Chevalier is a psychopath. He plays games with the lives of people like us for the fun of it. Most people think it's a lie, but ..."

"Is there a chance of anyone knowing about that letter before you left?"

"No, but there's a very good chance of it being discovered immediately after we were through the door. It was in the wine bar where all the parents meet."

"And Chevalier," said Ariette.

"Yes, the mentors drink with parents that first night. Why? We already know that Lisette and her friends are acting on it."

"We also know that Chevalier has a link with the outside world," Benedicta said. "For your brother to have been murdered."

"Does your mother know that it was murder? The letter accused Chevalier of many things, but did it talk about murder?" Ari asked.

"Does your mother know?" asked Benedicta, to reinforce.

"She knows Bob is dead," Data said. "She saw me carrying his body home. She doesn't know he was murdered."

"I meant about the genetic elements."

"Almost no-one knows. They're working on it because it's possible we can let a few more people into our little universe if we know what genetic markers to exclude. And we can maybe have regular trade. It changes things."

"So, you will be able to let more people out if you know which markers are liable to cause death."

"My brother and the new kids muddied those waters."

"We have to prove they were murdered. We know they were, and it hurts every time I think of it, but we don't have enough evidence."

"We have to, but do you?"

"Maybe my people don't need that proof, but we can't exclude links between these events until we know more about them. Also, the emotions matter. Do not kill people: it's the law. We will work together on this."

"We need to get back to London."

"We're in a car and on the way there," Data said. "I have no idea what we're going to do next."

"Right now, Chevalier and his people are running the show," said the Merlin. "We need to take control."

"How?" Ari asked. "We've got information but no direction."

"What happened in Dover? Why didn't you trust your own people?" the Merlin asked.

Chapter Eight

There had been a balloon. It had run a bit wild, rolling along the grass sometimes and floating above the statue in the park at others. It ought to have been a red balloon, or ninety-nine red balloons, or something that held equally dramatic symbolism, but it was silver on one side and said "Happy Birthday" on the other, and it was vaguely heart-shaped. The park was in Dover, but it could have been anywhere.

"This is where we find your people?" Benedicta asked for the third time.

"For goodness sake," said Ari. "We've only been waiting ten minutes."

A dog snapped after the balloon with a kind of random joy, then two children began to chase the dog, and Data said, "That's what we look like right now."

"You're chasing your birthdays," Lisette stated. The others all turned to look at her. "I might have my sense of humour back," she said apologetically.

A figure waved at them from across the park.

"It's Benedicta," stated Data, just moments before everyone

could see that for themselves. "Did you lose your balloon? Why have you got a balloon, anyhow?" she shouted at her boss and gestured to the flying object. Benedicta nodded and walked over to grab it. "Oops," said Data.

"I feel as if we're in a children's story right now," said Lisette.

At that moment, the balloon burst, splattering Benedicta with green slime. Underneath her feet, the ground rumbled. Data and Ari both ran towards her. Data got there first, and, leaping on her boss, she pushed Benedicta off balance. They collapsed in a heap while a door opened where Bennie had been standing.

Lisette waited and came forward when it looked safe.

When Benedicta and Data had extracted themselves, the four of them quietly walked out of the park together.

"Are you OK?" Benedicta asked Data.

"Shocked, is all," she replied. "That balloon … And you were the one who nearly got sucked into a hole."

"A hole, that's what it was. A hole in the ground. I thought it was a doorway," said Ari.

Data nodded. "I've checked with your people, Benedicta. It's just a hole."

"But why here, and why now?" Lisette wanted to know.

"It's unlikely it wasn't aimed at us," Benedicta said. "Probably at Lisette, if they've tracked us this far."

"A warning," said Ari.

"There was writing on the balloon," Benedicta said. "That's what I was looking at. It's a system that I am, shall we say, familiar with." The paper had two symbols and the word 'Dover.' "Do not trust Dover," said Benedicta. "From my friends. Let's clean you two up while we wait for the car I'm about to call. I do not want public transport at this point."

"What about that doctor?" Lisette asked.

"He'll meet us there," answered Benedicta.

He drove the oversized sedan that picked them all up. It was old, but it was big, and it would fit all of them.

Benedicta sat in the front with the Merlin, and they talked quietly. The others were silent. Data was in constant communication with David.

"You could've been in that hole," Data informed him. "Maybe it's just as well you were left behind this time. Also, Benedicta got slimed!"

"I'm not sure I wanted to know that," said David.

"Sometimes you're too polite," Data informed him.

✡

One day, some time ago, there was a wind-up tin toy on the floor. It was a monkey, and it was old. The monkey carried a tin balloon that said "Bonne Anniversaire". It felt the effects of age, especially after it was wound up and set to leap. It did a walk, then a half jump, then a walk, then a half jump, then another walk, then a stagger as it hit the edge of the rug. The monkey toppled to its side, its feet walking nowhere through the air.

Ariette sat on the floor watching her favourite toy enter the unpredictability of old age. *I may join it one day,* she thought, *or I may be dead in two weeks, along with my friends.* She wasn't regretting choosing her perfect career. She was wishing that it was safer. That more than one in five of their group would make it through to France above. Even if she were the one who lived, ici-nous would be angry from here on in.

I'm going to be different, she resolved. *I'm going to help change things so that death is not a given. We've accepted it out of guilt. We survived. Our grandparents never made it to the death camps. They are listed as dead, and they never died. They lived here. We should not feel guilty. We can work for others to live. We can fight hate. We don't have*

156

to die. This price is too high.

Today was her birthday, and this evening there would be an uncomfortable family dinner. No-one would want to be there, and all of Ariette's life would be kept away from the table in order to avoid triggering an angry episode from a sibling.

Publicly, they looked like the perfect family. Privately, Ariette wondered. She wondered how much of it was guilt. How much of it was jealousy. How much was … all the stupid things.

I know what I want to do, she informed herself, and held her head a little higher with newfound dignity. *I shall rename myself. The family always calls me 'Ariette', so I shall be 'Ari'. Myself, but not the self they think they know. Everything I do today will be my farewell to Ariette.*

There was a knock on her door, and she picked up the monkey from the floor and opened the door in one graceful swoop.

"Monsieur Chevalier," she said, "I wasn't expecting you."

"I'm not part of the Envoy programme any longer, so I wanted to wish you on your way personally. It's such an important moment in your life and in the life of Tsarfat."

"It's very kind of you. Let's go downstairs and get you some coffee." She wondered why he'd been allowed upstairs in the first place, then realised he must have come in using the entrance for the car.

"What are you holding?" he asked.

Ari handed him the monkey, and he fumbled and dropped it. She watched it tumble down all the stairs. She followed it down and picked it up again when it finally stopped falling.

"You should have been more careful handing it to me," Monsieur Chevalier told her sympathetically.

Ari bit her lip politely at that time, but she asked every single Envoy from that day on if Chevalier had come to see them a few days before they went through the doorway, and he had indeed done so, and each of them had been tested in a similar way. Something had been broken, and he had blamed them.

For her, his actions immediately converged with the mild underlying disdain she received from certain family members. Home no longer felt like home. Her memory of home was safe and full of good feelings; but as a visitor, it was not those things at all.

Her new home, in London, was quite different.

What had sent Ari back into the past was an unexpected visit from Benedicta. It was Benedicta who had changed everything. Just when Ari had been full of despair, Big Ben had asked her for help.

"We need your tech knowledge."

Not her power, her knowledge. For a young woman who had lost four close friends, and for whom home was no longer somewhere she could visit without hurt, this was surprisingly welcoming. It was as if the door out of Tsarfat was a door into sorrow, and then Benedicta had opened a second door. A door into somewhere exciting. A door that gave her the income to set up her own place, free of the restraints that usually applied to Envoys. For three years, she had advised a university department on all the things she could advise without giving away where she came from. Benedicta had made that possible.

She had checked with home, and home had given her permission, and so it was all legal. The official word was that she had come from Earth1, that it was a limited door, an occasional door.

Oddly, this worked, on an emotional level.

It wasn't until Ari got to know Data that she realised this was due to Data's mother. Data's mother carried Earth1 with her. She kept up with TV broadcasts and played on the internet for Earth1, and so it was Earth1 Data's Mum had used when she taught her various classes. Ari had done two classes with her. One was English and the other was advanced preparation for living in Earth2. Both of them were lined with a feeling for Earth1.

Ari's personal delight was Earth1 science fiction. This was how she and Data had become sisterly so very quickly. That Earth1 affiliation had lasted beyond any need to keep Tsarfat so strictly hidden. Ari would always remember the day when she walked in on Data, and Data had streamed Earth1 material to an Earth2 television. Data had been expecting the worst scold. She had not expected Ari to say, "Be careful with anything that references *Anne of Green Gables*, for this version of Earth completely lacks Anne."

"I wanted to watch the Earth1 version of this anime precisely because it has a whole lot of Anne." Data said. "I've got a little list of books that I need to remember not to mention."

"We should compare notes," said Ari. "In the meantime, mind if I join you?"

Home was no longer Tsarfat. Home was sitting in front of any screen, in any place, watching alternate Earth versions of whatever television they were in the mood for.

"Why didn't Anne get to Tsarfat before it was cut off?" Data asked.

"Because Anne isn't such a French series of books and only Envoys and your mother are really interested in English."

"There are more English speakers than Mum!"

"Yes, but they don't talk about it the way your mother does. She keeps her home alive, and we got that from her."

"She used to watch something called 'Skippy'. I've never found it. Not in either universe."

"Your life is a bottomless pit of misery."

"It is!"

"That's why your hair is three colours this week?"

"I wanted my hair to clash with everything this week. That may be misery, or it may be that my hair has its own personality. I don't know yet."

"What do you think about Earth1 and Earth2 linking?"

"What?"

"We had a week when we could talk both ways, even though we chose not to. All these holes the terrorists are making. Door changes. One day, it could mean that Earth1 and Earth2 are linked."

"Preserve me from that day." Benedicta's voice came from nowhere.

"I think it would be cool," said Data. "I have relatives on Earth1."

Benedicta came out from where she had been sitting and joined the two in the lounge area. "Grandparents are a fine thing to meet," she admitted. "But have you thought about the difference in the two universes for Jews?"

"The big one is England, isn't it?" Ari asked.

"Yes and no. The big one is that there are enough substantial populations of Jews that, until the recent bombings and threats that went with them, we've been reasonably safe. Great Britain has worked with other countries. Have you thought how much of a difference that makes?"

"Not really," said Data.

"I've not had time," Ari admitted reluctantly.

"We took the history Tsaifat gave us for Earth1, and we examined it very carefully. On Earth1, there were big population losses in the Middle Ages, under the Ottoman Empire, during the time when the Inquisition was so powerful, and were much greater than they were here after World War II. Essentially, the two Earths share prejudices, but our Jewish population is ten times the size, and we are more able to defend ourselves. There is established Jewish power in the UK here, where there is not in Earth1. We still have to fight bigots. There are far too many people who believe lies. But if we had continued connection with Earth1, there would be every opportunity for those who feel vulnerable about their own place in humanity to blame Jews for their vulnerability."

"Why would anyone do such a thing?" Ari asked.

"Your family is in Tsarfat because they did such a thing," Data pointed out. "And I think you're saying, Benedicta, that Jews in Earth1 are like my family in Tsarfat."

"Some Jews. Those Jews in the countries where they are tolerated. Here, we have acceptance."

"Not universal acceptance."

"No, but …" Benedicta paused, and it wasn't for effect. This was something she found uncomfortable to say. "But did you notice that the portals that lead to worlds with a larger neo-Nazi aspect, like one of the London ones? That the whole attempt to find portals date to the same time precisely as …" She paused again. This time it was most definitely for effect.

"As what?" Data prompted, unwilling to wait.

"Tsarfat found a way of listening in to Earth1's airwaves and internet. Within months, we had the first incident."

"I need to see the timeline," said Ari. Magically, Benedicta handed over a paper. "We were talking about it. I thought it was coincidence."

"You would have reached this conclusion yourself eventually. You were edging your way towards it."

Benedicta was right. The incidents were not linked to knowledge of Tsarfat, but to Tsarfati knowledge of culture on Earth1.

"I would like to say that it's not linked to antisemitism," said Ari. "I would so very much like to say this thing."

"It may not be intended antisemitism. It may. What I am seeing is someone trying to grab at a cultural profile that denudes English Jews of a position we've held for centuries. They may not be doing it to hurt others. It may be that they hurt and don't care about the consequences for others. The outcome is the same either way. If I'm right about what they're doing, and if they succeed, then Britain will no longer be safe, not even for someone like me."

"That's not all, though," Data said. "Tsarfat would be endangered. I mean, the whole of Tsarfat. I may complain about being a minority and what that means, but ninety-five percent of Tsarfat is Jewish, and if someone works out how to get in and out and …"

"It's nebulous," Ari argued. "No-one's going to raise a hand and destroy Tsarfat because they don't like it being Jewish. That's impossible."

"Actually," Data said reluctantly, "it's what happened to Jewish Europe during World War II on Earth1. Over three times the number were killed there."

"We can't be certain," Ari said stubbornly.

"Of course we can't," said Benedicta. "We can work to prevent it."

"Is there anything we can do that we're not already doing?"

"I can think of something," said Data. "You're not going to like it."

"Go on," said Ari. "Punch me in the face with your idea."

"We can muddy the water. Make it look as if Tsarfat is impossibly dangerous to leave. Make Chevalier's mob scared of the door."

"It wouldn't be that hard to do," said Ari. "Given the murders."

"It would take Tsarfat right out of the equation," said Benedicta. "That's a good thought. If it's protected by the door, then we can work on protecting Earth2."

"How do we do it?"

"Superheroes," Data said. "Although, that means lying about Benedicta."

"I'm sorry?" Benedicta was confused.

"If we say that only superheroes can come and go safely, then there's very little rigging of evidence necessary. I can make it fit with the tests back home."

"I'm a problem how?"

"You're a superhero and not even your little finger is from Tsarfat."

"I'm not a superhero," she told Data firmly. "For how could I be? It's not a question of age or power. It's personality and choices. I live every day on the brink. Tsarfati heroes have a home to go to that is not riddled with this grief. The home is strange, but it's there. To be honest, I've always thought that the heroic is an aspect of the imperial and that I'm in the wrong profession entirely. Bureaucrats as the unsung heroes of Empire. We can make Tsarfati superheroes the only superheroes. We can leak your existence to the world and have heroes for Earth2 and superheroes from Tsarfat."

"Heroic professions linked to expansion of evil Empire. Got it," said Data.

"I did not say 'evil'" Benedicta said. "I was thinking of British."

"Evil for certain then," Data said to get a reaction. "Ari, can you guess the other categories?"

"You, Data, are an annoying child."

Data smiled at the compliment and pressed Ari until she answered.

"I know that list, I think. You'd remember it better than me. It was in the first year of our special education. Explorer, Soldier, Bureaucrat, Scientist."

"You're the scientist," said Data.

"Not really," Benedicta answered. "Empire theory only enjoys the Humanities when they are poets or in music. We don't have a soldier in our group, and all the explorers are from Tsarfat."

"Tsarfat's idea of Empire is possibly not a standard one, given we have no army and do not want to take over other countries. That's why this is not a standard narrative about challenges to Empire or about Empire trying to grow. We don't fit the classifications."

The three were enjoying themselves far too much by this point.

"Maybe our disloyal opposition fits those classifications. We've met the scientist already, and he was an environmentalist, so actually a scientist. Chevalier is the bureaucrat."

"He would hate to be called that," said Data. "He hates anything that diminishes Chevalier for even a second."

"I'd rather know if he's a key player than if he fits Empire theory," Ari answered. "In fact, the Empire theory is only useful to us if they're enacting it. Let's move on."

"It helps to know that Empire theory might work for those fools who bomb at the least excuse," Benedicta reproved.

"My people have to question the ethics of what we do, claiming to be ethical and then imposing our ethics. The Jewish experience is that one can't sit back and accept that others will be ethical. This adds additional burdens to large Jewish populations, especially the very establishment one in the United Kingdom. We have to be ethical the whole way through and not abuse our power. We're fallible and human and quite capable of doing stupid things and wrong things, but we have to try."

"Thanks for the lecture," said Data. "But it's nothing much to do with me. For me and probably for Ari, your whole world is against ici-nous. It doesn't push for other people as a part of its existence. This sucks. More people need help. Bottom line."

"It's complicated," Ari said, trying to reconcile the two before they argued a hole to the middle of the earth. "I know why this is so important for all of us, personally." Then her feelings took over. "But why are we spending so much time talking about it? Why aren't we doing something? We're linked to the world, and we don't have to just sit and talk and sit and talk and sit and damn well talk."

"First, we've just been through a bloody nightmare," said Benedicta. "That poor girl." They were all silent. "Second, we passed a kind of test."

"I thought we failed," Ari said bitterly.

"We didn't succeed. We passed. We need to move on, but we will move on at the same level and in the same direction if we don't reconfigure our approach."

"This is reconfiguration?" Data was fascinated.

"It is."

"Do you mean …" Ari paused, not intentionally, trying to sound out something that made both her and Data look stupid and that she really didn't want to verbalise. "That you've been getting information out of us this last hour?"

"Partly." Benedicta was not at all worried about being caught out. These girls needed to know her. "We're reasonably certain that it's Chevalier at your end passing information from your delightfully techo pocket universe to someone on this Earth of mine. The question is, who's he passing it to?"

"David should be able to help with that," said Ari, moving restlessly, "Let me—"

"Please don't tell him yet," Benedicta said. "We will tell him. He's one of us. But …"

"What?" Data's face had a slight flush of unhappiness. Not quite anger.

"He was sent to us. He's perfect for his job, and he's loyal to us, and he's a genuinely good human being. I don't intend to exclude him. I also don't intend to get him into trouble."

Data settled back in the chair, and her face calmed down. "What is it then?"

"Information between the three universes is carefully watched, is that correct?"

"Yes. I blame Mum for that."

"What did your mother do?" Ari didn't quite believe that Data's Mum would do anything.

Data sighed.

"When Bob was buried, I had to leave home. I had to heal. I can't go back for years. She was told this and then left alone. She had her students, but she came home to … nothing. She talked to me when they'd let her."

"How often was that?" asked Benedicta.

"Once a week. Every Friday afternoon, we were allowed to chat, but we were monitored."

"Monitored? That's just wrong," Ari said.

"I'm pretty sure it's been standard for a while. It's fair enough. It's making sure that we're OK. Not all the training in the world could make going through the door easy. Anyhow, they didn't know I could see it. When I was told that I'd be cut off from communications, I could see that they still monitored me. I could've cut them off, but I didn't; I wanted to find out how long I was watched. We're always watched. Me closer than most because my computing is attached to my body, but we're always watched. I kinda let Mum know, and Mum and I still talked, but it was stilted. We never got to deal with the big things, like Bob's death."

"Your mother was terribly alone," said Benedicta.

"'Terribly' is the exact word."

"What did she do?" Ari asked. Her voice was full of worry.

"She sent a long email to Earth1, telling them about Tsarfat and asking if they could come and bring her home."

It was fully thirty seconds before Benedicta said, "What happened next?"

"We lost the two-way link to Earth1 at that point. No-one has tried to restore it. They talked about it, but never did."

Again, there was time where no-one spoke. Three minds were working in three very different ways.

"Ethics." Bennie broke the silence.

"My mother?"

"Not your mother, the thing we're looking for. Chevalier and the man we just lost shared critical aspects of world view. One of those aspects is a warped sense of what's ethical. What else did they share?"

"A need to know things," said Ari. "What else?"

"Can we look at that need to know things first?" Data asked. "Because David has lunch with his supervisor once a week and doesn't talk about us, and he tells me every week how much his supervisor wants to know about what we're doing and what we know and what he's learned; and David's just pinged me to ask me to ask you."

"Timely," Benedicta said.

"Not so much. It's his fifth ping. We were chasing around and dealing with crises during the other ones. Anyhow, David's supervisor fits into the kind of thing we're asking. I think we should talk about him the way we were talking about the relationships between worlds, cement our understanding. Change our direction? Because I don't think that man is neutral in this. I never did. I still don't know his name, and I knew he wasn't neutral. I assumed he was on our side because he pushed David into the job, but then David hates him, and I trust David.

And, yeah, I think we should talk about this. Do we have time?"

"We've still got an hour before we even have to leave for the train."

"Who starts?" asked Ari.

"Auntie, would you?"

"What do you need to know?"

"What characteristics you're looking for, first. What you've seen and what's missing from the equation. I get why we're doing this; it's a type of profiling, and the addresses led to blanks, so we're reduced to profiling. Or not reduced. We know we're being watched. That means someone's watching, and if we can work out who, we've got a new lead."

Benedicta looked across and assessed Data. "Either you've grown in the last weeks or I missed certain elements of your personality."

"Probably a bit of both," said Ari. "She hid this side of her back home because it got her into trouble at school."

Data grinned. "Things were always easier when I was bubbly but not terribly strong, so I made myself bright hair, bright smile, bright words–everything bubbly. The other side of me has always been there."

"So back home, you're not fully known?"

"And right now, isn't that a good thing?" Data's brightness was a bit forced. "Monsieur Chevalier is the one who thinks he knows me, and he's in the middle of it. Whatever else we don't have, we have that. And me being alive. I have that gift too."

"Hmm," was all Benedicta said in reply. Data was right, however. What knowledge of this group did they have? "I would guess that typical traits of our opposition include the fact that they have privilege but feel that they don't. They want to take everything and make decisions for others. To be in charge."

"That's been obvious since they started trying to crack holes in worlds," Ari said sarcastically.

"Don't take that tone with me, young lady." Benedicta kept her voice amused and soft, but made her point. "In one way, they're like you. They need to know everything and feel they're special. The man we let go felt he had the right knowledge and the world was lost without him."

"You know, David's supervisor fits all that. But so does the Merlin."

"I like my cousin's ethics better," said Benedicta. "Bart is well aware of his privilege and has firm political ambitions to prove it. He's a pain in so many body parts, but he's a good human being."

"The Merlin's name is Bart?" Ari was amused.

Data was aghast. 'Bart' couldn't possibly be a real name. It belonged to English fiction. It needed its own cartoon.

"One of his names is Bart. His personal names were chosen by his father to annoy his mother. He avoids them whenever he can."

"I need to find all the names and share them with David," Data said dreamily. Also to tell him they had the nickname they were after for the Merlin.

"Go for it," said Benedicta. "They're in Debrett's. Don't come to me for help if either of you call him by one of them, however."

"The difference between the Merlin and David's supervisor, whose name also never gets mentioned, is whether we can come to you for help? Is this a thing with male UK names?" asked Data.

"I forget names. Is this a problem?" Benedicta asked.

"Anyhow," Ari stepped in, quickly, "The difference is that David's supervisor puts different kinds of pressure on David to your cousin. Your cousin persuades everyone to walk alongside him; David's supervisor pushes to get David to go to those meetings, and he never walks away from them happy."

"This is interesting," said Data. "It means he has the same kind of self-importance as Chevalier."

"More," said Benedicta. "Bart will write about anything that opens up a path he needs. Rupert would do worse; I've seen him take private material and destroy privacy." She noticed that Data didn't react to the missing name but Ari wrote it down instantly. Data had been pretending she didn't know until someone officially told her. She might look trusting, but Data demonstrated fascinatingly divergent behaviour.

"You'd not put it into context before?"

"More that I didn't think anyone from my own damn circles was relevant. He still may not be. We're after someone who would be willing to murder culture and intercultural norms, however. That man would do those things, perhaps, if it meant he got what he needed and wrote about it and made a big name. He disclaims destruction in so many ways while using it to push his career."

"I hate him," Data interrupted. "I would never, never, never do a thing like that. And I hate him for it."

"What did he do to David?" Benedicta asked the obvious question.

"He made David into one of those TS Eliot wriggling things, being examined. He doesn't care about David's career or about David's life in any way. He sends David messages about everything, all the time, and expects answers from him about confidential stuff we are doing."

"And David doesn't reply?"

"You know how David drifts off in the middle of conversations? He told me that his mind takes longer to get places sometimes because he dreams along the way. David pretends he misses things when there's someone he doesn't trust. He doesn't trust his supervisor. He and I developed a whole line of things that he could talk about in meetings with that guy—dragons and sea creatures and stories of magic tourism and its failings. He keeps his stories straight, and he uses real interpretations to mislead his supervisor."

"What if Rupert comes to me and doesn't get the same stories?"

"I'll ask David to copy you his notes. He doesn't trust himself to remember everything from scratch. Besides, he thinks I should write some fiction, and he thinks his ideas would make good starting points."

"You want to write fiction?" Ari marvelled.

"I don't know yet. We were talking about it, that's all, because we didn't want to waste all the notes David's making. They're great notes."

"Have you two started dating yet?" Ari asked.

Benedicta laughed at Data's discomfort. "Enough. We need to leave."

"Can we have ten more minutes? I mean, do we have ten more minutes? Because I thought we did, and I've done some thinking, and maybe you need to know it." The talk about David had made Data charmingly defensive. Benedicta wished she had been as charming when she was that age.

Ari looked at the time, then at Benedicta. Benedicta nodded. "Go for it," Ari said.

"Wait," said Data, "Are we in British time or French time?"

"Dammit," said Ari, and they all ran.

Chapter Nine

They caught their train, barely, and talked about nothings the whole way to London, because the whole way to London had too many nearby ears. That nothing had some useful effects.

"We need to find people like the ones we're talking about," said Benedicta. "Or experts in fields that will take us into that scholarly area. I have an idea about that."

Data took up the conversation when David joined them at Benedicta's office. "I think there's a thing we're not talking about," she explained. "I got it a lot back home because I'm not Jewish. I find it very strange that here it's because people *are* Jewish."

"Your homeland was settled mainly by those who fled much worse persecution than we're suffering now," Benedicta pointed out.

"True, but even they, even we haven't avoided these problems." Data was surprisingly relaxed, given the subject, settling back into her comfortable seat, her head leaning gently into David's hand as if David was himself leaning on the chair entirely by accident.

"Explain them," Ari said.

"It's usually Her Maj who asked us to explain," David chortled to himself.

"What did you call me?" Benedicta Beja's eyes narrowed, and David felt a rush of worry. How did the thoughts in his mind escape to the wide world?

"Pretend he didn't say that," Ari said into the small silence caused by Benedicta's evil stare. "Let's hear what Data has to say. We need to understand if we're to handle this without loss of life."

"*More* loss of life," David corrected gently. *We're all so damned gentle*, he thought.

"It happened in stages," Data said. She wasn't looking directly at any of the others. In fact, her gaze was shuttered and inward looking, and for the first time, David could see that she was as much private and European as Australian and open to the world. "A lot of it happened before I was born. My mother's story. My father's story."

"Superhero origin story," murmured David.

"What's got into you today?" Her Maj asked him.

"I think the zipper on my mouth is broken," he answered.

"Well, mend it!" Her tone was sharp, but more amused than angry.

"And you know," Ari added, "We aren't superheroes, and I really hate it when anyone calls us that. We're an Envoy team from Tsarfat. That's all."

"Tsarfat does embassies differently to other nations," Her Maj added, then cast a sidelong glance at David.

He decided this was permission to not feel guilty.

"I am a superhero," Data proclaimed. "I decided this all by myself, yesterday. And if this is my origin story, then so be it. Let me start again. I don't want to talk ..."

"I don't want to talk about my parents. What happened to them before I was born, I mean. I need to go home to find out if I even know the half of it. I don't think I do.

"I know that Papa was murdered because his parents were German, even though both of them fled to Tsarfat because they had protested the whole National Socialist movement. Papa had an uncle who was Jewish, and Mum always said it was because Papa's parents saved that uncle's life, but I hardly remember him. Mum always said, over and over, that we should not hold the murder against most of Tsarfat because it was a minority group that did it. That's where I'll start, then. When we were in our late teens and recovering from Papa being so suddenly gone. That's where we came in, my brother and myself.

"We both had Australian names. That was Mum. She always wanted to go home. She had come to Tsarfat by mistake when she was twelve, and she never wanted to be there. We were the only things keeping her from walking out that door."

"Why didn't she do that earlier? Why did she stay so long and get married and all the rest of it?" David walked into countries when he wanted to. He was curious, and so he went places. He couldn't understand anyone staying somewhere they didn't want to be.

"We don't talk about it much," Data said," but a lot of people can't survive the transition between worlds."

"That's how your brother died," Her Maj said gently.

"I don't think it is. I think he was murdered, like Papa was. Maybe even by the same people.

"I've known it for a while, because his symptoms weren't right. My research is stuck. I can't work out any more without help. I've compared every case we have with his. I've been working through the rest of it, and I am only halfway there, but my halfway says that he was murdered. If he and I could both

174

live, then it's possible that Mum might too. But they won't let her. They're still telling her that leaving Tsarfat would kill her, and there are people watching to make sure she doesn't even make the attempt. It's not because she's Australian, but it may be because Bob and I are the only whole family to get through and survive, and someone killed Bob, and I'm out of reach. That's why I asked to be on this taskforce. I think what happened to Bob is linked to what's happening here."

"Off track," said Ari. "But important."

"Sorry. I didn't want to talk about my parents. Anyhow, if we skip to the time after Papa was murdered, our friends and teachers pushed us to leave Mum alone. They said she needed healing time. They told us what to think and how to grow into proper adults. We listened and did all the duty in public, but in private, we were still those Australian children who had never seen Australia and never tasted Vegemite. If someone had asked me which country was home, I'd've said Australia, not Tsarfat. Now I'm a bit from both countries. There's an inner home that's Australia, but I am all Tsarfati.

"We were so pressured to become Tsarfati that this was inevitable. We stopped playing cricket in the yard when we reached our teens because that would've made more kids give us a hard time for being different. Just a little bit different was worse than very different, I think."

"Why?" David asked. "I'm not asking why you didn't rebel. Being a good citizen in public and oneself in private is part of who I am. Why did you know you had to do this?"

"We didn't know who it was, but someone was making it harder for Mum every single time we didn't act purely Tsarfati. No-one expected us to be Jewish, but everyone expected us to behave as if Jewish was our everyday. We asked Mum about this, and she laughed, every time. She tried to make it seem small and unimportant, even though it was killing her emotionally. She can't talk emotions, not really.

"Mum said that it'd be the exact opposite in Australia. Anyone Jewish would have to toe the cultural line the way we toe it in Tsarfat. She told us it was fair, it kept a culture going, but that it hurt. When Mum admits something hurts, that's so bad. She never says she hurts.

"I'm not convinced that it's fair. I'm also not convinced that it's a sign that Tsarfat is doing things properly. I discovered William Blake last year and thought about that worm in the apple. I think that some of the pressure was deliberate. Someone wanted us to disintegrate as a family."

"That's why TS Eliot," said Benedicta. "You're finding cultural roots."

"I'm trying," Data said, then she grinned. "Very trying."

David cuffed her very, very gently on the top of the head, more like a whisper than a cuff.

"When we were well-behaved, opportunities would be offered to us at school. We were given excursions and treats. Bob and I talked about it, and Bob wondered why. He was the one who started looking into what made the door work the way it does."

"It's not the door."

"I know. It's the transition. The thing is, the scientists back home have been looking at the genetics of the shift for fifty years now. They've noted who could leave comfortably and who was killed. They were putting together data so they could work out who was affected in advance. That was the data I was just sent, and I'm still processing it. By the time I had left school, they'd worked out that anyone who came from this universe was more likely to die on re-entering this universe. But Mum ... Mum was the very last person to come from Earth1. She came through just weeks before that explosion. She wasn't fully green until she was fourteen. They hung onto her and kept her close to the Envoy scheme because her biodata was this big mess of information. They introduced her to Papa, and we were damned lucky it was a love match."

"You think the murder …" Ariette was aghast.

"I can't know. Tsarfat isn't that big. We're less than a million people. Papa was beaten to death in a popular shop in a popular street. There were no witnesses. I think it was very odd that the youths who murdered him were never identified or caught, and that the moment he was dead, the pressure on Mum to conform grew. I also think the timing is suspicious."

"How?" Bennie's eyes were again narrowed, but this time with concentrated fury at what had been done to Data and her family. When she had told the girls about her secret group of friends, she had unofficially adopted them. The 'Auntie' she insisted they call her indicated a real relationship in her life.

"We were old enough to think about the younger entry point for the Envoy scheme. We finished school with that in mind. You were there, Ariette, you saw it happen. Am I right?"

Ari looked across at her and nodded, reluctantly. "It fits. I wish it didn't, but it fits. What also fits is the way the rules were changed so that you could both be trained. The way Monsieur Chevalier–who everyone knows hates your mother–was your mentor, the way …" she drifted off into reflections.

"Mum had a special name for our mentor." Data's face looked suddenly irreverent. "I think it's why Bob did his own research into things and wrote that letter. She said it wasn't fair to call him by his real surname because it was an insult to all Christians in Tsarfat, so she invented a nickname. I still use it."

"The missing letter," David said solemnly, focussed on what mattered. Nicknames were interesting, but missing letters were exciting.

Data nodded. "The missing letter."

Her Maj was less focussed. "Out with it. What did your brother call this source of all evil?" Benedicta Beja would have fumed if there was someone who deserved the fuming. As it was, if she ever met Monsieur Chevalier, David was certain it would be the source of all evil who would rue the meeting.

"Does Earth2 have any Centres for Disease Control?"

"In America," David hazarded.

"Yes, in the US," Benedicta agreed.

"Well ..." Data's voice built up to a little climax. "Chevalier's initials are CDC. He's the Disease."

"That calls for a tea break," Benedicta announced. "We will get back to your story and to the theories you were going to propound. I need to hear them."

"That's a big thing," Ari whispered. "She was only being polite early on."

"I thought so," Data said with much irony. "I was telling it to David anyhow."

"To David?" Ari was puzzled.

"David has a higher need to know that the rest of you."

"Are you going to tell us why?"

David blinked at the level of denseness in the room, which had been full of intellectual sparks five minutes before. "We all need that tea," he said.

"I've been thinking about this," Data began when cups of tea had been found. "And I need to stick to the theory a bit more so we don't go off-track. I've broken it down into stages. What happened in our lives first was amity, when everyone was nice to us so that we didn't question being treated differently and so that we didn't believe Mum when she said things were wrong."

"Wait," said Ari. "I can write this up."

AMITY she wrote on the wall, which was also a whiteboard.

178

David loved that wall and wanted to take it home with him. His best possible superhero power would have to be shrinking objects like this wall, putting them in his back pocket, quietly walking out with them, taking them home, then growing them again. Gods did that in Chinese fantasy dramas. They shrunk things and hid them in their sleeves. His superhero power could link his cultures.

"OK," Data continued, sadly, David thought, unable to share his mental image. *Superpowers aren't what the comics say they are. They don't grow into infinity as you get to know the superhero. That's their biggest drawback in real life. If you want to be as powerful as Superman, you've got to start off by being Superman.* "Next came insults that we got that no-one else got. They couldn't see what we were reacting to."

"Who was doing this?" asked Ari.

"Later for detail," said Benedicta. "Write that up as 'dog whistling'; it's a standard aspect of a certain type of racism."

"There are studies?" Data asked.

"There most certainly are studies," Her Maj said firmly. "David is going to get them for you."

"I would like that." Data was nearly diffident in saying this. "I would like to know what it is and that it wasn't us. I want to learn how it wasn't us. All I know is that there was a pattern, and Bob and I got wise to it, and I got angry, and Bob got even."

"Got even?"

"He played practical jokes on the perpetrators."

"Not very wise."

"Maybe, but no-one could accuse him of ill will, just as no-one could blame the dog whistlers. It was a strange little war."

By this time, DOG WHISTLE was up on the board.

"I can already tell you why this might be part of our broader problem," Benedicta offered, "but I'd like to hear the rest of the list first."

"The rest was us reacting. Me especially. Everyone knew that when people annoyed him, Bob would play tricks on them, but only the nasty guys knew why. Me, I lost my temper a lot. I walked out of meetings. I ... was told I was a drama queen. That was the turning point. Bob and I were left out of social functions, just like Mum had been. It was like our whole family didn't belong in Tsarfat. Nothing we did was acceptable. We were respectable, and we were invisible, both at once. I was told I was a nice person, but never invited to parties or dinners or even to the picnics our old school friends organised. We were terribly alone. If someone had offered us a chance to enter normal society and become a part of it, we would've leapt at it."

"They didn't offer you that?" asked Ari. "I knew you'd been left out after your father died, but I was part of a meeting where everyone decided that the rest of us had to pull our weight and reach out because you were bereaved."

"You went through the door at that point, didn't you?"

"How did you guess?"

"Because you didn't see that we weren't invited to anything more private than the *bal musette*. I'd walk down the streets around lunchtime, skipping lunch. Everyone lunched *en famille* behind their shutters. Bob used lunchtime to do research that other people wouldn't notice. Mum worked through lunch because people kept on giving her more and more work. So, I'd walk past each red brick house and look at the different ornamentation, and I'd wonder if I knew the people inside. At that point in my life, I didn't know it was possible to be more lonely."

ISOLATION went up on the whiteboard.

"That was the Disease's moment."

"The disease?" asked Ari.

"Bob's nickname for Chevalier," David explained. "We had

it a second ago." Everyone looked at him. It was odd being the centre of so much attention. Data's look was the one he liked the most, he admitted, since it was a slightly silly grin. He noticed Her Maj notice the grin—light went off, and a faint 'Oh' escaped Her Maj's lips. He added slightly defensively, "She knows what I call my supervisor."

"I'm so glad," said Her Maj, more sarcastic than gracious.

"What did the Disease do?" Ari asked, falling into the nickname as if it were made for her to use. David reminded himself that Ari needed to hear things three times to remember. He wondered when the missed conversation was.

"He offered us a way out. Or rather, a way back into society, to find careers and to be respected. He arranged for us to get the training and to go through the door. Both of us. Even though it was improper. With him as mentor, even though he hates Mum."

"How could you ever accept any of that?" Ari demanded.

"He was our saviour at a time when no-one was talking to us. We didn't know that he had probably set the whole thing up the way he'd set all the earlier stuff up for Mum. We worked it out before we went through the door, but that was too late."

"Everyone's entitled to draw back, even right at the door. It's a rule."

"We were told that the rule had been changed. That's why Bob wrote that letter. The missing one. He didn't know how far the Disease had played us, or what lies we'd been told, and he wanted to get everything documented."

"He wasn't stupid, your brother," Benedicta said thoughtfully.

"He was very bright. You and he would've been dangerous together. All brilliance and brain and wanting to make the world better. If the rule hadn't been waived, he would've been the right person to be an Envoy. I am not nearly as perfect for this job as he was. And I think ..." Data stabbed her stylus into the arm of the chair as if killing the chair would help. "I think that's why he was murdered. They thought they had us both. They really only had me. When they killed him, they lost me."

"Losing you is a good thing, right?" David asked uncertainly.

"That's a very good thing," said Data, giving him her sweetest smile. "They knew I had trouble hearing, but they didn't know my super talent was going to be computers. I was going to be their poster child for sadness and loss. Now I'm going to send them on the path they sent me on."

"Except the end of it for them will be a trial. I promise you that, Data." Benedicta ruled the room, always, and at this moment, it was very clear why. It was not her position nor her ancestry nor her magic; it was her. Every word she said carried an enormous strength.

Chapter Ten

David handed a set of comics to Ari.

"Why do you want these, anyway?" he asked.

"I need to collect ones that have influenced our thoughts, and you're a new component in them. Your superhero interests feed into the way you work and affect how you react to us. I'll annotate these and scan them for emergencies."

"What kind of emergency uses these comics?" asked Data. She was having a lovely time flicking through them. Comics had been a part of her life for a long time, and there were two Wonder Woman comics in this pile. "This is my Mum's favourite," she noted.

"You can't borrow them," Ari said. "Get your own. This is head-of-mission work."

"How is it head-of-mission work?"

"It's showing the way we each build up our various suggestions at various times. It's a lot easier to send these across annotated than the regular approaches. We have no time for the regular approaches."

"We have time for talking," David said. "In these comics, the superheroes don't have time for talking nearly as often as you make us chat."

"That's one of the reasons you're represented by the comics. You compare us and we fall short, often as not. I also chose comics for you, David, because you're always listing the superhero powers you would have if you could."

"Hey," Date said, "that was confidential."

"It's fine," said David. "I don't mind being known by comics. It fits the way I examine the world in my research."

"That's what I thought," Ari said.

"I'm missing why this is so important," Data said. "I thought you collected ephemera for yourself. This is not part of that collection, then."

"It is," Ari said seriously, "and it isn't. We're on close-down. They say the door is shut because of the most recent deaths. I can't get the physical copies through the door and have to send in electronic versions. Also, I want it to look as if all our outside operations have ground to a halt. I don't want any traitors to have even an inkling of what we're doing."

"*I* don't even have an inkling of what we're doing," Data declared.

Ari ignored this and continued to talk about comics. "I have an actual collection in storage, but the likelihood of any of us surviving here if the policies at home change and exclude us is low, and so I make sure that if I die, my more meaningful thoughts go to my successor and they don't have to start from scratch."

"I didn't know those policies could change. Why aren't we safe?" Data asked. "Also, I thought we were over the worst. Now that we know the threshold's restrictions, we've solved everything."

David didn't know whether to be amused or astonished. He opted for astonished. "Data, she's saying that Chevalier and all his best friends are probably going to target you or have someone else target you when you stop being useful to them."

"Or when the gaze of Tsarfat is not on us. Data, your mother has been cast out from society. My family has cast me out. Each alone is not a strong argument that we're in peril, but when you add the Green family members who I have confirmed are still working for us ... there's a lot of casting out. We're in danger. It's the price of being ethical and in our circumstances."

"How closely is our project linked to the foul betrayal? Will working on it help my mother?" Data asked this hopefully, David noted.

"At this moment in time," Ari said, "unless the man in Amiens who recognised you is linked to the bombings, I have not the least idea. I'm taking precautions and adding to my collection of ephemera as a part of our work, in case. I want us represented in the archives if our lives are destroyed and for enough material to exist there for someone to reach in and research and find out what we did and who we are."

"Secret codes!" Data was too enthusiastic, David felt. She was ignoring that the secret codes were brought into being by personal peril. The anxiety of the everyday was taking its toll. He was very glad that this world was his home and not a little Green pocket universe. He yearned to visit Tsarfat, but Singapore was a safer place all round.

Ari shifted the conversation sideways. "Here, read some Wonder Woman. I need quiet."

"You should just switch off your ears," Data said.

"I noticed you doing that at the pub last night," Ari admitted.

"How could you tell they were off?"

"The colours changed," David said. "I didn't know why at first. I shouted at you before and after, and you couldn't hear me either way."

"There was simply too much noise. I went internal."

"Internal?" David asked.

"Computer stuff," said Ari. "We're the land of techo, remember?"

"I don't get to see your techo much," David complained. "I thought it was just you misusing English."

"I like that," said Data. "You thought I was saying techno all wrong."

Ari was more sympathetic. "Next time you see that colour change, whisper to her on the internet. She gossips a lot there."

"I do not gossip! I have friends!"

"I thought your phone was the advanced computer," David said. "That's why I heard techo as 'techno.' I thought it was a new release I'd not seen. I had no idea I was typing directly into your ears."

"It's not actually a phone," Data said, handing it over for him to examine. "It's my emergency backup for everything. Mostly power, but backup."

"You carry it—"

"I need something to hold to my ear and then frown or stare at wisely and nod the way you do. Camouflage."

"Is it that your hearing aids are attached to a computer or that your computer is attached to hearing aids?"

"Neither. They're separate. The earpieces are to show people I have them; it's a courtesy because I prefer to read peoples' faces to checking the disturbed airways for sounds and then decoding them. Reading lips mostly works, and reading airways only works occasionally. One of the advantages of my late father's job and my mentor's normal work was that they specialised in advanced communications."

"And they're tiny. I mean your earpieces, not your parents." David felt stupid for explaining and stupid for mis-saying it and … just stupid, he guessed.

"Micro rather than nano, and mine is unusual in how far it's connected, because my power turned out to be linked. No-one else's system operates quite like mine."

"You said that like the boast in *Beauty and the Beast*. I want to call you 'Gaston' … no-one's ears glow like Data's, no-one's—"

"Shut up, you," Data said, cuffing David in a friendly manner.

"I shouldn't tease you. Not after what my supervisor did."

"I didn't mind what he did because I didn't like him. I correct people I like. But him, I don't want to chat with him; and if he thinks that less hearing equals less intelligence, well, that's in my favour."

"It wasn't just the earpieces. He hated your hair. And he said something about you coming from a failed universe."

"Now that's interesting," Ari said.

"The hair?" Data was still mischievous.

"The hair is always interesting, although I'm not certain about today's striped challenge, but I meant the failed universe."

"I don't see how Tsarfat is a failed universe." Data's tone became stubborn, and her chin lifted, ready to fight.

"Not Tsarfat. Earth1. No magic there. And now, no superheroes. We're here."

"I'm not from Earth1!"

"Your mother, you said," David said. "She was the last person to cross into Tsarfat. But that means the whole of Tsarfat is tarred with Earth1, just her a bit more so."

"Let's not have your supervisor as our enemy," Data said lightly, "for he won't care if we all died, since we're all linked to that failed universe, eventually. All of Tsarfat came from there. Every single one of us."

"What does he want, your supervisor?"

"In a theoretical way? He did a paper on it last year. He has an ideal political system that would work in a pocket universe.

A perfect place. He's writing the structure of it now. Economic and social theory. Scholarly world building, he describes it as, theoretical and a useful way of understanding how societies work. He's good at breaking it down into common English and sharing it as a dream. He has groups of followers in the most amazing places."

"I bet," said Data, "that he knows I'm hard of hearing but doesn't quite believe in the rest of it. That he thinks I'm a bit stupid and that my earpieces are accessorised hearing aids. He thinks he knows everything and is on top of everything. He was consulted and let us take his student away to use as slave labour, but we're another group who is supporting his theory. He doesn't treat us like real people from other worlds."

"That worked until a few weeks ago," Ari pointed out. "Until those fractures. David, don't tell him anything. He's a theorist, but if he's communicating with others and one of those groups is linked, then we're stuffed."

"That's a problem, though," said David. "I mean, we've just cut ourselves off from the most obvious link for information from those circles."

"And if he's linked to the terrorists?"

"Surely not," David said.

"I don't mean he's in with them," Ari said. "He talks to the office here, after all, and has gone through all the security checks. It's just that he's popular, and you said he's good at talking. If he knows things about us he should not, and if he brings that knowledge into his theory and then talks about his theory, it could compromise our work."

"I can think of another reason not to talk to him about any of this, and it's a reason Her Maj wouldn't see."

"Why do you call her that stupid nickname?" Data asked.

"Because I like it," David replied smoothly. "Do you want to know my reason?"

"Give!" Data said.

"I think he hates Jews. He talks differently about anyone Jewish when there aren't any Jews present. It's not that he's careful with it. It's a deep part of his language culture; he adjusts his adjectives according to the level of Jewishness in a room."

"Why such a strong word? Hates is big."

"I once heard him making an ashtray joke."

Ari was silent from shock.

Data was silent from Ari's shock, but after a moment said, "I don't think we have ashtray jokes in Tsarfat. What are they?"

"We were saved from ashtray jokes by escaping to Tsarfat," Ari said, her voice quiet with pain. She didn't answer Data's question. "So, we avoid David's supervisor whenever we can and for as long as we can, and we tell Benedicta why. And that we need to take our earlier hypothesis about him quite seriously."

"Not formal communication. We can't use paper or the computer," David said. "He's done a lot of shared work with Beja's Office. He's quite proud of knowing what's going on here."

"I'll take care of it," Ari said. Her voice was resigned. Her face was entirely missing spirit and life.

✡

It took Ari a half day to get in to see Benedicta Beja and let her know. Beja was doubtful about the antisemitism, but agreed that chances should not be taken once Ari pointed out that her privilege might be masking problems and pointedly called her 'Auntie'. Data, in the meantime, had been sent off to collect more information about the earliest incidents. She dutifully went to each part of London and talked to locals.

She couldn't simply use her techo. Data had to catch buses

and trains and walk from shop to shop and chat to the police and
to people on the street.

When Ari returned to their rooms that evening, she found
Data sitting in the big chair. That window was always right.
Their lodging was in a busy part of London, and a well-lit part
of London. The brightness hadn't worried Data before, but that
night her back was resolutely facing that window.

"Did you find out anything?"

"Not much," Data replied. "People were very nice to me.
They wanted to help me because I'm disabled. They were being
so damned helpful they didn't listen to what I wanted, and they
were full of information we don't need. They didn't notice that
my damned hearing aids work very nicely, thank you, and they
condescended like buggery. I wish someone would turn the
lights off so that I can cry in peace."

Chapter Eleven

Data's problem with people not listening to her was the first in a whole series of tiny nuisances. Little things, each of them, but they were relentless in their combined effect. From phone lines going down to failed hacks on servers to more rudeness (about Frenchness, about the shape of eyes, about … all the things) to calls on Benedicta's and the Merlin's time that took them both out of operation.

The small and the stupid continued and built up, and within a fortnight, everything was delayed. The team had not hit a brick wall. They were operating in a never ceasing deluge of slime-filled balloons.

David set up a whiteboard, and he and Data classified everything.

Some of these small irritants were political, some were straightforward "This cannot be done because," and some were interpersonal.

The moment of most pique came when Benedicta took Data shopping. "We need a break," she said, "And you need respectable clothes. I can't be seen with you at functions in what you're wearing."

Data grumbled at her in the way one grumbles at a favourite aunt. She didn't care about Benedicta's preferred clothes, but being shopped for by Benedicta was a nice thing, she thought, especially if they had high tea afterwards, which Benedicta had promised. There was a new place Bennie wanted to try. The moment she put on her 'Bennie' friendliness, Ari resolved to watch out. The friendliness was genuine, but so were the agendas.

"I've never had high tea before," Data said with enthusiasm.

"The others can join us there."

"We'll have to have high tea later, then?"

"The service changes over. They'll have dinner. We'll have high tea," Benedicta said. "My assistant has booked it all. There's a reception in the evening to honour a couple of musicians. We'll go straight from one to the other."

High tea, Data jubilated all day. *With Auntie. Real English high tea. Mummy never got to try that. I will tell her all about it. High tea!* Her earpieces distracted everyone so much with the flashing that Ari asked her to turn the colours off.

"I can't concentrate," she admitted.

Data turned off the lights and joked to herself about being in the dark. Behind those thoughts lay the comforting words, *High tea in London with my Auntie.*

Underneath these words was the dawning realisation that, somehow, Benedicta had moved from being a distant, cold boss of supreme rank and respectability to being an Auntie who would take her to high tea and buy her clothes. She decided not to tell anyone this. It would last longer if she didn't annoy Auntie Ben.

High tea was lovely from the moment they entered the door to the exclusive new restaurant. Staff bowed and led them in and gave them the menus and Data said, "I didn't know we got to choose."

"There are six choices for each type of dish," the waitstaff explained, her face glowing with happiness to help. "And twenty choices of tea. When you finish a pot, of course, you may choose a different tea. There are pots of chocolate, if you prefer, of course, or cups of coffee."

"I don't want coffee at all," Data declared, matching glow for glow. "I want tea. Auntie, I like all the dishes here. Choose for both of us."

"Meaning you have no idea of what half of them are?"

"You're so very English," Data grumbled at her. "Of course I don't know what half of them are. I can look them up, or I can trust you."

"I could explain," the amused staff suggested.

"When you serve them, I would love that, thank you; but first, I want Auntie to surprise me with her choices," Data declared.

"All right, then," said Benedicta. "If we exclude all the dishes that have ham or its close relatives, that leaves us precisely the right number. That's a large number of dishes to have that single ingredient, but it makes it very easy for us to choose."

"So simple," Data said.

In front of them, the young happy woman ready to help … changed. Her smile looked forced and her politeness was cool and restrained. "Thank you," she said. "I will arrange this."

"She didn't take our order for tea," Data said. "I've got a list of all the ones I want to try. If I drink a lot, I can get through, what, three?"

"When she gets back, you can give her your list. Or when someone replaces her."

Benedicta was right about a replacement. Tea was brought with the food by a new staff member.

"We didn't get to choose our tea," said Data, aggrieved.

"We have run out of everything except English Breakfast. I'm terribly sorry," said the older woman who had replaced the younger. She put everything down quickly. Neatly. There was no fault to be found, except that the difference between the grand welcome and their treatment now was unmistakable.

"Do you get this a lot?" Data asked when the waitstaff had quietly gone.

"I don't, no. Was this booked in my name?"

"In Ari's."

"Good. That is what I wanted. These people have no idea who I am and are serving me as an older Jewish woman who is visiting with her niece. Can you report on this to young David? As we go? Tell him he may talk on social media about any aspects that he finds give him interesting insights into British culture."

"Is he allowed to use phrases like 'my girlfriend and her auntie'?"

"Girlfriend?"

Data nodded nervously.

Benedicta sighed. "Very well. Honorary auntie, however."

"Done," Data said, and they started enjoying the food. "Is this part of our project, then? I can't see it, myself." The sandwich was poised between her plate and her mouth, for the thought had temporarily taken over Data's need to eat. "Or is it something just for you?"

"You needed time out, and I heard rumours about this place. I wanted to find out for myself."

"Oh," Data said. "My mother got so tired of it all that she only ever goes to two places. They're run by the parents of friends of Bob and of me, so the staff can't isolate her."

"That's why I wanted you. You know the difference between mild ostracism and normal poor service."

"Oh," Data said, feeling strangely vulnerable. "This was made hours ago," she then said as she bit into the sandwich. "That's why it came out so quickly. It was not made for us."

Benedicta helped herself to the equivalent sandwich and bit in thoughtfully. "This was made hours ago too. So dry." Her mouth puckered, and she took a quick sip of tea. "Teabag," she guessed. She opened the pot, and there the teabags lay. "Tell David, and tell him about the difference in the way our table is treated."

Data looked around and saw that other tables were treated as if the diners were special.

"I bet their sandwiches were made for them and not ahead too."

"I think we're eating someone's untouched food from earlier." Benedicta noted. "Review it for David but don't say that. Find all its strengths and all its faults. Be brutally honest."

Honesty was easy, for they didn't see a staff member until one visited fifteen minutes later to present the bill.

"We've only been here a few minutes," Data said.

"I'm sorry, but we're short of space." The apology sounded authentic, but ...

"I booked for dinner as well," Benedicta stated, her face showing worry. "That's why we have a table for four."

"I'm sorry, but there was a mistake in the reservation."

"I would like to speak to your superior."

"I'll go get him."

"Are we staying?" Data asked.

"Certainly not. I want to let him know that we've let the whole world know about this. That's all."

"A courtesy."

"That's right."

Ari and David were told to come in and collect them. Benedicta put her card in the wallet and waited for a response. Nothing. Or rather, everything. Simply a return of the card and a receipt with an extraordinary tip added to the receipt.

"Excuse me," Benedicta said, "I choose how much I tip. Take

my card and try again. With no tip." The wallet came back the moment the others appeared. Benedicta opened it and examined it and put a note in the wallet explaining that bad service and poor food concerned her and she would not be visiting again. Given this, she wrote, she was including a generous tip to make up for the loss of future custom. She added cash. Before she had finished, three friends had joined them.

"Why tip them at all?" Data turned to the person closest.

"Damn Jewish stereotyping. If she doesn't, no matter how deserved that no-tip was, she would be guilty of being mean."

"I thought that, with England being so very Jewish ..."

"Bigots exist of all kinds in all places."

The Merlin sighed. "She does this all the time. Instead of intimidating people, she depresses them."

"What would you have done?" Ari asked as they left the new and illustrious dining establishment behind them forever.

"If I were Benedicta, I would have gently dropped my name."

"But as you?"

"I never face such things."

"If you did?" Ari prompted, curious.

"Magic," he admitted. "I would have made it very clear that those who discriminate against me face consequences."

"Everyone else would then have to face consequences you've set up," Benedicta said. "I've said this so often, and you never understand. You and I are privileged. We have the choice to experience or not to experience slights. Other people are not so fortunate."

"The social media," said Ari. "That was your way of handling it."

"How many people know that bad behaviour is not rewarded with continued support?" Benedicta asked her.

"At this moment? 4,512."

The Merlin sighed. "All the anti-Semites will now visit that restaurant for high tea."

"They have a right to," Benedicta said. "Just as I have a right to fresh sandwiches and to feel special in a place one only visits for the experience of that treat."

"It's more than that," Data argued. "I've seen this type of thing back home. If only those who are bigoted turn up to a place, then the owners know what their choices mean."

"How did you experience this at home?" Ari asked.

"My father and I, when I was little. And I don't want to talk about it. Hatred might hurt, but being treated as a second-class citizen hurts too."

"I've always wondered why you took up the Green dreams when you're not Jewish and your mother has never really belonged in Tsarfat."

"It's because the Green dreams help address for others the causes of Mum not being allowed to belong. I love my Mum beyond anyone, and she was hurt and is still being hurt. No-one should have to go through what she went through."

"You know," the Merlin said conversationally, as if paths of great depth and sorrow were not being trodden, "it's like misogyny in a Christian environment. I have no idea what Tsarfat thinks of women, but here, how one is treated as a Jew, being not quite acceptable, is how many women are treated outside the Jewish community. I need to research this. What did your world give you in terms of misogyny? Do you read John Chrysostom, or does it come naturally?"

"You reduce personal experience and discomfort to research projects, so I'm not going to answer that," Data replied.

"Good," Benedicta said. "Besides, he can observe for himself, given where we're going."

"Where are we going?" Data asked. "You said a reception?"

"Officially, it's for musicians. My daughter set it up. They're obscuring the fact that it's for your people," the Merlin said. "You'll see. You won't have time to eat there. Let's get some food."

It was a very comfortable kind of reception. Tea and coffee rather than alcohol. Groups of chairs rather than enforced standing around. Two musicians met everyone at the door. One of them was Ari's favourite singer of Gilbert and Sullivan. She wasn't as round in person as she looked on stage. In fact, she resembled Benedicta. *A relative*, David thought, as the polite handshake he had received folded into a hug when Benedicta came close.

Five rescued Tsarfati Envoys felt welcomed and, for the first time since they walked through the door that left home behind, safe. One of them was Lisette. They couldn't go home until the problems were solved, but they were safe.

Data and Ari were there to provide the feeling of safety and to welcome them to England and …

"Why are they all here now?" Data whispered to Ariette when they had a moment in between groups. "And why are there so many British government people welcoming them? I didn't get anything like this."

"They've all been checked and are not talking to Chevalier or anyone else. We can't use our own offices, so we and they are part of a new group that works with the British on particular types of problems."

"You're the international superheroes," the Merlin said behind them. "I don't know if I'll maintain this over the long term, but it will certainly be useful for the next few years."

"Next few years?"

Data was confused.

"The sort of thing those fools set up with their bombs and their recruitment of people into random groups to commit their acts for them will have consequences. Too many people have discovered the joys of hurting others to fuel their own grief."

"And this can't be done purely by your government?"

"We have a history," the Merlin said drily, "of not being entirely perfect in this."

He walked away at that point, leaving Data puzzled.

"Look up bombings over the last century or so," said Ari "Anywhere British. That'll give you a dozen reasons why the government wants to stay out of it."

"Is it good for us? I mean is it good for Tsarfat or the Green dreams?"

"That's difficult to say. It depends on us. It's the sensible path at this moment, however."

"Wait, I get it," Data said enthusiastically. "This is why we've worked with the most senior people. In their offices rather than of their offices."

"Plausible deniability," Benedicta said quietly from behind them. "I'm sorry it has to be done this way. For you, for these other children."

"We're not children," Data pointed out.

"I know. That's part of our marketing. You're the Green Children, and you will save us from evil."

"You needed to know who could be trusted or if we had to work outside our own offices," Ari said in accusation. They were speaking in hushed tones, as if there was a world of listeners.

"We did. The moment you sent that message, wanting to meet with me, this was a likely outcome."

"I'm not sure I'm happy with it," said Data.

"We're going back to my office after this. David's there. And you won't like his briefing at all. Make these five welcome, for you may need them."

Chapter Twelve

David was not only in the office, he had brought in good coffee and an array of gourmet cake.

"What's this?" Ari asked.

"If I'm doing the briefing, you need sustenance," said David.

"Bribery to stay awake," Data said.

"That too."

Benedicta sat down behind her desk. "I'll be listening," she said, then proceeded to her paperwork. The tap-tap of fingers on the keyboard and the occasional rustle of paper was all that anyone heard from her for the next hour. David's thought when he realised this was how quiet her breathing was and how creepy such quiet breathing was. He had dreamed of his grandmother again, and in that dream, her breathing had been the same as Benedicta's right now. His grandmother had said nothing. She had sat in the chair next to his bed, and he could hear her breathe while he lay there.

He tried to put it out of his mind, but it haunted his presentation. The first bit of the briefing was easy.

✡

I'm going to tell you about two incidents. The first is one that took place a while ago but only just came to light. I'll use it to explain where we're up to and the results of the work I did while the rest of you were doing ... other work. Then I'll update you on today's incident.

There's a hill in Somerset. The first paper in the background papers I'm giving you now (Data, couldn't you wait 'til I got it to you?) is a map of the region. Several of those hills are thought by tourist traps to be fairy mounds. They're not. They're hills. Geologically speaking, totally hills. Not barrows. Not secret places where the good folk live. Hills. Hills in a hilly country.

That's why this old incident is part of the briefing today. I've been pulling together the evidence for all the incidents, and one thing they have in common is that all the places have popular belief that matches the door thing. That's the unifying factor. They do not match up with ley lines, with magic locations, with great moments of history. They match up with the folk traditions you read about in tourist brochures.

I'm using this particular incident to highlight this fact because the hills make it so very clear.

I interpret this as indicating that if there's someone central to the whole series, they are unlikely to be local to any of those areas. We're talking someone who started in England, and who is making it spread outside England, but who is not actually English. Why they are unlikely to be English will become clearer soon.

I've traced the popular traditions, and all the ones that link to incidents come back to tourist brochures. Even the Embankment incident can be traced back to a tourist brochure. That's page two of your handout. The tinted page for you, Data. That tour of Victorian London plays with the idea of doors to the past, and the tour guide uses the Embankment as the place where they stand and declaim, "If we went back to the past at this point, we'd see a different England."

I interviewed the guide. They asked me not to identify even their gender. I'll explain that soon.

They said they were going to use Soho and talk about sex, but a group of children were part of an early booking, so they changed the route and talked about the Embankment, and that brought in other things, which I'll get to shortly. The illustration they used for the Embankment was the sixteenth century and how most Jews in London were still hidden at that time.

I asked them about Milk Street, and they said yes, they used that too. "This is the centre of Jewish London in our universe," they told me. "In an Earth with fewer Jews, it might be gobbled up by the financial district. In another universe, where Hitler won, the street would look very different."

I asked them what they thought of those two incidents, and they said they were scared.

At this point, you should note that I've used no names and no gender. This person is an independent scientist. They couldn't get a job after their PhD because of the cutbacks, and they didn't think they were suited to industry, so they settled down in other work and thought it would be fun to run tours describing alternate Londons based on their research. Real Earths brought to life while my source walked tourists through our streets. Those tours never took off. My source replaced them with tours of London from various periods, and they started riffing off their research because of the children and Soho.

The subjects obscure the fact that the PhD was in physics.

I asked where those ideas came from. I told them that nothing they had said so far explained why they were so scared.

They had met two members of the Green family. One of them had informed them about Tsarfat. They had used Tsarfat as a base point when they were still researching. They hadn't believed in Tsarfat, but they thought it would be interesting to use the concept. When they were in between jobs and bored, they redid all their calculations concerning other worlds using what they'd learned from the Greens. They used this *for their tour material.*

I asked them how they knew about the Hitler thing, and they gave me a set of calculations showing different factors and different distances from our Earth and what factors need changing to reach that particular one.

They're terrified of whoever it was that bombed the way into something that for them was a scientific exploration. Now that they've passed us everything, their calculations, their notes for the tour, they've gone into hiding. I can't find them anywhere, and I'm hopeful that whoever did the bombing can't find them anywhere either.

They helped me check a random set of incidents, and only three others match their work, and all of the incidents we checked were used to add 'colour' to their tour in London. I take this to mean that the science behind the bombings is largely experimental. The bombings, then, have real calculations behind them but are based on extrapolated data, with the information from the tour guide being used to give a head start. This explains why it all looks so very random. It also explains why some places, like the one in Somerset, have delivered nothing more than a hole in the ground.

An outsider is using material foreign to them.

Now we get to when you were in France. Some of it made news.

Twelve deaths. The church. The pit in the middle of it that was full of brimstone and fire. That was an early one. I've done what I can with the notes from my source, but I'm better with words than physics. From what they said, though, I'll lay odds this is not an Earth close to us in the scheme of things. It has more factors changed than any of the other calculations, then. I don't know how, but I can guess why. The narrative of the incidents is that much clearer.

That hole opened up beneath a church. The British default modern culture is Christian, and the incident in the church had all the hallmarks of a hell mouth from Medieval tradition. I have a briefing from your people, Benedicta, and they say that every indication is that this is not a part of ancient Britain. This mouth has transgressed, in other words, and shifted space as well as time. That is why two flying lizards came out of it. They were hurt by the flames, which suggests that they are not hell beasts.

"I can't believe you're saying this all so seriously," Data said.

I wanted to be sarcastic. Truly I did. But people died.

I'm not going to get emotional about this bit, even though it's very emotional. I represented the Office at one of the funerals from that first fire and brimstone incident because I'm Christian. Other bits of government did other funerals from this incident, but that one was mine, and I don't know how people do this kind of thing as a regular part of their job. I was there at the back, thinking about how terrible it was that this person had been killed. The people in that church on that day were there because of an explosion. I looked around and wondered what else they had in common. The explosion was one of the useless ones. It hadn't created a gate. It had killed a person. If there had been a change on the streets, someone more senior would've gone.

I know it was just another door to just another world, and I ought to be sophisticated about this by now, but this one hurt me so very much. That funeral ... I've never been to anything so sad. It wasn't for one person. It was for the whole family. Three generations were there to cry about their lost boy. Whoever plans these things has won my eternal hate.

The service was short, because no-one else could take it either, but we all stood around in the church afterwards, and we cried, and we talked, and we cried, and we talked. It was as if I'd known all of them forever. I didn't know any of them and won't ever see them again. But it was strange. We were all together, hating whoever did that thing and wanting to bring the family back and wanting to go back in time and wanting so very much.

While we chatted, that other hole opened up. A hell mouth. A gaping maw. Things flew out of it and flew into walls, through glass, into *people.*

When someone found out that it was me who had brought the Merlin in, it all became too uncomfortable. I never closed the hell mouth. I was there. I made a phone call. I didn't save anyone.

That's going to hurt me for the rest of my life. Can I finish reporting the incident without the emotion, please? Thank you.

The creatures that emerged have been determined to be non-human. Quite possibly related to birds. The material used to determine this was gleaned from the church when everything was over. There was a bit of a fight with the two of them as they flew out from the hole. The congregation sent me their version of events, telling me that it was wings of darkness bringing shadow to the world.

As everyone knows, I saw them emerge. I rang the Merlin, and he was there thirty seconds later. Both birds exploded into puffs of smoke that smelled like brimstone. The Merlin and I and everyone else who felt official helped get everyone who was still in the church out. No-one was hurt after he arrived.

We didn't know what to do with the hole into hell. The Merlin made explosion after explosion using his magic, and eventually, it sealed. The stone floor looked as if it had melted. There were more body parts. I don't know how much longer I can brief you on this before I explode.

Chapter Thirteen

"Good," Benedicta said. "And well done." She looked up from her work and started to pack up.

"What now?" Ari asked.

"We need to feed David cake," Data said.

"We'll have to take it with us," Benedicta replied. "David, I would prefer you came with us. We're going to need everyone this time."

"More deaths?"

"Not at all. There was another door. It remained open for precisely two hours. Why I wasn't told about it earlier is beyond the fathom of humankind. We need to hurry."

"What happened?"

"We have two hours' worth of refugees from a warzone. The trucks with help are on the way, but there's a certain lack of hands when something is as classified as this."

Two hours later, they were at the site. It was a cliff by the sea, the sort that would normally appear in a BBC drama. The cliff itself was the usual shape and size and texture, except that one section–maybe four metres across and eight metres high–was oddly flattened. Nothing crumbly about it, nothing flaky. The rock looked as if it had been polished, which was impossible.

"Too much of this looks impossible but is a hundred percent real," David said to Benedicta. They were a team. She was the source of all decision making, and he was documenting it. This gave him time to look around. The level of the shore was wrong. For metres and metres around the flat stone, the land was higher, and it was rubble rather than weathered stone. Crumbly rubble. Rubble from the cliff face.

"The explosion sheared it off," he said to Ari as she came back to check in. "Look."

"That's a door, then?"

"I think an old one. Someone has done this before."

"And it closed. But how?"

They wandered over and investigated.

"I wonder if it's self-closing," Ari said.

"Or if there's a switch on the other side."

"Either way," Benedicta said, catching up with them, "this means the door was made on the other side. We need to shut it in, pronto. There's a war on the other side of this portal, and a beach full of refugees is as much as I'm willing to handle of someone else's fighting."

Data helped hand out rescue packages. Her big eyes took it all in, and her techo sent everything back to all those who needed it for processing. She had already worked out that there was no happiness in this safety. The door itself was clearly not able to be used safely. Even if it could, home was not safe for these people. They might have special abilities in this world, or they might not, but they didn't speak a local language, and they were not quite as European in appearance. They would not be able to put makeup over the green skin and hide.

Her thoughts were interrupted by the order to empty the

beach and get everyone to safety. "Stay here," Data was told.

This surprised her. Data's task was to get pictures of any of the incident-makers so they could set up a new trail. None had appeared. They weren't interested in a door that led to a dangerous place, nor in refugees who further pushed their importance to the side. That, at least, was familiar. Only now she was recording ... something else.

"We need your eyes and David's computer hands on this scene. Ari's going to make sure the refugees reach a local hall, where we'll hand them over to Immigration."

"What am I looking for?"

"Watch and see." With that, Benedicta strode away, big steps for a short person, to tell others what to do.

A huge, dense metal mesh was dropped from the top of the cliff. A team of builders went in and padded it with ... something. Looked like cement, but it couldn't have been. This sealed off most of the cliff face around the door, with maybe two metres extra on each side. Another layer of ... something ... was slashed on top, quickly, as if time was critical, using a combination of machines and men in slings. Within an hour, that whole area of the cliff face, and some more besides, was covered in stuff. Dark stuff. While the cliff was being covered, another machine was brought onto the beach itself. This was tricky, for the tide had come in. The moment the tide was out far enough, the machine positioned itself on the sea-side of the slope of fallen cliff and blew the rubble back onto the cliff face. Where it stuck. Throughout the process, engineers checked and talked and checked again.

At the end of the long evening, Data was too tired to leave. In the dark, looking at an engineer in a sling, half-lit by spotlight, checking the rubble that had been blown back to where it had been only a day before, she saw only a dark blotch against the pale stone. She found a rock to prop herself up and looked at the lights that kept this place 'safe'. Inside her brain echoed the words, *I wish they'd turn the lights off so that I can cry in peace.*

There are times and places for everything. Some times and places are not appropriate for dwelling on personal sorrow. Next to a door to a tormented land is one such place.

Data's eyes framed the cliff as part of her inner world. She saw the spots of lights climb up and down and the lights from the beach flicker on and off as the cliff was slowly secured. She wished there was a fixed camera on it that was not held by her eyes. She wished she were back home with her mother and brother and that the last years had not existed. She wished that Earth2 was fictional and that she'd never walked through a door.

Data smiled a little grimly to herself as she realised how much further she'd come in resolving her past. Until tonight, she had been unable to wish at all. Meanwhile, people walked around her to fix and tidy the base of the cliff, people sat on their little mobile rope-chairs and checked the cliff face over and over, and a smaller number of people worked at the top of the cliff.

Data divided the big picture into scenes. Her eyes might be able to see more now that the tide was going out, but it would come in again, so the rock she was leaning against was still the best place to be. Data's brain needed to stop being on overload, she decided. Time to break this epic adventure into its component parts. Her eyes traced how one person checked the cliff face from bottom to top. When she reached the top, or rather, when the person checking the rock reached the top and the chair was moved a bit for the next check to begin, Data began from the top and worked her way down. A new specialist took up the chair.

The way he moved and the way he analysed the chair before he sat and the way he sat reminded her of Bob. There was something in his movement and in his shape. She smiled less grimly.

There was something different about this one. The person at

the top wasn't controlling the machinery in the usual way. The rope took the person down the side very quickly. It jolted and bumped against the new rock, swung in and out and bashed the seated engineer against the cliff face. Within a minute, it was at the bottom in a heap.

Data ran the twenty steps to reach the person. It was a man about Bob's age. He was dead. His bones were broken and crumpled his limbs in impossible ways.

Data froze. Physically and mentally, she froze. Electronically, she froze. Her techo stranded her inside her own brain, and she relived the last few moments. From the moment she thought this man looked like Bob until the moment she stood over him, crumpled on the beach. Her techo hit repeat and repeat and repeat. His death became Bob's death. That moment was her whole world.

Chapter Fourteen

Ari found Data at the bottom of the cliff at dawn.

"Benedicta and David have already gone," she said. "We've got the car to get ourselves back."

Data didn't answer. She stood very still, staring at the ground near the cliff. Ari assessed the situation.

"What happened here?" she asked one of the last people on the beach, a woman collecting litter.

"That's where someone fell," she said. "The word is that he was killed."

"Killed?"

"His ropes sagged, and he fell down the cliff. I don't know any more."

"He was collected a few minutes ago," said someone else, joining the conversation because it was a conversation. "They said there was tape of what happened and there would be an inquiry, and we were told to clear up everything and move out."

"What about the police?"

"They've been and gone. Everyone's been and gone."

"I was at the top of the cliff the whole time, and no-one called me." Ari felt savage.

"They called the police." The statement was supposed to be helpful, but it was also final.

"Did the police or anyone call someone to help anyone who saw it?"

"You'd have to ask them."

"Thank you," Ari said, but her mind was saying *No thanks at all. To any of you. How could you leave a person standing there and not take her to safety?* Ari was furious at the position her little sister had been left in.

Ari moved closer to Data, ready to put her arm around her and comfort her away. Above them both, the cliff was crumbling.

"Data, I need you. Tell me why the cliff is crumbling?"

I need you pulled Data out of deep freeze. "The cliff? It was patched up … and … "

"Look at the specifications Benedicta sent you. The way the repair was done. Is there anything missing?"

Data's eyes turned from blank to introspective as her techo unfroze, and she scanned.

"There was rain predicted, and it didn't come," she said. "The cliff needs gentle water. Not big rushing sprays. Soaking stuff."

"Rain," Ari said, depressed. "How long before all the work crumbles?"

"Not all the work. Just down to the mesh. But the mesh isn't as secure by itself as they'd like because it wasn't given enough time to dry."

"Rush job, botched job?"

"Pretty much," Data said more cheerfully. "Except the rain would've solved it. Fixed everything for a long time."

"I bet not. I bet it's a temporary fix, but I'm sure the Merlin's office can handle it if it's a bit more stable. I need to call some rain. Then we should go tell Benedicta so that she can tell him."

Data checked with Benedicta, and she was there. Her chief assistant said so and said they were all going to be there forever because there was too much work.

"I know it's too much work because she's turned into an ogre," the assistant mourned to Data. "This doesn't happen very often at all."

"Today it has happened. We're leaving the beach in about fifteen minutes. When we get to London, we'll take care of you."

"Bring us coffee!" the assistant instructed.

Ari felt comforted that she was subverting the firm rule of tea in Benedicta's office.

Fixing the wall would have been easy enough on an ordinary day, but Ari had been up all night helping process refugees. It had been arduous for everyone. "Make sure no-one's watching me," she told Data.

"I can do that." The small task made Data stand taller. Good. There would be an unravelling later, to sort this mess out, but right now, Data being more confident would suffice.

Ariette Green reached out with her mind and with her body and felt for gentle rain. The sort that lands light upon the landscape and moistens slowly. She changed the winds and the air density and brought that rain to the beach and its surrounds. A few miles of coastline would have a damp day without much wind.

Exhausted, she said, "Data, can you drive?"

"I'm not sure it's safe," Data said apologetically. "I'm a lot better than I was, but I'm still askew."

"Can you drive us to the station?"

"I don't know."

"Can you let Benedicta know we're catching the train and she'll need to send someone to pick up a car?"

There was an agonised two minutes before Data said, "Done."

Ari sighed and drove them to the station. It only took five minutes, but those five minutes lasted forever. They spent all their coins on junk food and drink from machines in the ten-minute wait for the train, and they ate this breakfast all the way to London.

A car and driver waited for them in London, so they bought the coffee they had promised at the station. They also bought far too much cake. The two of them went straight to Big Ben's office, bearing coffee and cake.

Despite being the one who had talked to Ben's assistant with such apparent cheer, Data didn't want to go. Data wanted to find a quiet corner and test her techo again and make sure it was fully functional. She also wanted to test her limbs and make sure they were fully functional. She already knew her brain wasn't fully functional. Data wanted to finish expressing her sorrow. She didn't want to see Benedicta or her people. Data didn't trust Earth2 any longer.

Also, she needed time to sulk. Data admitted this, very loudly.

Data placed the coffee and cake carefully on the reception desk, then Ari dragged her into the office unannounced. Data calmed right down. David had not been in reach using her headset because he was here, talking about folk things with their boss. He hadn't been attacked. This universe still sucked, Data noted, but it wasn't entirely comprised of suckitude.

They walked into the middle of something.

Benedicta said to them, "Wait a few minutes, please. This is important."

Data used that time. David was there: check. Then she began on the slow techo verification. Each part of her system that was tested and fixed made her feel more functional. At that moment, she quite understood why Ari refused to use her particular skill unless under duress. It was horrid being so dependent on it.

She sent a silly message to David for him to find when he got out of being the centre of attention. She even grinned at Ari and then grinned more wickedly when she saw the slight frown that always showed when she freaked her friend out. Data snuggled into the big leather chair that she always took as her own in this office and waited for life to return.

✡

David wanted to write a scholarly paper, but he didn't have time. He also didn't know what Her Maj's obsession with this subject was for. He'd been given direction in a way that was quite particular to Benedicta Beja. She had told David, "No hungry ghosts" very strictly.

"No hungry ghosts" was Benedicta Beja's shorthand for "nothing that belongs to Singaporean culture or flowline unless it came from England." They had this discussion every other week. David saw two-way influence. Her Maj didn't care about two-way. Her world emanated out into the universe, and the universe was assumed to never talk back.

He knew why she demanded this approach in these circumstances, but it was wrong. The portals she wanted to understand and the people from underground might be linked in some way with places she knew, but they weren't the only people and places.

He proposed another verbal briefing. He said in an email, "It'll take less time for everyone, and you can ask me any details I didn't know you needed."

This was cheeky of him. He hadn't expected to become cheeky in this environment, but it was happening, and he wanted to blame Data. David's briefing seemed so irrelevant by comparison with the way her face looked drained that he felt guilty drinking the coffee she brought and eating the cake. He had hated leaving Data alone at the beach and was so worried when she came in late and bereft and full of shock.

There were too many briefings and not enough action. Either that, or his models for superheroicness failed in real life.

Chapter Fifteen

The briefing he gave didn't contain any of the amazing list of superhero powers he'd yearned over during its making, although he was tempted to add one where one walked over historical land and instantly knew everything that happened there. He also wanted to create one where Data was everywhere, but that was a different kind of power and far more personal. Life trended that way.

What David spoke about was portals to other worlds. That was what he had been told to focus on. "We know the science. We need the lore."

He talked about sleeping knights and kings and Ogier le Danois (who was both). Annwyn had its own explanation as another world that was historically attainable from various places in the British Isles.

The questions his panel of intimidating females (like his mother in that important way, he thought) rapid-fired at him were solely about portals. Doors to other worlds and places where shifts in reality could occur. They wanted to know where they appeared and what they did. They needed to know what the evildoers were evildoing using popular stories. He had to explain over and over that different cultures, even in Western Europe, treated these things differently, which argued for most of them not being actual portals.

"There is no such thing as an instant answer," he said firmly. Years of being questioned by his mother had been exceptionally good training for this moment.

"How about when they come and go and where they come and go?" Ari suggested.

David spent ten minutes working through some of the folk stories and showing how the mentions of doors and portals and paths from one world to another were too vague to be useful. The Japanese bridge of stars was easier, he suggested, but not appropriate for England.

He felt obliged to point out how much more relevant the questions about green children had been. The different accounts of those children had overlapped in the detail to give solid results. Contemporary writers had observed the same set of incidents, which made it useful testimony.

Almost everyone writing about doors in other contexts wrote about it in different ways. There was no strong evidence of the kind the team needed.

This third time of saying the obvious finally led to a result.

"So, we can't pin down actual portals to other universes by using folk stories?" Benedicta asked. This was the best she could do in terms of settling on a simple answer after twenty minutes of description and analysis by David. "It's not like what happened in Newcastle?"

"That's a really good question." *We can move on*, his inner self rejoiced.

"Why is it a really good question?" Benedicta asked pointedly.

"It gives us the context we need to understand how we interpret folk stories." David paused long enough to discover that this was not an explanation for the others when, for him, it said everything.

He was rather pleased that he turned the pause into a dramatic one and continued. "Let me explain. Whenever someone writes down a folk story, they classify it. Sometimes it's as a folk story, sometimes as a local tradition, sometimes as a funny story about a place or a stupid story that people once believed in. The whole notion of 'folk stories' involves a set of definitions. When I studied this in Australia, the big issue that cropped up over and over is that the West defines things as 'folk' that are often nothing of the sort to those who are from non-Western cultures. I'm using your parameters for my searches, and I can see why you want the folk element in it because those are the stories most likely to be written down in this cultural environment. Folk, superstition, popular stories; there's a whole range of material I can access if I use that approach."

"So why is it a problem?" Ariette's interest was piqued.

"These stories are classified and even changed by the writer during the process of being written down, by people retelling them, by people studying them, by the very fact of writing. They are changed to suit the classification method and in the retelling. Their shape tells us a lot about them, and that's sufficient for so many uses, but not so much for ours."

He stopped for a moment, took a breath, and took a swig of coffee.

Ari leaned forward, her chin cupped in her hand. "Let's start with what is a portal–a door that leads to another universe. That's simple enough, surely? We know what they are. We've seen them in reality."

David felt that he was floundering. "How is that simple? You've given me a word in one language and a definition that fits the way scientists like to sum up pages of equations so that they can describe research but that has very little to do with the word. How are other universes connected to the word 'portal'? How do we match that across languages when we're looking for stories, not science? I can find folk motifs that demonstrate related concepts, but that simple construct isn't so obvious. In a story where a house is changed by magic wishes from a small house to a big house to a small house again, are portals involved? They're probably not, but we can't be certain, for the story I'm thinking of has been 'improved' by the person who wrote it down and aspects that don't fit a Christian reality may have been modified. Only some kinds of portals even fit into Christian realities, and other ones fit into Jewish, and then there are those that fit into both but don't show anything outside the two. This is just with that one story and those two religions. Other stories carry other religious and cultural baggage. We can't be certain if there was a portal involved or not in the story about magic wishes because it crosses all these points at various points in its history of being written down and written about. Honestly, we don't even know if it was fictional or not. It looks fictional because no-one can use wishes to change big objects like houses in that way, even if those wishes come from ubersources, but what if it's a type of craft magic or locative magic that has been forgotten? I am comparing versions of the same tale to redress this, but it's difficult."

"Sometimes you annoy me," Benedicta said reflectively.

David felt he ought to be annoyed himself at this reaction. They wanted him for his knowledge and so he was explaining why they were being stupid. It was all fair and just and ... he wanted to go back to university, where life was safer. Where actual portals were hypothetical and the subject was mostly owned by scientists.

Or maybe he wanted to be part of a novel, where portals were simple constructs easily explained and had strong and obvious cultural outlines. They had to in most novels because novels were cultural constructs just like folktales and they had their own restrictions and …

Yes, he might annoy Benedicta, but Benedicta's views annoyed him.

He had drifted into irrelevancy at that point. He thought he'd cured himself of dreaming in the middle of conversations.

"What do you mean it's difficult?" Data's look was very curious. Give his girlfriend a problem and she'd solve it eventually, if it were solvable. Maybe. She thought she would.

David gave her more information towards the hypothetical solution. "Not enough overlap. Not enough texts for some languages. We can't do a comparative hermeneutical analysis of the words. We can't know if the sort of door to another universe leads to one, or if it's a folk tradition or something else."

"Tell me a bit more," said Benedicta. "What can we know?"

"We have more information on two types of doors than on others. The first is doors that lead into fairy mounds, which archaeologists say are barrows or other buried monuments. They include doors, however. And some of them may well be magic. In fact, we have evidence of magic doors in Ireland, around Tara. I need more information on the Irish doors; there may be more of them."

"So, we could go to them and measure and find out if there is any legacy of real portals that match the ones here," Data said.

"I guess so," David agreed.

"I'll get my people to do that," Benedicta said. "That's data rather than advanced research."

"Was that a joke?" Data asked suspiciously.

Benedicta merely smiled. Her mere smile revealed nothing.

"The other category?" Data pushed David. It was easier than interpreting her temporary boss.

"Places again. One with traditions of being doorways of one sort or another. Some of them move. I was thinking of a particular type of doorway, to be honest, but it escapes me."

"Think of it," Ari said. "Otherwise we never get lunch and you're stuck drinking cold coffee forever."

David looked down at his coffee. He hadn't realised it was cold.

"What, never?" Data asked wistfully.

"No, never," Ari said.

"Gaping maws," David said quickly before the two could break into Gilbert and Sullivan. They were fixated on the operettas, and they broke into song just when a sane person wouldn't. Like now.

"Explain." Her Maj was back to being curt.

"The hell mouths depicted in, oh, all sorts of texts. None earlier than the ninth century. Maybe none. Maybe just almost none. The hell mouth in modern fantasy derives directly from the thirteenth century version of the ninth century one, possibly. The vast bulk of the early material is religious literature. One is a fake gospel. I can't be more precise than this because the Medievalists got angry when I tried. I received a bigger theoretical lecture than the one I gave you a few minutes ago."

"Places?"

"Not fixed. Not certain. Same problem as with other things. There isn't one single set of terminology. The hell mouth is better understood than most because Latin texts cross across a lot of Europe, and the same phrase leads to Christian interpretations that link all the versions I've seen. Some really great ones are plays from the Middle Ages, but a lot of texts in a lot of places. Wherever the church is, we have stories of hell mouths. It's integral to the Christian view of magic's links with other realms."

"May I say," Data said, "that this is kind of a mixed blessing."

She had found herself again. David found himself about to burst with an irrepressible bubble of joy.

"No, you can't," said Her Maj, "for it would not be amusing. At all."

"Just as well I didn't say it then." And Data smiled at her very sweetly.

"You have notes on the hell mouth? Or do we need to consult with my cousin?"

"Probably a bit of both," David said cautiously. He didn't want to consult with the cousin. No-one in their right mind wanted to consult with the cousin. Or eat cold pizza with him.

"That's enough," said Benedicta. "I see the problem. Texts alone won't give us the solutions, and the longer we rely on them, the further we'll be delayed and possibly misled. We need to find material at sites where incidents have occurred and give it to you to locate in texts."

"That's the bottom line," David said.

"Then we're done with that," said Her Maj. "We need a break."

"Dinner!" Data exclaimed.

She and Ari linked arms and led the way to the nearest pub, singing the captain's song from *HMS Pinafore*. David suspected he'd never hear it sung with French accents again. What never? Well, hardly ever. These two sounded as if they'd sung it before, after all. Many times. In front of him they mainly sang *The Mikado* and *Trial by Jury*. He wondered if there was meaning in this as he quietly followed the others to dinner.

Chapter Sixteen

The next day, David's heartfelt wish to never meet the Merlin again was rudely ruined. The day's redeeming note was that his grandmother had not appeared in his dreams the night before. He missed her, but every day without a warning was a good day. Or maybe simply a less bad day.

To reach the Merlin's office, they disembarked at Embankment Station, walked right past the mess from the incident, and then turned in to the legal district. It was a long walk from what David regarded as civilisation. Except the Temple Church. One of his favourite authors loved it and so it remained civilised. Also, it hid some great stories. Definitely civilised.

The district itself was felt as if it were in itself an ancient monument. It was also intimidatory. The grandeur and heaviness of power weighted the air, even in those spots that didn't look as if they owned groups of people so influential that Singapore would not have been given independence if they hadn't agreed. Technically, Singapore was all about its relationship with Malaysia, but in reality, these people played a part in all the places that were once Empire.

David noted the way no-one actually looked at each other.

"Lawyers," said Ari.

"Ah," said Data.

"Can we go into the Temple Church?" David asked, but it was closed. His tourist dreams were foiled.

They walked through lawyer central and didn't talk too loudly. Everything felt cream and overbuilt, even the trees, of which there were too few.

Down the street, round a very small bend, the buildings changed. There was a second pocket of the Middle Ages that had nothing to do with the surrounds. Romanesque and beautifully proportioned. Not a castle. Not a house. Not a church, but built with the same stonework as the Temple Church.

"This doesn't exist in Earth1," Data said informatively. "This building has its own unique spot in our corner of the multiverse."

"Well, it's where we're headed. And are you checking up everything?" Ari asked.

"Is he the same person the building was built for?" Data asked back. "For if he is, it is old."

"It's old." A person sitting at a front desk just inside the door gave them all a start when he spoke unexpectedly. "However, the current Merlin is a descendant of the original. May I help you?"

"Ms Beja sent us to see him. We have an appointment."

"Ah."

Paper was written on in an old-fashioned, lawyerly way that placed this office very clearly in its wider surroundings. Benedicta's people were far more casual and immensely more dynamic, David thought. *I can deal with the Merlin.*

"He's been called to the other office by an emergency. Give me a moment." The elderly man sent a text and sat with his fingers at the ready to text back should it be needed. It wasn't. He read something, nodded, and wrote a note. "He says to come to him.

Here's the address. I suggest you hurry. If you go out that door,"
his head tilted very faintly to the right," and through the hall and
then outside, I'll have a car waiting for you by the time you get
there."

"Thank you," Ari said, and they hurried, and yes, a car was
waiting for them.

Data looked at it and asked David, "When did we enter a
secret service film?"

"Tell me about it!" David agreed.

The Merlin was avuncular as he welcomed them into an office
that looked as if it belonged in a film set in an old university.

"Playing the educated old soul act, I see," Ari said.

"Respect, young lady."

"I've given up respecting the English, it's too much work."

His spectacles were halfway down his nose, and he peered
down them, still in professor mode. David did not understand
this man. He had brought them out of one of his offices into
another, a mere ten minutes away. Why? Why was he at his desk
when his staff had said he was handling an emergency?

"The last few days were as bad as they looked?" the Merlin
asked.

"Worse," Data replied, then sat herself down inelegantly on
the biggest leather chair she could find.

"I'm relieved you're still helping us, then," he said gently.

David caught himself looking deeply to see if it was an act, but
the warmth was real. If this man were genuine more often, maybe
David wouldn't object to seeing him. Benedicta was brusque and
could be rude, but she was always honest about emotions.

"I've been given a briefing," the Merlin said, "but there are
some things I wanted to check. Data, that film of yours. You
were right. Someone did cause that poor fellow to die on that
cliff. My people have looked at other events, and there are other

226

potentially intentional deaths."

"Any patterns?" Ari asked.

"Left-wing intellectuals."

"That's not what I was expecting to hear," Data said. "I was expecting it to be religious or racial or random."

"It's only five people, so it could still be random, but I doubt it."

"What did they have in common besides being left-wing and known for their intelligence?"

The Merlin was suddenly very wary. "That's why you're here. We don't know, and as a group, you see things."

"It isn't that you want to poach us from Auntie," Data said sarcastically from the shelter of the big wings on her oversized chair.

"Oh, I do, but not right now. Right now, finding perpetrators is rather more important than me making arrangements with Tsarfat or recruiting new officers. Bennie and I have agreed that you'll work with whichever of us needs you until this is over."

David was fascinated. "I understand how this would work for me, but how does that work with people representing a foreign power?"

"One to David," said Ari. "And Benedicta beat you to that. David works primarily with Data and can only be seconded with her agreement. They both work for me. It wasn't Benedicta you needed to consult with." In the silence that followed this statement, David appreciated the honest and open look of worry on the Merlin's face. "I am happy to work with both of you, however, but …" Ari was enjoying the tension. "I call the shots about who works where. I'm not going to have either of these two caught in political arguments or in assumptions of whose office they're in."

"Tsarfat is more political than I realised," the Merlin said glumly. "I was hoping ..."

Data laughed, almost manically.

"Dammit, Data," Ari said. "We need to get you time out to recover."

There was a thud and then an explosion in the background, muffled by brick and stone. It contradicted Ari's words.

The Merlin picked up his telephone. "Is it finished?" He listened for a moment and then gestured to the others. "Come and see. We were waiting for it to be over. Safer in here until then."

While they were all admiring a beautiful stone wall on the building opposite, which had been brick minutes before, the Merlin said, "I'll copy you the names and biographies of the five. See if you can find a better link than we could."

Someone proudly informed Ari that the failed portal had left them with some nice new medieval stonework. David wondered why Data was standing there. Her earpieces were not on fire. It was as if time was paused around her. He went to her and asked, "May I?" She nodded and he held her close.

Data shuddered and then relaxed, then she said, "Thank you."

"What was it?" David asked.

"Damn PTSD. This was an aftershock. Not so bad. I was in a terrible place after the thing at the beach. I don't know why being hugged helped, but it really did."

"Some people use cups of tea," David said. "Some need isolation. We learned about it in training. Grounding is what the tea brings, and time out to recover is what the isolation brings. I think this means that grounding helps you. I'll watch, if you want, in case it happens again."

Data looked at him with such hope in her eyes that his heart thudded much more heavily than the echoed explosion.

This new incident left David thinking carefully. He was glad he had been able to handle Data's PTSD on the spot, without causing her any problems, but still, it needed thinking about. Post-Traumatic Stress Disorder wasn't something one should leave in the dark and hope it didn't return.

David knew this from too close. National Service and his thankfully short time as an officer cadet meant that he knew a bit, but he had seen it at home as well, for his grandparents had each developed their own forms of it. Occupied Singapore wasn't something that Europe tended to talk about. He wondered whether English people even knew about it. Benedicta did, but Benedicta didn't think of its side effects, or of its long-term. David had grown up with the long-term, and that had helped him help Data.

Still, I'm not going to bring the subject up, David thought. *I'm not going to talk about my grandfather and his trembles or my other grandmother and the dark enclosures that trigger her symptoms. They've earned their privacy. Also, there is the respect thing. I love England in so many ways, but respect is different here. I can help Data without anyone knowing that my family has its own heritage of hurt.*

He felt there must be a way around this that let Data know what she was dealing with. The problem was that she had grown up with Holocaust survivor families, and her whole childhood had probably had something of the tone of his, where she went around knowing the regular pain she and her family had to handle was nothing compared with what the survivors had endured. David hated that so many people hurt, and he hated that one person's pain was compared with another to create a hierarchy of hurt.

No-one could deny the Holocaust and its appalling nature. But there were other ways of hurting at the same time, and it was a particular type of hurt–personal damage that caused PTSD– that Data needed to understand. She needed to know she was not alone. Her people were supposed to help her and counsel her, but David guessed this was another thing that had quietly been changed. This man who hated Data must be a real piece of work, vicious and petty, both at once.

That gave him an idea.

"I can't talk about this," he typed to Data, "because there's family history involved, but my family's been through stuff, and some of the problems you've got in handling some situations relate. I mean, I feel as if I've seen them."

She became very still. David wasn't certain if she was a rabbit seeing headlights or if this was a breakthrough moment. He should not have typed. He should have spoken aloud. They were standing there doing nothing, after all, while the Merlin's people did all the grunt work.

"Tell me then," appeared on her screen. "Is there something I can read?"

"Changi might be a good way in because it includes Australians," David typed. "The history of the place and what happened there. There are studies of it and of Australian soldiers there and—"

"I'm going to hate this, aren't I?" she asked.

"Yes." David was miserable. "But you have PTSD, and I want you to see that people have had it in the past and many of them find ways of handling it. It stops you from being you now, but maybe, later ..."

"Yes," she said. "I will look up Changi and PTSD. But I'll do it slowly."

"That's best," David said. "Don't force yourself. I ought to tell you to go and get psychological help, but ..."

"We don't know who's been compromised, and I'm top secret. I've gotta do this myself. With help from your hugs. Thanks."

David thought Data looked a bit more hopeful.

"That's all we need," Ari said, "A method to get you out of the brain freeze."

David wondered when they had stopped texting and started talking. He hadn't noticed the transition.

"It's not a brain freeze," Data said in objection.

"It was, you know," Ari said. "A brain freeze that pushed your tools into a data freeze."

"It felt like a labyrinth."

"We need to play Ariadne. We need a long thread from wherever you are to the exit of the labyrinth. Like that cup of tea David talked about. Something that brings you home. Can you place something in your tech that will work that way?"

"Make it go to a friend who's on the computer all the time," David suggested. "That way you've got someone to talk you out of it, the way Ms Green would've done at the event that triggered it the first time. The one that caused today's aftershock."

"I didn't actually talk—"

"Good idea," Ari said. "Is there anyone around twenty-four hours a day?"

"I have gaming friends in lots of time zones?" Data sounded oddly hesitant. This was uncanny ground and did not make her comfortable.

"Good. Do it. Now. We can wait."

While Data's earpieces flashed rainbows as she set up the new elements, Ari asked the Merlin, "Does this meeting mean you've got a lead? That there's an expert we can tap into to get into the right circles?"

"I think so. In fact, I'm pretty sure so. You two are going to a conference. How many have you been to?"

"None. Not outside home."

"Then David should go with you so that you can act as if you belong."

"You want us to be invisible?" Ari was amused.

"Not distinctive will suffice."

David was amused now, for the Merlin sounded exactly like his cousin. He suspected this was the Merlin's natural voice.

"What do you want us to find?"

"I said that already. An expert."

Chapter Seventeen

This is how the three of them found themselves in Cambridge with Benedicta's permission. None of them knew Cambridge. Data and David wanted to explore, so Ari let herself be dragged around by David with a tourist map ("What? I like paper.") while Data tested her rebooted system. They compared notes the whole time.

Every corner, every old building, every time they crossed the Cam (five times in all). Noted. Annotated. Compared. The comparison—as Data liked to say and said often, for it entertained her to say it—was in triplicate. The GPS system showed a straightforward map once based on the work of the Ordinance Survey. Data's own map was the same, in theory, but interpreted through satellite. Then there was the map Ari whipped out on her tiny computer to upset the applecart.

"Should we see what Cambridge looks like in Earth1?" she asked.

"I can't connect to Earth1 today, dammit," Data said.

"I can."

"Show off."

They compared all three in such detail that they used up

their whole day before the conference. They'd planned to go to a historic hotel for lunch but never made it. They'd planned to eat tourist food and had forgotten to look for it.

The differences were notable in some cases, mysterious in others. As they walked past the Colleges of the Jews, they found that in Earth1, it had been replaced by two more modern colleges. The women's was Lucy Cavendish in Earth1.

"We have a Lucy Cavendish too," David said. "I have a friend who went there."

"It's further out," Ari said, "and the building is huge. Very corporate."

"So there are more women's colleges in our universe?"

"One more. Earlier than the others because it wasn't catering to the religious. The Jewish colleges were founded as 'of the Jews' rather than for rabbinical study so that the whole oath aspect wouldn't tangle anything. Jews could get university education but couldn't take public office."

"What?" Data asked.

"Don't worry. It's history. Let's see what else changed the map."

So they kept going, and David managed it so that they ended up in the right building for the conference, and the conference organisers had managed it so that there were coffee and biscuits waiting once they had signed in. That was the moment when Ari looked at Data and said "Lunch," and David looked at Ari and said "We forgot."

"Too late," Data said. "Quick, have another biscuit." They were still eating when everyone was ushered into the hall for the opening session.

The building was terribly nineteenth century on the outside. Back then, it was part of the great glory of the British Empire. Inside, that hall had been covered with modern trappings, much of it made of plasterboard, and it was almost entirely without character and, David noted, without acoustics.

Ari passed a note around that said, "This building is not in Earth1. Lucky Earth1."

David wrote on the back, "It might be a good building under the refurbishment."

"You two," Data wrote. And that was the end of their notes for fully five minutes, then Data added to the bottom of her comment, "Remind us what we're looking for?"

Ari's sigh was audible. She whispered, "We're recruiting. The Merlin thinks we've hit a brick wall and that the right person will tear the wall down. That person has to know stuff we don't. This is a gut feeling thing, not a find a mastermind to solve everything thing. We're not in the movies now. Wish we were. I want neat answers and happy ever after."

"OK," Data said. "Now shush so that I can listen."

"She does it on purpose," David wrote in a note to Ari. "It's entertaining."

Ari sighed again.

David paid very close attention to everything about the first speech. He remarked on the thud of the words as they hit the null space that was the walls and ceiling, the short and snappy high and nervous tone of voice. David noted how those blue eyes went from person to person, and he realised that the reason for the nerves was the presence of certain people in the audience. This speaker had written a paper that referred very heavily to the work of others, which was fine in and of itself, but it shaped each reference as if the work of others was supportive of his own work, when that other work was the main scholarship on the subject. David didn't have to know the subject matter to work this one out, for the speech itself had very clear structure showing that there was not a single scrap of original thought or interpretation in his paper.

Every single time the speaker talked about how his own labour was in this book by that famous author-artist-scientist-academic, how this person's work reflected his own work and was linked to his own work, his gaze would get trapped in one spot, as he looked guiltily at someone in the audience.

I never want to give a paper like this, David swore to himself. *I will not do this thing. Not even once for fun.*

"Shiny," Data said, "but totally useless if we want to use them in any way. If this were in a movie, those first ten words would've got us in, though."

"Except as a target," Ari suggested.

David looked at her, surprised. Her face showed deep distress.

"Why a target?" was all he could think to ask.

"Shiny," Data said. "Those first ten words."

"Visible and noisy and clearly intellectually aggressive without putting in the work. Perfect to attract attention and no loss if they get hit in the crossfire."

"You know someone like that," David guessed.

"Data's mentor, Chevalier."

"Oh," Data said.

David had assumed that Chevalier was a mover and shaker. This was food for thought. The next speaker began before anyone could explore this any further.

This speaker was quite different. A woman who came from London and watched too much Australian television. Terribly Estuarial in an odd way that would pass as the leaves drifted in autumn. David rather liked his simile. He didn't like her accent. Her language was no better.

He noticed that Data took copious notes. David lowered his eyes, but not his head, to see what Data was saying without giving himself away to her as reading over her shoulder.

"Use of Hebrew words in this English is like Hebrew in Tsarfati," Data noted. "This means the English here have cultural groups that overlap with us. We can seek them out if this useless conference continues to be a raging bore." David was very proud of his influence in all respects. Data was not only taking notes, they were thoughtful and sarcastic notes. "Don't look so smug, David," Data's notes continued.

David opened his notebook on a new page and wrote, "? About content not about my smugness."

Ari answered him. "I'm wincing," she wrote back, "because the intellectual content is fine, but the cultural understanding is a wallop of negatives."

"?"David repeated on the page, and Data grabbed it from him and wrote, "Yes?"

"Pronunciation of Hebrew words. kh is sh–it's ugly."

David wrote below the question, "Look at audience. They hate it too." He saw Ari and Data both turn to the audience for more information and rested his notepad. His work here was done … for the next few minutes

Ari felt that she owed David a drink for pointing out the audience. The faces taught her a lot about the type of person at this conference. She noticed a woman taking notes voraciously, her face reflecting the *amuse-bouche* that this talk was to her. The note-taker didn't like the Hebrew, but it entertained her. *I need to meet this woman,* was the mental note Ari made for herself. *She's amused by matters that ought to be amusing, and I like the way her face shows it.*

Ari reached for David's notepad and wrote "I wonder what this would sound like if the speaker understood the full meanings of the words and where they came from?'

"Yeah," Data wrote back, "this one isn't for us."

This was not entirely true. Data noted, "He is so much the

centre of his own universe that he wants to be a specialist on his own writing."

David wrote, "Bigot and a snob. Impressive."

Ari wrote, "All the famous people he claims to know personally supported the recent push to bring the government down."

"Was he on our list?" Data handed the reply to David, who handed it to Ari.

"Yes. He knows a few people who look as if they'd be useful."

"That's why?" David's question was in his much neater handwriting and made the other looped writing look careless. Ari nodded, and David kept writing. "His language suggests he knows some of these people but not from within an inner group. He's big-noting himself."

"He's one of the people we're here to assess."

David allowed himself inner sarcasm, *Thanks for telling me.* "Maybe," was his more public response. "Public face doesn't equal intimate. Do you need public face or someone with knowledge?"

"He's write," Data scrawled. "Pun intended."

David smiled and handed the note on.

The speaker changed direction. He stopped speaking about the important work of those he respected and said, in much shorter terms, that the work they'd been doing had been threatened by government cutbacks but was continuing. "We found a supporter. There will be an announcement in due course." Then he finished.

"Can we ask him?" Data leaned across David to talk to Ari directly.

"Not until we've checked him out. I don't want him to know about us without clearance. Even if his supporter is at the centre of things, we can't use him in our team if he really is that limited."

"My supervisor knows him," David volunteered.

"Good," Ari said, "but don't ask yet. I want to run background checks first. Your comment suggests a hierarchy, and we need to tread carefully until we know what it is and who's in it. Maybe the other speakers will be more useful." Ari's note took her past the introduction of the last speaker.

Her name was Carolyn Jane Smyth-Joness, and she was the most regular academic yet, Ari realised. Smyth-Joness was also the *amuse-bouche* audience member from earlier. This woman's paper demonstrated that she was no piece of fluff, but her sense of humour infiltrated every aspect of her talk. Her paper obviously had overheads purely so that she could smile at the faces of the audience when she talked about herself.

Data passed a note saying, "Ego much?"

David nodded and passed it on.

Ari laughed aloud and wrote, "Maybe ego. Maybe exceptionally funny. I think she's satirising the others while analysing what they do. Let's bet."

Ariette was certain she'd win this bet. The speaker was passionate and thoughtful and intellectual. In Ari's eyes, Dr Smyth-Joness was a near-perfect human being.

"I think I'm in love," she noted to Data. "And I won the bet."

"I think she's our person, and you won the bet," Data noted back, "Even though I think her sense of humour stinks. You get to find out if you have a crush or true love."

"You're too young to be so cynical," Ari wrote. "Shall we ask David to ask her to join us?"

"Please very much."

'Dr Smyth-Joness' was apparently the pseudonym of Professor Leah Israel. "My name is so very Jewish that it satirises itself, so I chose an equivalent English name."

"Why the pseudonym?" Ari asked.

"I work in several fields, and I like to keep one subject clear of the other. It's like pen names."

"I've seen your work in folk studies," David said.

"Actually, we met at a folk studies conference, two years ago. You don't remember?"

"Two years ago, I was overwhelmed by the UK. I buried my head in my thesis and was polite to the world but not connected to it."

"You're still not connected," said Data.

'Does that mean no dinner tonight?" David asked wistfully.

"It probably means you've not paid her enough attention," Ari suggested. "Dr Smyth-Israel, have you ever met Benedicta Beja?"

"My Mexican grandmother calls her the Bruja and is one of her friends."

"You're a magician?" Data asked.

"No, but my grandmother is, and she told me three of her people would look for me today and that I should say 'yes' to whatever you asked me to do, for in it, I would find my destiny."

"I don't know that form of magic," David said, as bubbly as Data over the thought.

"I'm not surprised," Smyth-Israel said. "It's not at all European."

"It's the sort of magic Americans put in fiction," Ari offered.

"True," said the magician's granddaughter, "so I've agreed to who knows what, and the only one of you I have even a name for is David Chan."

"We're classified," Data said in a dignified fashion.

"She's cleared," Ari said, looking up from her phone. "Apparently, our people know her already."

"I just explained, my grandmother ..."

Data and Ari looked at each other and burst out laughing.

"We're not from Benedicta's office," Ariette explained, full of sympathy. "Not properly. Just connected."

"We're Green Children," Data said helpfully. "And what

should we call you?"

"Call me Elsa," Catherine-Leah said. "But Green jokes are not terribly new."

"Ms Beja had me looking into the Green Children stories when these two appeared in the office," David said to their new recruit. "Is it an English thing to play practical jokes of this sort, or is it something to do with your crowd?"

"Their crowd," Ari said. "English Jewish left-wing intelligentsia is notorious for thinking themselves funny. This puts us in a bit of a spot, for we are," and she turned to face their guest, "actually from the Green Family. I'm not sure that it matters today, however. We'd like to work with you on one of Benedicta's projects, but it really doesn't matter if you have no idea who we are."

"Suddenly, I find it matters," Elsa said.

"Suddenly, I find it matters that you have so many names. I'm Ariette Green."

"And I'm Rose Data, you know, like Rosie the Riveter and Data from Star Trek."

"My fake names are at least easier to think of as real," Elsa said.

"Ariette is my real given name. I'm Jewish."

"And obviously from France," Elsa finished.

Data said, her voice full of unholy joy, "I'm loving this. Let's not tell her where we're from. Let's let her guess."

"Yes, let's," Ari said almost grimly.

"You expect me to work with you?"

"You've implied they're fictional in two different ways," David pointed out. "They're only giving you fair return for your disbelief. She's OK, really," he told the others.

"How is she OK, really?" Ari asked. "By which, I mean what specific thing do we want to ask her?"

"She can find us contacts in groups. We can find out who's doing stuff."

"What stuff?" Elsa asked.

"Terrorist stuff."

"You want to join it or to stop it?"

"Why would we want to join it? You don't have to believe that we exist, but do Green Children work with anyone whose aim is to destroy?"

"Green Children are superheroes in all the stories."

"All the stories," Data echoed. "I need to find them. Stories!"

"You do not need to find them," Ari said. "I don't want you wandering around thinking you're that kind of superhero. Besides, they're all wrong."

"I'm not a superhero of any kind," Date said. "I know that. I'll always know that. It's a good joke, though, and I want to know where everyone thinks we come from and what they think we can do. I want to be in a comic and able to punch the sky and fly. That's what I want."

"You're from various mysterious places," David said. "None give you French accents."

"All of them say the Green Children are from another universe," Elsa said.

"I need to look us up." Data was stubborn. "If people are trying to create doors into universes, then we need to know the stories of us."

"That's what I should be researching," David said slowly. "Not fairy tales or magic."

"And I'm beginning to think we need lunch and a good sit down to talk," said Elsa.

"Alcohol," Data said. "We need alcohol."

"Do your superpowers require alcohol?" Elsa asked ironically.

"No, my superpower has checked with Big Ben, and she said

that you're normally righter than this and we should give you time."

"Techo is not superpower," Ari objected as they started walking towards food.

"My techo may as well be. And you don't use your ability, anyhow. Once this month. Just once. It's a sorry excuse for superheroicism."

"I don't even know what hers is," David confessed. "I've seen it, and I don't understand."

"Weatherish," Ari said dismissively. "Of no special importance."

"Who are you? Don't answer the Green Children."

Ari stopped and looked up at Elsa (who was astonishingly tall–the two of them next to each other made David feel he was in a forest of tall women) and said, clearly, "I'm the Tsarfati Envoy to the UK and to France."

"And I'm her temporary evil aide," Data added.

"My right-hand superhero?" Ari suggested.

"I hate that term, to be honest."

"Can all of you stop?"

They did. Literally.

"Not like that." David said. "I mean, take this seriously. It could be fun, but it isn't. People are dying."

"Fair enough," said Ari. "We're part of a team from our country that's helping the Office for the Non-Natural and the Office of the Merlin work on the terrorist problem."

"And why do you need me?"

"We've hit a dead end. We need your knowledge and your contacts. Your academic self, whichever name it's using on a given day, is an expert on refugee issues. One of the possible reasons the explosions are happening is to create pocket universes for refugees to live in. We already have one pocket of refugees from someone else's war. We were hoping you could help. One of your other selves might also be useful, the one that researches underworlds and networks. We need to locate one person or one network."

"Probably one network," Data interrupted.

"One network to find out who's committing these crimes."

"Why you?" Elsa asked of the two women.

By this time, they were sitting down at a small table in a quiet corner of a café.

Ari and Data looked across at each other, and Ari shrugged.

"Want me to tell her?" asked Data.

"Do it," Ari said, looking very tired.

"We were telling the truth. I like telling the truth so that no-one believes it. It amuses me. We don't come from France. We come from Tsarfat. It's a pocket universe. An exceptionally stable one with a clear link to this Earth. In fact, it's the only one anyone knew existed until the recent events."

"The explosions set up temporary links. We need to stop them before they do real damage." Data was firm.

"Thirty-five people dead isn't real damage?" Elsa queried.

Bingo, David thought. *We have her.*

"What do you think?" Ari asked.

"Fine," Elsa said, "I'm listening."

She was listening, but not seriously. Elsa herself still thought she was there to flirt with Ari.

Ari was having fun, David realised, which was rare, but two hours into the conversation, he decided they'd spent far too long not doing anything useful. He quietly took out his phone and texted Data, "If we want her to do real work any time soon, and if she really knows Her Maj, get Her Maj to ring her and tell her to stop wasting our time. Also let her Maj know that she doesn't believe in you. I feel aggrieved that she doesn't believe in you."

Data nodded and messaged him back. "All done. And why didn't I think of this?"

Soon, Elsa excused herself, stood up, moved away, and listened intently to her phone, speaking very occasionally. Three minutes. David timed it. Three minutes. Elsa's end of the conversation was mainly, "Yes," "I understand, "Oh," and "Yes," "Yes," and "Yes."

Data whispered to David, "Your Maj is in a mood."

"Understandably," David replied. "You're *her* superheroes. She can mess with you all she wants, and she will boss you and order you around and even talk down at you, but if anyone else even doubts …"

"She rips you one," Elsa said from behind.

"You believe us, then?" Ari asked.

"I have to act as if I do, even if I bloody well don't. I'm working with you, even if I don't give a damn."

"But why?"

"Don't all the names give it away?"

"We're all foreign," Data said cheerfully.

Elsa sighed. "Auntie Ben says I'm to meet you in her office tomorrow. You can find out for yourselves before then. I'm not mollycoddling you."

"Auntie Ben?" Ari asked.

"Honorary Auntie."

"Same class, same background, children probably went to school together," David felt impelled to explain.

"Close enough," Elsa said, looking weary. From Ari's body language, Elsa looked divinely weary, even when she'd just insulted them all.

One day, David swore, he'd understand English gentry. Today was not that day.

✡

Two hours later, Elsa was flummoxed. "Let me get this right; the descendants of Jewish refugees from another Earth are here as the Green Children to save the people who left someone else's ancestors for dead."

"That's not the way I read the records," Ari said.

"How do you read the records, then?"

"We help human beings who are in trouble. The fact that some of their ancestors were warped excuses for human beings in any universe is irrelevant."

Elsa started laughing but stopped long enough to say, "The superpowers are real."

"Also irrelevant."

"Are they superheroes?" She turned to her aunt.

"She just calls us that to get a bite," Data said.

"Both are true," said Benedicta. "If I'd known you were back from Canada, Elsa, I would have sent them directly. I didn't know this was your new area of interest."

"I was a replacement. I can't see how I can help you anyhow. You've told me your latest secrets for no reason whatsoever."

"Not no reason," Ari said. "All of you at the seminar came from a particular background, and you have links we need to access. One of our suspects also comes from there. An environmentalist."

"You want me to contact this person?"

"No," Benedicta said in dismissal. "We've already got what we can from him. We want you to trace back through the thread begun with that environmentalist until you reach someone who is responsible for the mess. Then it will become dangerous, and we'll pull you out."

"You need me to hook you up with terrorists? I'm sorry, but I don't know any."

"Ari, can you help?"

"I can," Ari said. "But will I be polite, that's the question."

David noted how very firmly this was not a question. Ari's interest in Elsa didn't stop her brain short.

His thought was interrupted by a distraction. Data's earpieces sparked and did their own style of Mexican wave.

"Data, your ears?" David asked.

"I was wondering if I could do diagrams of all the links from the seminar people and those five names from the other day as their victims, and I can, but they're not showing us what we need to know. It's a mystery."

"Show me," Elsa said.

"Turn your laptop on," Data replied.

David grinned at Data's cleverness in trapping Elsa with her own fascination with knowledge.

"Data, send it to all our machines," Benedicta ordered.

"I can do that, boss, or I can send it to the wall over there."

"How?"

"David's computer has a projector."

Ari asked the obvious. "Is the projector techo?"

"He needs it," Data argued.

"What for?"

Data laughed, and David looked down at his toes.

"Nothing illegal," David muttered.

"Techo?" Elsa asked.

"Do you believe in superpowers?"

"I believe," Elsa said with sufficient gravity.

"Now we're baking bread," Benedicta said.

"Not quite," said Ari. "I'm pretty sure she thinks we're secret Jews from your France."

"I'm not even Jewish," Data grumbled. "I'd rather be accused of being Australian."

"Benedicta still doesn't believe you're Australian," David

informed her. "Not even half-Australian."

"Stop telling me that," Data said, then put her hands over her ears, saying, "La la la."

Elsa laughed aloud. "I'm sorry I started this. Tell me where you're from."

"Tsarfat," David said. "They're from Tsarfat. Still. Same as before. Me, I'm from Singapore."

"You're from Tsarfat." Elsa looked as if she actually believed.

Data turned to Elsa. "My mother was from Australia. My father was from Tsarfat. Both parents were from an exotic cultural-religious minority."

"She means they were Christians," Ari said.

"Where in France are Christians a minority?" Elsa was fascinated.

"It's not where we are from that's important," Ari said, picking up what David had picked up. "Besides, when we're here, we're trained in silence for when we need to fade. Data is not very good at this, but otherwise, we live secretly, the precise way many Jews in countries other than this live. Politely. Quietly. Not drawing attention."

"You're political," Elsa stated.

"It's impossible not to be political. We exist in politics, and we've done this ever since the Shoah. How we're different to Jews in most countries is that only a few of them are visible. We are political and visible in the place where we live. In fact, we're the culturally dominant group."

"We know the Shoah." Elsa was both dignified and hurt. "Some of us are descendants of Survivors."

So that is part of her background, David thought. *She's not entirely from Benedicta's establishment world, and not all her grandmothers are Mexican.*

"You're survivors and children of survivors, grandchildren,

great-grandchildren of survivors. We're descended from those who fought the Nazis. It's a different heritage."

"Same but different," said Benedicta.

"Yes. And we wake up needing to make sure the world is stable and everyone we know isn't suffering. You wake up safe."

"That's not the problem. The problem is getting the ordinaries to join in. There are so few Jews left, and there never were many to begin with. We need the rest of the world," Data argued.

"We, here, are what you call the ordinaries," Benedicta said. "This is Britain. Not your Britain."

"I'm sorry?"

"You went in one world and came out the other. Here, we have magic and we are thirty percent of the British population. Jewish Britain runs the gamut from establishment Jews to working class Jews. It is not the Britain you know. It has prejudice, but it's not the Britain you know. Should I say this one more time?"

"How did you ..."

While she sported a I-have-a-display-I-prepared-earlier grin, Benedicta's tone was sober. "I've been thinking about this ever since we ran into each other that first time. You inherit the magic from us, but your burdens come from another world entirely. Our Shoah was appalling, but not as appalling as yours."

"I think I might be missing something," Elsa said.

Benedicta grudgingly said, "Tsarfat is a pocket universe, mostly peopled by descendants of Holocaust survivors from an alternate Earth. Is that what you were missing? They've told you six times, at least."

"Yes, that explains it, I think."

David was fascinated. Elsa had to hear it from Benedicta. This showed her privilege. She didn't have to listen to the stories of others or the evidence given by others, or ...

He pulled himself back just in time to hear Benedicta ask,

"Will you help?"

"I should at least help them help us save our world. Let's network those names." Now Elsa looked the academic again. She turned her doubt into drudgery and developed a methodical networking system with the others being her team.

This took two days. What they found in those two days was both a lot and not very much at all.

The five targeted victims all had similar public profiles. Data discovered this, and she also discovered that they moved in the same circles as some of her friends.

"Explain," Benedicta said when they returned to her office to brief her.

"Well, it's like this ..." Data hesitated. David suspected it was seeing her friends made public. "I don't know any of them personally, but a lot of my friends read their online material. They were public."

"What did they say?" Ari asked.

"I can answer that," said Elsa. "They were all given the same label, you see."

"I hate that side of things," Data said vehemently. "They were called Politically Correct Dummies and were accused of saying nothing in a very loud voice. I made a list of other PCDs who could be targeted."

"Are any of them your friends?" Benedicta asked.

"All of them are linked to my friends. Not six degrees of separation either. Three at the most. Probably just two. In some cases, one," Data said. "I was too busy chasing villains to see all the obituaries, but they went mega."

"And how long is your list, Elsa?"

"Too long still. Over a thousand names."

"Then we need to find more from the attack end to hone it down. We can't protect over a thousand people."

"We could protect the biggest names?"

"That's an idea, Data, but it's better if we protect the targets. The Dummies tag could be another overlapping piece of information and not the reason they were targeted at all. What does the other network look like?"

"It's impossible," Ari said. She didn't say this bitterly, David noted. She said this authoritatively.

"She's right," said Data. "We've got a lot of names that feed into the flash mob thing. We don't have names that work outside it."

"Do we have any information on interests?" Benedicta asked.

"Yes, a bit." Data sounded a bit grudging. David knew why. This was close to home, with people who knew people affected and yet not much information. This was just the thing that provoked Data. He'd won a game against her by causing that same grudge.

Those dreams took him to the online game, and he re-entered the conversation when Benedicta said, "Then set me up a game. Play it. Find me someone who actually knows what's happening or is directly linked to someone active in this garbage pail and bring them in for questioning."

David felt that he was in school as he raised his hand politely. "What do you mean by a game?" he asked.

"You'll see," Elsa said darkly.

They spent the rest of the day trying to work out what place and space they should be using for the game. Only a small part of it entailed explaining the game, and none of it at all entailed explaining to David why they called it a game. *Some historical precedent* was the best he could get.

"But it's important," said Ari. "It means we can find targets for crimes. People who are not criminal in nature. People who are ethical. People who can give us a way into the world we need to get into. That's why the game works."

"It means we're taking advantage of them," Data said. "Trapping them somewhere they've gone on a day off."

"Yes, in a way. Acknowledging the difficulties they face, in another. It depends on how we handle this."

Finally, the combined brains of all of them except Benedicta (who caught up on paperwork while they wrote all over her office wall) found that the best kind of place was the kind of place where people with difficulties went for refuge. A place where they could be themselves.

"The modern version of a molly house," David suggested. This drew so many blank looks that he just shook his head and didn't explain. He didn't know enough about molly houses to be certain that they were escapes, anyhow.

"Elsa, do your thing," Benedicta ordered.

"Sometimes, Auntie, I hate you," Elsa said perfectly cheerfully and went outside to make a call.

The next day their next step began. They had identified potential sources of information with all that datawork. "Datawork means Data worked," said David.

"Shut up, you," Data retorted. "I have no idea how we go about doing this thing."

"Maybe you just don't want to volunteer to lure someone into a life of sex and crime?" Ari suggested.

"That too."

"That's what it is? This game?"

Elsa sighed and explained again. "I thought you understood," she complained, her tone suggesting they were millstones for forgetting. "It was a trick used in the nineteenth century to trap homosexuals, back when it was illegal to be normal. Someone pretending to be a prostitute takes a client to a room, and before anything too dramatic happens but when the client is definitely exposed, the other half of the team crashes into the room and makes blackmail demands."

"So, this party we're going to?"

"It's run by actors. There are dozens of social groups of actors on the verge of success or failure or playing with the idea of acting or trying their whole life. There were four names on our list that came from just one group. Two of the Newcastle bombers come from that same circle. I doubt if the leader is in that group, but I would lay odds on the used car salesman aspect of leadership being part of it or linked to it."

"We're meeting someone, though," David said.

"And which of us is going to lure whoever into illegal whatever?" Data asked, supremely cheerful.

"The Merlin is our missing member, but he can't come in because he's too well-known. So am I, in this context."

"Me?" David asked.

"Not if your supervisor's potentially involved," Benedicta said. "I think Ariette."

"I think someone other than Ariette," Ari said, her voice full of certainty.

"Too bad," said Elsa. "You're it."

✡

Ari looked good dressed for partying. David thought this and saw how Elsa watched every movement Ari made as if she were tracking prey. "I don't know if this is wonderful or terrible," he texted Data.

"Ari needs romance," Data answered.

David found himself imagining the statement as one of her firm, quick, entirely unchallengeable words of sometimes-wisdom.

"I think we should be aware, though. This Elsa is complicated," he said.

Data nodded, and they both returned to admiring Ari in party get-up.

Ari attacked the party grimly. She put on a suitable face and chatted up anyone that she was told to. Her brain did more of the work than her capacity to persuade people.

"Not a game player," Elsa noted. "She looked as if she could be."

Data was sitting opposite her and stared, her mouth open with astonishment. "That kind of people game is wrong. We don't do that back home. It got my mentor into all kinds of trouble each time he did it."

"And he's still your mentor?"

"No, he's still our arch-enemy," Data retorted. "It's complicated. The thing is, he played those games because he knew that no-one would stop him. Ari would never do that. I bet she gets our result, but I bet she gets it honestly rather than by tricking someone into doing something illegal, immoral, or stupid."

"If she can do that, then I'll have to fall in love with her," Elsa said almost casually.

Data was about to reply, then stopped.

Ari ignored the outpouring of instructions from Elsa and, after fifteen minutes, took off the earpiece entirely and put it in her clutch bag. She went around the party methodically, telling people she had a bet with a friend that there would be just one person who met a particular profile exactly, but ten others who came within a degree of it. Within minutes, she had a small crowd, trying to see if the numbers added up. Within a half hour, she had identified the single person they needed to speak to the most.

His name was Bill, and he was a rather right-wing politician.

"Maybe the lure-and-blackmail was a better idea after all," Data said. She was keeping an ear on things through the muffled earpiece, and things didn't sound good.

Bill had walked Ari to the terrace, definitely interested in her. When Ari didn't react in quite the right way, he informed her that she was a French lesbian.

Ari had said, 'That is nearly correct."

Bill used the same power Ari had used—the power of a crowded party—and called a couple of friends over. Everyone was beginning to spill outside and that 'couple' became a half-dozen within a matter of seconds.

'I was interested in talking with you," Ari explained.

"Talk to all of us," one of his friends said. He loomed. He wasn't going to listen. He was only going to loom. Something was very wrong.

"Why are you all here? Are you friends of–"

"Friends?" Bill laughed. "We were looking for people, and you're the first of them."

"People?"

"People," and his voice went very soft, "the world will be better off without."

Ari panicked and tried to call the weather. Heavy rain to force everyone back inside and into safety. All that came down was a few drops. The men didn't even notice. Ari felt devastated. She stopped standing tall, and the men around her started moving her out, step by step, away from the safety of the party.

Data noticed. She had to turn up the volume to get the whisper, but she noticed. While Ari was trying to call up rain, Data called for the Merlin. "Emergency," she texted, adding the address. "Ari's been taken outside. They're threatening her."

The Merlin arrived before Ari had been shuffled out of the

gate. He invoked ... something. Like Ari's rainstorm, nothing materialised.

Bill laughed. "I'm glad you're here," he said, welcomingly. "We can demonstrate to the world that you interfere in private matters."

Data heard all this. She switched the device in Ari's clutch and shouted into Ari's hip, "Fuck it! Just run!"

Ari did that and was followed by the Merlin.

This was by far the best move. The men couldn't chase them without it being very obvious.

The car was close, and the Merlin brought both of them safely back to Benedicta's office. Along the way, however, the mobile phones were talking.

Benedicta was furious with Data, for she thought Data had forced Ari to lose her cover. She rang Ari, to make sure Ari was fine, but didn't ask for details. She rang the Merlin, and he made Data look even more to blame, for he did not explain that the politician and his men were protected against magic. Then the Merlin apologised. Not on behalf of himself, but as if he were protecting Data.

By the time they reached the office, Ari's arms were crossed and her face was angry. Data had been forced into silence. David stayed close to Data, trying to let her know that he knew what happened. Benedicta had moved on from blame and was analysing what would come next.

"He'll put something in the press," she informed her cousin as he entered. She ignored Ari. "I don't know if it will make you look stupid for running or make Ari look guilty or something else. I don't know what his play will be. I do know that he will have one."

Halfway through a heated argument, there was a knock at the door. The door opened before anyone could answer the knock.

Rupert's head peered around. "It's me," he said. "I was passing and thought it would save time to drop in now and see if David is on track. I couldn't help but hear the argument. I can help, if I may."

And he did. He rang Fred's wife then and there and explained. "Your husband's got himself into a bit of a pickle. He had a run-in with some senior civil servants."

"He's going to make a fuss, isn't he?"

"I'm afraid so," Rupert said. "It could cost him the next election."

"I'll talk to him."

And that was that.

Everyone dumped all their doubts, for Rupert had used the speaker phone and saved the day, both at once. Not quite everyone. David noticed that Rupert's body language was odd around Ari. He needed to know why.

Ari didn't notice anything that evening. In her mind, an evil mood swirled round and round, tighter and tighter, like a cyclone with words at the calm centre, *I can't be a super hero. I can't even be an ordinary hero.*

Chapter Nineteen

Another incident. This time, a door had magically appeared in a brick wall. It was made of wood but had a fine bronze overlay. That door was made to impress. It borrowed a bit from Germany and a bit from Ancient Rome. It sat there innocently in the middle of Cambridge. It felt fairy-tale and looked tempting.

Some people had come through it, the locals said, but they had left.

It was locked, and no-one was willing to break it down. No-one knew what was behind it. Another Tsarfati team was brought in, and they calculated where it came from and what explosions might close it again.

Benedicta's office recommended that nothing be done just yet because an explosion in Cambridge might damage the natural environment and the heritage and environment and pretty well everything. The Tsarfati team were sent back to London to work on the Embankment and Milk Street problems but asked to add to their work the task of finding the least damaging way of replacing the door with the stretch of ancient wall that it had itself replaced. In the meantime, a watch was kept on the wall.

It was the least exciting incident, but it clearly demonstrated to the team they were progressing nowhere fast.

✡

The moment Rupert reached the sanctity of his own office, he typed notes to all and sundry. Every now and then, he'd stop, refer to another file, and sit a while. Every time he stopped and thought, the notes changed their target.

An analyst might have thought he was trying to avoid the attention of the Non-Naturals. The reality was that he had a running file from someone who worked in the Office, showing Benedicta's movements. It was not a big thing to keep Benedicta from being caught by a portal shift ('portal shift' was his personal term for the explosions and their side effects; he kept no tally of the dead and injured) but he still had a fondness for her.

She might not have a fondness for him, since he had lied about everything, almost, but she was still the woman he would have kept, in a universe that was less all to pieces.

Their lives still contained its strange harmony, for while Rupert spread his germs and thought of Benedicta, Benedicta was thinking about him. She, too, was in front of a computer.

The file she had just opened contained an update on his personal history, discovered through the game. She may have fallen in love with him all over again for saving her people, but she was no innocent. It took longer for Benedicta to reach the level of distrust David had formulated, but when she reached it, she used that distrust to re-examine all the files Data and Elsa had left. She had seen his name on several of the lists, but according to the data set, he was a minor player.

She called up her expert in the secret web and gave them Rupert's name. An hour later, there was a file.

Benedicta was not at all surprised the reason for the file was because he came from Tsarfat. She had guessed his persona as an Englishman among the English was fake before she had split up with him twenty years before. She was very surprised, however, to discover that he wasn't Jewish.

He knows a great deal about Judaism. From the inside, I would have thought. I am the deception. She was silenced by her own thoughts. Bennie took a deep breath and kept reading.

Rupert's original name was Pierre Chevalier.

I can't email this. We need to keep David out of this loop until we find out more.

It was a bigger shock to find that David might be one of the corrupt members of staff than it was to discover that her ex-partner lived a lie.

One thing she noted was that when she knew someone (like Rupert) who was likely to be part of this terrifying and dangerous rebellion, they had strong views on magic control. She brought out the lists her team had brought together. She was right.

"I'm right almost always and I hate it," Benedicta said to herself, the feeling of self-hate for being so very wrong about Rupert welling up inside her. She quelled it.

What did these people want? Maybe she could pin it down on paper.

They were male, for the large part, and all the people they supported publicly were also male. Not all men were part of the group. Not every man wanted to change the world and bring the borders between worlds and magic under their control. These were, however, the subjects common to the public discourse for all those they had public discourse on and indeed every single one of this group were on an internet forum devoted to the subject. Now that the idea of social change was on the table, it shouted at her from that table. They thought the current regulation of magic use in Western Europe was unsafe. They said over and over again that they wanted stable people and strong people to sort out an obvious mess.

This was Benedicta's breakthrough moment. She sent a message out to bring the team back in. The whole team. Including David. Then she sat down again with her papers.

The next document she had to handle concerned a group of refugees. The public was talking about it.

Most of the reactions were to be expected. Benedicta wrote down actions for her people to take, or she simply filed the reactions as interesting but not serious.

Benedicta had compartmentalised all her emotions regarding Rupert and David and moved on. She knew she'd pay for it later, but there wasn't time for the luxury of anger at this point. One announcement circulated on social media brought all her good resolutions to a grinding halt.

She took a deep breath and read. The headlines informed her that this document was not going to be good reading.

The refugees were not the group she knew of, those who currently lived in a hall near that reconstructed beach. These were different people entirely. "In central Europe" was all the broadsheet said.

Benedicta called it a broadsheet because it had so many of the makings of one. The shock and the 'we are telling this story for your good' and the trashy writing and misused apostrophes. Benedicta found herself writing *'apostrophe's'* on the paper and was angry at herself. She stood up and walked around the room rapidly until she had calmed down a little. Other people threw things. Benedicta made bad jokes. The worse the joke, the greater her distress.

The broadsheet held the first public claim about a particular group being responsible for all the crimes. It claimed to be by that group. "We represent several religions," it said. "We do not hate the Jews," it said. "They live next door to us and they run our society. This is not to be tolerated."

"A door opened to an alternate Earth that is not dominated by world-owning Jews, and several people came through to talk to our Earth. That door closed, and none of these Jew-riddled governments are doing anything to re-open it. Help us help those innocents who were lost on our side of the door after it closed. The government has brought them to London. Help us get them home."

For the next ten minutes, Benedicta scurried, checking the briefing she had been sent by her staff along with the broadsheet, discovering that it lacked any sort of information on antisemitism or other kind of problem. This was why the broadsheet had not been at the top of her briefing for the day. She told her secure team (again) to hurry. Then she sat down and nutted out (the hard way) the science and geopolitics that were needed to address the broadsheet.

It felt cathartic and therapeutic doing the work herself and not deputing it. It helped her think through the enormous problems that were Rupert and her own Office being corrupt. As an aside, she worked out how to handle David, since moving him would alert Rupert. *And besides, he may not be the problem.* She had a good feeling about him but still had to take care.

When she had done all she could, Benedicta made a call to a friend, and the friend took it from there. She warned the friend about Rupert and her own Office.

"I'll tell the others," the friend said. "You hold the fort here."

"I want to do more than hold the fort. I want to carry this fight into the outside world. It will make waves."

"I'll let the others know, and I'll get this back to you as quickly as I can. I'm glad you called in Elsa, by the way. I hated that you were alone in this."

"I'm not entirely alone. I can't trust one of my Tsarfati people entirely, nor the student Rupert is lending me, but I have the Tsarfati Envoy."

"Not a lot against the world."

"Not a lot. I'm going to use my two unreliables to bring in more people."

When she came back to her work, she found that two of the 'innocents' in the broadsheet had been brought to see government officials, to argue their case for being given refuge in England. *Someone's put a lot of money into this,* was her first thought. Her second was, *I need to meet them with my whole team. I can see how Data and David react to them while we all find out what we can.*

She had a reason for the meeting the moment her scientific friend reported back. The message, backed up with scientific argument and documentation, left her white hot with rage. Her compartmentalisation failed.

Benedicta went for a very fast walk to calm down.

In the end ('the end' being ten minutes later), she took herself to the place where the innocents were being held. They were not in central Europe at all, unless Threadneedle Street was quite differently placed in that other universe.

David's argument for known places for events was looking increasingly reliable. She only wished the young man himself had no link with Rupert. This was an impossible thing to ask, as it was Rupert who had suggested him.

There were eight people, and they were in a warehouse in the Docklands. Their trail from Cambridge was littered with reports about them. Their intrepid journey in an alien world had been brought to a halt when they reached the Docklands. They were found right next to what was once a warehouse and was now the museum. Canary Wharf was too many rail links from her office, and one too many types of rail, so she ordered her car.

"Wait for me here," she told the driver. "I need to be back in time for a meeting I called a half hour ago. I'll be as quick as I can so that you don't take up the delivery zone too long." She cast a quick look at North Dock before she went inside, and there was nothing happening. One boat, no people. Good.

Benedicta loved the architecture of this museum. Industrial architecture, but with beautiful proportions and detail. She could feel herself unwinding just a little as she marched in to take charge.

One of her people was waiting for her at the entrance. "They're in the Pocahontas Classroom, ironically," Fred said. "Do you want me to get your driver to go round to the schools' entrance? I checked; there's space. It'll save you that walk from the carpark."

"Do that," Benedicta said, then turned to make her way downstairs.

The room was guarded. She introduced herself, flashed a card, and walked right in.

"I'm the Permanent Secretary for the Non-Natural Environment," she told the assembled group. "I'm here to find out a bit more about you so that we can consider what to do."

"Send us home," said a tall man. "We didn't expect the door to close behind us. Not after we were invited."

"First we need to know where that door came from and where you are in relation to our Earth. Anything will help."

"We're from London. That's why we came here," he said. Obviously, he was their spokesperson.

She looked around. Some of the others looked nervous. Benedicta decided to tread carefully.

"But not this London," she articulated.

"No." He frowned. "Someone from this London talked to us over a three-day period. We were discussing a trade agreement and other things. Your London has some problems, and we offered to help."

"That's very kind of you," Benedicta said. "What happened after three days?"

"The contact with your universe went dead. There was an explosion resulting in a door in Cambridge. We came through, hoping to establish everything quickly. We could not do otherwise. You really are in a lot of trouble, you know."

"That's exceptionally generous of you," Benedicta said. "How were you planning to help?"

"We needed to know more about what happened and how it got this way. We decided that we will act on our understanding immediately. That's why we sent a delegation. Some of us are able to talk trade, but five of us are military experts."

Those last words gave Benedicta an unholy shock. Five of them. Only two guards outside. She needed to find out what they thought was wrong, but she also needed to be prepared. With her finger and its glow hidden behind her other hand, in her lap, she wrote herself a protective charm as she talked.

"If you can give me the names of your contact people, that would expedite things at our end," she suggested. There was a silence from the group in the classroom. "Is there a problem?"

The leader strode forward and yanked her necklace off. Pulled hard. No excuse, no gentleness.

"You're part of the problem," he said, holding the Star of David up to her eyes. "Jews taking over the world, that's what we're here to prevent. We can begin with you."

He leaned forward again, this time with violence in his eyes and raised fist. Benedicta quickly finished coding her magic, and when the fist landed, sparks rang off the barrier around her. He backed off, clutching his arm.

"Witch," he said. "Witch and Jew. They were right. This place needs our help. There will be fires here that will rival the fires of the sixties."

Benedicta was out of the door before the words "They were right," were finished. She heard the rest, but she also said to the guards, "These people are dangerous. Very dangerous."

The door handle half turned and failed to open. The sound of crashing and banging grew.

"I've called for help," one of the guards said calmly, tapping on his radio. "You should leave this to us."

Benedicta nodded. She took out her phone on her way out and rang Data first, telling her to tell anyone she could reach that this place needed more people.

As she got into the car, she saw the 'innocents' flooding after her. The guards were with them.

"Damn," she said, "Get us out of here, quickly."

"Data," she said into the phone.

"Still here," said Data.

"The guards let the prisoners out. Tell everyone. Also, can you track all the mobile telephones from that location?"

"There are two," Data said.

"Follow them. Not literally."

When Benedicta was back in her office, breathing safety, she found one small item that reassured her. She called the Merlin.

"I've been updated," he said at once.

"Was that a pun?" Benedicta asked suspiciously.

"Maybe," Bart prevaricated. "Are you all right?"

"Shocked a bit, but not much damaged. They took the necklace you gave me for my twenty-first."

"I'll try to get it back. I'm on this one now."

"That's why I rang you. I have something you need to know."

"From your experience?"

"From Tsarfat. They've analysed that door for us already."

"And?"

"And whatever you decide to do with those racist misogynist bastards, they can't go home."

"Why?"

"That door should never have been opened. It destabilises our world. The Tsarfati scientists say that it might be the reason that hole appeared in the floor of the second church. The timing fits, and apparently, the seismic echo. If that door is opened again, for any length of time, Britain will become the land of the volcano and the earthquake."

"My men will get those idiots back, and we will clean this up."

"Another thing you need to know. What they said. There were burnings in the sixties in their Britain. Jews and witches, they said."

"That would destroy us."

"I want to know more about what it did to them, and I want to help survivors, but—"

"We can't open that damned door. All we can do is prevent those fools from bringing their hate here."

"They already have. The guards …"

"Bennie, when this is sorted, I'm buying you dinner. You can't afford to carry it."

"You say this every time."

"And you say it to me. It happens to be my turn to provide a shoulder. I know a good place to eat. I'll ring you when I'm through."

Benedicta didn't ask what the Merlin would do. He had his faults, but at moments like these, his peculiar mix of abilities and charisma and rock hard toughness got results. Even if there were traitors in his team, nothing would get through.

She hadn't seen him like this in years. He had been grooming himself for politics. The grooming had fallen away softly and silently. All that was left was Bart.

Benedicta wanted to remind him that their favourite poem when they were ten was "The Hunting of the Snark," and she wanted to tell him that he was a Boojum. She couldn't, but she could think it, and the thought comforted her.

Comfort was essential. It was her fault this hate had been brought to Britain. She needed to lift her game.

"I need a cup of tea," she said on the phone to Ari. "And I need to brief you on what just happened and what your people have done. Then we're finished. It's been handed to another department more suited to the complications." She sounded like her normal self, but inside, she still shook.

✪

The Merlin was furious. There were lines deep within his soul. And they were absolutes. Anyone who attacked Bennie crossed those lines. All of them.

Once his people had rounded up the delegation and their accompanying guards, he left them all stewing in the most secure place he could find. Eight hours he gave them, then he turned up, personally, to make an announcement.

The Merlin arrived with pomp. Many staff, much fuss. He had, in fact, dragged all the available staff along. Everyone senior. Everyone able to handle crises.

For the first time that year, outside meetings, he combined all elements of his portfolio. Quietly placed among the rest were six staff members from the military arm. These six officers might be hiding in the shade of the other sections, but they were very well-trained and had significant amounts of experience.

Britain mostly forgot that Benedicta's office was the path

of peace and his was the one that dealt with war. He called it 'international relations' and so it was … up to a point. Everyone forgot because the government wanted it that way. Not all countries had magical military forces. His office had taken on the role in 1915.

This was no longer a game.

When the full pageant of his staff was present, the Merlin made sure that they were all in order. To his right was a more junior female officer, and to his left, a more junior male. Both were geared up to impress, with arms and magical equipment. The Merlin walked in, his heavy step demonstrating his anger.

He held up his hand in front of the tired room, demanding attention and brooking no words from others.

"You have let us know clearly that you will not accept working with the Non-Natural Office nor will you work with the Permanent Secretary. You have also let us know that you do not accept the authority of the British Government. Given that you are in Britain and that no other country on the planet has any interest in you, that is an unfortunate decision on your part.

"We have no interest in re-opening a door to your universe.

"Your case falls under a specific piece of legislation. My people will give you copies to peruse at your leisure. You will most certainly have leisure for the perusal. You will be moved into individual holding cells in prison on a temporary basis. Each of you will be questioned. Those of you who might prove a threat to this country and its people will not be accepted into Britain."

"Where will we go?" the spokesman asked.

"We have an offer from a pocket universe. It's a pleasant place, I believe, culturally Jewish. Quite civilised. If this suits you and you suit it, then you will have a second option. If not, we can negotiate space for you in a refugee camp or you can remain in isolation in prison until you can find a country that will take you.

We have already made inquiries into this latter, however, and you will find a welcome difficult."

The Merlin's people had rung officials from twenty countries who they knew would be not interested in giving refuge to them. The Merlin left very little to chance when he was angry.

The reaction to this was immediate. Furious. Violent. The Merlin's offsiders proved their worth, and each and every 'innocent' was taken into temporary custody in very short order. The media was not informed.

Questioning brought out information that helped tie everything together: the timing of contact with the Earth of the diplomats had been linked to Tsarfat's contact with Earth1.

✡

"While we're passively watching Earth1," Data explained, having talked to the researchers, "we don't interfere with the relationship between realities, but when we set up that two-way link … we interfered. I mean, the scientists think that we distorted relationships and more doors became possible. That and the work that was done from here to find those doors made the one from Nazi universe possible."

"Don't say Nazi universe," Ari said. "Please. Call it Earth3."

"What I don't understand," Data continued, ignoring Ari's request, or pretending to ignore it, "is how anyone on Earth2 knew. It wasn't one of us."

"Have you lost people?" Benedicta asked.

"You know we have."

"Not to death. Over the years. Has anyone disappeared?"

"You don't mean just anyone, do you?" Ari faced Benedicta head-on. "You mean someone who might want to change the status quo."

"Let me be blunt. Has your Monsieur Chevalier lost a cousin?"

"The Disease lost his brother. That's why he keeps creeping back into things. Everyone's sympathetic."

"How old would this brother be?" David had been silent because Benedicta was ignoring him, and the ignoring meant he was distressed and trying to work it all out. But between Benedicta's unhappiness and these questions, suddenly a few things he thought he was imagining … "Would he be in his late fifties?"

"Yes," Ari said. "You know someone."

"I was pushed by my supervisor into working with you, and he wants more information than he should. Also, he turned up that day. And …"

"What?" Benedicta was sharp, but in a good way.

"It's his accent," David said unhappily. "It's too Eliza Doolittle."

"Too Eliza Doolittle?' Data was puzzled.

"Too perfect," Benedicta said softly.

"Too much within a stereotype. Magic, maybe. Conforming, or languages." Either of these was a superpower of envy. David added them both to his mental list. He and Data had been using his list to create their own comics. This was their path to understanding what was going on. It wasn't useful just now, however.

"You knew it was him." Data looked accusingly at Benedicta.

"I've thought he was involved. We still don't know if he's central. We do know, however, where these people get their science from."

"Home," Ari said bitterly. "The very country set up to survive people like that."

David spoke up reluctantly. Dwelling on comic book heroes had been safer. "It makes sense, you know."

"How?" Ari's voice sounded as if her world had fallen to pieces. Only a small part of it had, but that small part was enough.

"First, it started here and went to France." His mind was still on his comic books, and they were usually set in a place because it was famous or colourful. This was no comic. "That means that England is the first target and France the second. Tsarfat is under France, so France makes sense, especially as the French attacks were all in your region."

"OK," Data said. "But what about England?"

"Something that everyone we've encountered has manifested," David said reluctantly, "is a degree of antisemitism. My supervisor has it, but tries not to let it show too much. He doesn't take on Jewish students for higher degrees, and his comments on my drafts were unexpected and troubling. It's something he camouflages, and it took me a while to realise what he was hiding. I'm sorry," he said to Benedicta, "that I didn't see it. I'm not Jewish, and I'm not from a place with a big Jewish population. We really don't know that much about these things back home. I felt uncomfortable enough to not talk about things with him, and he's been unhappy about that, but I told him it was classified and …"

"Stay on track, David," Data said. "Tell us why England."

"I am telling you. It's difficult, though. Talking about hatred is not … right." He took a moment to compose himself. "If my supervisor is one of them, and if that tendency to antisemitism is constant—"

"It is," Benedicta said.

"Then the difference between the England in Earth1, which all the Tsarfati know, and Earth2, which all the Tsarfati have been hearing about since 1972 …"

"Yes!" Data shouted. "That's it."

"Spell it out a bit more," said Ari.

"In Earth1, England has a moderate-sized Jewish population. Also, three million more Jews were murdered in the Holocaust. The people there don't call it 'murder.' They call it 'extermination,' as if Jews were insects. It's several grades more uncomfortable for anyone Jewish there than here."

"How do you know this?" Benedicta asked.

"Me," Data said, lifting her chin. "He was working without all the information because he's an outsider in England. Outsiders need to be copied into things. I say this was one."

"So, you gave him access to files about us," Ari said.

"I copied him in," Data said stubbornly. "Punish me later. Let him finish."

David began uncertainly. "Here, the Jewish population is big. England is one of the intellectual centres of Jewish thought, Jews play active roles in society, and there's even a British Jewish Establishment."

"Me," Benedicta said bleakly. "Going back to the fifteenth century."

"Think of someone who hates anyone Jewish and …"

"I know this," said Benedicta. "I didn't know that Rupert was an anti-Semite."

"Is it possible he wasn't one when you first met?"

"We nearly married," Benedicta said bluntly, "So I hope not."

"May I add something?" Data asked. Everyone turned to look at her. "It's a personal note, from my life experience. People who want to be seen publicly as good people will pretend to emotions. Or someone trying to get into a position of power will ignore the things they hate about someone."

"That first …" Ari said, "Is your childhood?"

"Very much so. People tried to take over our lives, Bob's and mine, and they didn't give a damn about Mum. The other one too, though. When I started my Envoy training, a couple of people came onto me because of Mum because Chevalier was our mentor. They wanted special treatment."

"This is very pertinent," Benedicta said. "Your Chevalier and our Chevalier …"

"Same bloody values," said Data.

"And same capacity to hide it."

"I'm missing something." David hated the way his voice sounded small and plaintive. "Our Chevalier?"

"Your supervisor's real name."

"Oh bloody hell," David said. "No wonder you leave me out of some things."

"I trust you now," Benedicta said grimly. "Although, that was a very British turn of phrase."

"Australian too," David suggested, feeling reassured. "I lived there for a while."

"All this is well and good," Ari said, "but do we have enough hard evidence to arrest the man?"

"Not even close," said Benedicta. "We can't use him to lead us to whoever the central party is in this because of my past with him. He's corrupted our information lines just by existing."

"You didn't swear. I would've said 'just by absolutely bloody fucking existing'," Data said admiringly. "I need to learn this skill."

This earned a hard-given smile from Benedicta. It felt as if the missing piece of a jigsaw puzzle had been slotted into place. The team was back together.

They had to bring Elsa into this new game.

"We want to make jokes about the game being afoot again," Data explained, "so we need you."

"The networks didn't solve it?"

"They got us a long way," said Benedicta. "But we need to find missing links."

"I know a bar," said Elsa, "where quite a few people on those lists hang out."

"You've been doing more work on it," Ari stated.

"I couldn't stop there. If we didn't need it now, we'd find it useful at trial time."

"But we need it now. What do we do with this bar you've found?"

"Give Data a fake name and fake ID and put her at a bar and watch."

"What?" Even Benedicta was surprised by this suggestion.

"If someone knows something at that bar, then she'll find it. First, the bartender will ask for proof of age, then they will flirt with her, and then ..."

"Flirt?"

"Yes."

"What if the bartender is the wrong gender?"

"Gender is not relevant," Ari said, for she saw where Elsa was heading. "They will want to spend the time with her and will pay for it by dropping tidbits. Other people join, and she creates a party and gets all the information. It's a bit sad," Ari reflected, "but that's why she's here and will remain here until we don't need her anymore, even if she might be able to return home, physically, in a few months. Her capacity to win information from a stone meant she's out here for as long as we need her. Sad, but very useful."

"Sad?"

"She hasn't seen her mother since she brought her brother home."

"I hate you too," said Data.

"Who would've thought your accent would have been more attractive in that kind of setting," David said.

"My accent sounds French; hers sounds like a softened

Australian. An Aussie with French parents. Total sexpot."

"You think so?" Elsa asked.

"No, not really." Ari laughed. "It's what the inhabitants of bars think. All that sorrow and all that anger and all those inner sparks and all those curls. It's emotional entrapment."

"You taught me that," Data said, ducking in and out of the conversation purely to annoy them. David knew this for she sent him angry little text messages the whole time.

"Basic training—and it means I don't have to do it." Elsa sounded smug.

"You're not a pick-up artist at all, are you?" Data asked.

"And you are?" Elsa was curious.

"Not really, but I'm a bit of a drama queen," Data confessed. "I love pageant."

David thought of what he'd been told. Data had not simply returned home from her first adventure in this world outside the door. She'd walked back, endangering her own life, carrying her dead brother over her shoulders as if she were carrying the burden from the darklands. Drama queen and lover of pageant weren't the half of this young lady. No wonder he loved her.

¤

Data enjoyed her assignment. She reported on a conversation where a group of young men asserted vigorously that "We will bring them down! We will improve this country. We will not mistreat Jews, for we are not cruel; we will diminish their power, their status, and, if necessary, their number. We will take their magic. We will then send them away and develop the white ethnostate we should never have lost." This was her summary, not their words.

Unfortunately, the circle wouldn't let her in, and she had to listen from the bar. "My earpieces are on max," she texted David, "and I'm going to have a shocking headache in three minutes exactly. I need to return to lipreading."

Data noticed that one of them was taken out of the circle by a woman her own age. When he stood up, it was obvious that he was middle class. He and the woman wore rings. He left the group, took an order for drink from the woman, then wove his way to the bar.

Data followed him. She started chatting and within minutes was sitting down with the couple, talking about her holiday in England. Fifteen minutes later, she had their address, for she was the missing person they needed for their dinner party the next night.

"We're short one," Jane confessed, "and I like looking around the table and seeing the genders balanced and mixed and interesting people having fascinating conversations. Please join us."

The next night, Data was bewildered. Why was this dinner party so very entertaining?

The host was the same person who had dressed up and acted out when she had talked to him in the bar. Mark and his wife were delightful people, in fact. Charming, well-read, thoughtful. She was making pleasant small talk about the latest superhero comics, and no-one treated her differently when she admitted being hard of hearing. They had not admired her hearing aids the way David had, but David was David and her favourite person in the whole world.

She mentioned her Singaporean friend and half the table had been to Singapore on the way to Australia. The whole table was full of suggestions as to where to go in Australia when she visited her mother's country. Charming, well-read, thoughtful, well-travelled, and kind.

Was she really on the road to finding an arch-villain? Or had that amazing gathering led her astray and into the world of gentlefolk? Data needed help. She felt lost in a sea of unexpected kindness.

"David," she texted. "Help solve this riddle? Are these people kindness personified, or are they the link we thought they were?"

"How privileged are they?" David asked. "What position do they have in society? Are they Jewish, minority, or Christian? Where do their parents come from? Where did they go to university? Ask them about themselves, and we can profile them. Pretend we're in a police procedural story."

"Sounds like fun ... NOT," Data texted back, but asked questions anyway.

The conversation turned instantly to reminiscence. Data was the odd guest, the outsider at this dinner party. Christian-but-not-Christian was her assessment of the religion. Not active, but ... "Christian by default?" David suggested.

"Church of England by default, maybe. They like me because I'm Australian and secular, but ..."

"Their framework for seeing the universe is still Christian? That means they're majority culture and see the whole universe from that perspective. Good start."

Data built on that, and the profile showed prosperous and thoughtful people who cared about the world. Just as she thought.

David read it differently. "Privileged majority," he said. "Will want to support those who need help and won't have any sense of whether the person they support is a good human being or not, or whether the cause they support is going to hurt others. Find out who they support. Find out how they want to do good in the world they live in."

"I hope you're wrong. If you're right, it's damned depressing."

"?"

"The thing everyone believes in in Tsarfat is a Jewish thing. Even people like me follow it. So I get where you're coming from.

But our thing is tikkun olam, leaving the world better for you being in it. This thing of theirs would be something like that except …"

"They're possibly supporting people who want to destroy stuff?"

"Totally. Good people doing the right thing in the wrong way. I don't want that to be a part of all those people dying."

"Check it out."

Data was silent online for a bit and paid very close attention to the childhood stories she heard. These were the nicest people. Their childhoods were so much better than hers. She wanted their pleasant lives and pleasant personalities and kindness and all the things.

Finally, someone said, "When I was young, I was a Boy Scout. I loved it."

"My mother was in Brownies," Data said, quite truthfully. "She loved the charity work she did."

That was all she needed to say. Everyone talked about charity work and volunteer work the rest of the evening.

Her report the next day was that two of the people at the dinner party were more political in their support of charities than the others. They gave their money and time to those who they felt had been hurt through emotional abuse by society. What they did with that money was support performative expression to help the world understand what was wrong. They took on projects one at a time. One project had been to get a group of writings published so that the work of these people was visible to the rest of the world. It was partly voices being heard, Data explained, and partly the world understanding that there was a problem and that these people hurt.

"How do you see good people doing good work as leading to death and destruction?" Ari asked.

"Everyone at that dinner party was a good person. Every single one of them does good work. They all focus on unheard voices and addressing abuse. It's where the work leads that's the problem. Those two supported groups heavily dominated by people on our lists."

"Performative art?"

"I took a look at some of it on the way home. It's acting, singing, photographic–creating modern performative art. Not a thing wrong with any of it except ..."

"Except?" Benedicta never used ten words when one might do.

"It's one group. Just one group. They get all the attention and a lot of money. They still complain that the world is terribly unjust to them."

"Isn't that true of everyone in the Arts?"

"Not in this way," David said. "I looked up the overlap too. Every single person who is in our lists and in that group has a history of asking for public support and being unkind to other artists. They accuse them of conspiracy or claim they have undue privilege or ... it's always something. One member of the group has been accused of a particularly nasty kind of bullying, and two others, of harassment. Some of them do well and some don't do well at all, but they always act like victims."

"How does this lead to the explosions and the murder?" Ari still couldn't see it.

"We don't know yet," Data said. "We only know that it does and that good people are entrapped. This whole thing just got a lot more difficult."

"Tell me specifically," Benedicta instructed, "of one good person who has been entrapped."

"Elsa," Data said. Everyone turned and looked at her. "It's in her biography. Her work on these groups. She's sharing her biography online, chapter by chapter."

"Under which name?" Benedicta was sharp and troubled.

"The name she uses when she mixes with those people. The ones who think they're suffering but have only suffered from privilege."

"She can't be one of them," Ari said slowly, spelling it out to herself.

"It's probably a project she's in the middle of and didn't tell us about," David suggested.

"It's perfectly normal to write about events this quickly," Benedicta argued.

"It's a privilege. She's no less safe. Look. Read this. These people are all dead due to other people exerting privilege and feeling entitled. How many more will die because of what she gives away?"

"I'll call her," Benedicta said.

A half hour later, Elsa was the target for what Data had taken to calling 'the forces of evil'. "You set yourself up for it," Benedicta said firmly to Elsa.

"It was not for this precise reason."

"Nevertheless, you set yourself up. You will talk more publicly about your book, and you will be their target. That's settled."

"Her Maj really doesn't like it when people do stupid things," Data said to David.

"She so doesn't."

Chapter Twenty

The purpose of Elsa's book was to flush out government corruption. Elsa argued vehemently for an hour about the importance of keeping it secret until publication. This was despite her having accepted leaking it to become a scapegoat. Finally, she gave a reason for her stubbornness.

"I want documentation," she said. "There is antisemitism and other racism carried strongly within government circles, and I need to identify it and handle it."

"We can document what we find," Benedicta said. "Data, will you and David do this?"

"Sure thing," Data said cheerfully.

"That's American slang," David complained.

"You're a toad," Data informed him cheerfully.

"Have you two stopped dating, then?" Ari asked. "I am living in hope of this."

"I was turning him into a toad. That's not the same thing as not dating," Data informed her, lifting her chin slightly to indicate huff.

"Tell us about this book of yours, Elsa," said Ari.

"It will reveal all. The corruption, the racism, the mob

282

incitement. Your explosions and other worlds are the icing on the cake. There is an inner group in government that has been looking for those means for a while. I am pulling it all together to write an exposure. The government will change."

"Thanks to you," Ari said acerbically. "And newspaper columns."

"A book," Elsa said defensively. "The press will support me."

"That's privilege," Data argued. "The notion that press might support you."

"It will," Benedicta said.

"Check. Find out. You know what happens on Earth1 when Jews are targeted and the government doesn't do anything to help?"

"What?"

"In most countries, not a damn thing. In some countries, the government is part of the problem. In a handful of countries, the press will let rip and the world will say 'Look, Jewish conspiracy.' I might feel aggrieved about so many things in this, but I'm not going to hand the whole thing over to bigots in the hope it will persuade them to do something."

"You're not even Jewish," said David. "How can you know this and think this?"

Data gave him a withering look. "I know because that's what happened to Mum, to Bob, to me back home. This behaviour isn't related to being Jewish. It's human bigoted behaviour in any place. In every damned society on either version of Earth. I don't want it. Not for me, not for anyone. You shouldn't have to be hurt by bigotry to see this, dammit."

At that moment, Ari hated Elsa and Data hated David and the world was falling to pieces. Data expressed this for everyone else by taking the book, leaving the room, and slamming the door after herself.

Benedicta said, "I'm not going to improve the situation, David."

"What?" David asked, hoping she was addressing someone else.

"Your supervisor."

"Oh," said David, wondering what Benedicta could say that would make the day worse.

"You know that Rupert loves George Bernard Shaw."

"He quotes him all the time."

"Yes. He also copies his behaviour. Rupert changes according to the company he keeps. I left him because of the models he uses for those changes."

"George Bernard Shaw," Ari said.

"GBS. One of the great writers and intellectuals of the twentieth century," said Elsa. "I love his work. *Major Barbara*," she added informatively. Benedicta's words brought her down to earth.

"My mother met him. He hated strong women."

"That was of his generation, wasn't it?" Elsa's voice contained merely the least bit of tentative sound.

"Only if you exclude the British monarch, I mean, pretend she wasn't a woman," David said fully tentatively. He turned to Ari and explained, "He lived for just about forever. He was famous in Victorian England as well as in the twentieth century. I should read his work or something."

"Let me tell you how much Rupert likes Shaw," interrupted Benedicta. "When he's alone in a room with a woman he dislikes—and that's most women—he turns his back on them and recites one of the prefaces to a play. He explains this as modelling good behaviour in a Shavian way."

"He tried this on you, Auntie?" Elsa was horrified.

"Not at first. He would tell me where he was up to in

memorising the prefaces. He said it was good for his diction to recite them. It wasn't until we broke up that he showed me what he actually did with the damned things."

"What are you saying? Aside from him being a prick, that is."

"I'm saying that we've been seeing things the way Rupert showed himself to me when I first knew him, not the way they actually are now, because my view of Rupert is … out of date."

Ari sighed. "We've wasted a lot of time in angst. Can't we keep all that in mind and set out and save the world?"

"Now that we know a bit more about what we're up against," said Benedicta.

"Time to set out," Elsa said. "If I have to leak bits of my book, then so be it."

"We can't save everyone, but if we can save these powerful few, they can help save more."

"It's always about the powerful few."

"It's a damned narrative, and it would better if we didn't get to a place where it's the only one we can apply. We need to show people humanity, and for that, we need someone who doesn't just tell the right story. But who is the right story?"

"There's someone back in Mum's world. Not Tsarfat, Earth1," said Data, who had quietly returned. "She was a teenager who was shot for wanting education, and she's become a spokesperson and stands up for all sorts. Is this what you mean?"

"Yes. It's not how our community does things. We all work together. But this isn't our community, and we have no luxury of time. We've identified ten people, and each of them has the abilities to find change in different ways. Get all of them out, and more people live. Get any of them out, and some people live."

"That doesn't help," David said. "It really doesn't."

"What do you mean?" Data looked at him fiercely.

"It means we have to act," Benedicta said. "Our slowness is

hurting people."

"We need to change our genre to action," Data said, still looking at David.

"I'm not sure about that," David said. "I've been looking at the narrative of the Chevaliers, and they are assuming action. I don't think we should go there. I don't think Elsa should be put on the line."

"It has to be done." Elsa shrugged; her whole demeanour changed. "There's a meeting I can go to and reveal myself. Have everything set-up to follow me from there. This is endgame."

David realised that all she had needed was that challenge. He bit his lip so hard it hurt, for he couldn't see what sort of story everyone thought they were in. This event was beyond his planning.

"What can I do?" he asked.

"You're part of the team that observes," said Benedicta.

Elsa chimed in with, "Go to the British Library and do some of your own research, but stay in touch with Data and send her anything she needs to know. Be prepared to drop anything and join us if you must."

"Why the British Library?" David wasn't game to challenge Elsa's bossiness. She was a lot like Benedicta in that way.

"The meeting is in the hotel at St Pancras. It's all close, and it's all straightforward."

"You should not have said that," Data muttered darkly. "I'll go with David."

"I need you with me," said Benedicta. "Ari, you too. Bart's people will run protection for Elsa, and we need to be ready to manage anything unexpected."

"Why is David in the library, then?"

"In case we need him. It's very close."

"I can do work on my PhD," David said. "It's about time I got back to it. If Rupert is using the Library too, I can ask him real thesis questions of the obscure but terribly genuine variety. I've got several."

"But why?" Data was persistent. "And why alone?"

"Distraction. Rupert may not be the main game, but the more I look at what we know, the closer he is to it. If David's alone, then David's a potential distraction. He's also safe. For as long as Rupert thinks he's excluded from our core, he won't be targeted."

"The more David's supervisor thinks that David knows, the more danger David's in," Ari concluded.

"IhatethisIhatethisIhatethisIhatethis," Data muttered.

"Three times would've been better," David said cheerfully. "I don't mind being in the library. It really is time I got back to my real work. I'm not made for adventure."

"Don't say things like that. Not safe," Data said, looking at him directly and accusingly.

"Real life," said Benedicta. "This is not a movie."

"Even in real life," Data said.

"She's right," David said. "In that we take a lot of our everyday cues from the stories we read and see. So much of the work of the people we're investigating is based on the stories they read."

"They can't know why you're in the library, though," said Ari.

"Especially since I've been kept out of a lot of the action so far. From the outside, I look like someone who doesn't matter."

"But you do matter," Date said, still accusing. "Just you remember that."

"You be careful too," David said. "I worry about you all the time."

"Let's get a move on," said Elsa.

Why is she so uncomfortable? David texted Data.

She was married to B's daughter. Did you know that? B's daughter left because Elsa did dangerous things. B's daughter is that musician we met.

She's uncomfortable because we talk about how unsafe it is?

Or because we are openly a couple?

You're using whole sentences.

You're infectious.

Benedicta herself texted the Merlin saying, *D-Day, I think. Have your people ready in case we can solve this damn thing.*

Texting? Her cousin texted back.

Blame the Green Children.

Before the big adventure, Benedicta ordained that everyone would have a quiet night. She did not ask who would spend the night with whom.

"There's a song," said Ari's amazingly tall girlfriend, "that sums up this moment precisely."

"Why are we talking?" Ari asked, then kissed her.

"Wait …" Elsa thrust Ari away just enough so that she could reach her phone. She was gentle, but with her height came strength. Ari didn't like feeling feeble, but accepted the moment as it was. Weight training was in her future, she swore. "This isn't from our world. Data gave it to me."

"Data is bad at abiding by rules." Another moment in her future would be explaining (yet again) that just because Tsarfati could see into another world didn't mean they had to share it.

"Shut up and listen."

They snuggled in bed together and listened to Francoise Hardy sing about the first happiness of the day. The sun fell on Ari's shoulders as she looked at her new love and smiled at the now perfect moment. "Don't say that this is how the whole day will go," she said, "for it won't if you say that."

"However the day goes, we've had three perfect minutes."

"Shall we play the song again?"

While Ari and Elsa were falling in love, David was dreaming.

It was his grandmother's birthday, so he was not at all surprised to find her sitting in her favourite chair, beckoning him over.

His grandmother said to him, "There is death soon."

"Whose?" David asked.

He woke up before she could reply. "It can't be her birthday today," he muttered to himself. If it was, then what she said would be true. There was no avoiding that. He looked at the date. It was his grandmother's birthday.

Death was coming.

Chapter Twenty-One

The next morning, everything went wrong.

"David's missing," Benedicta said to Ari and Data and Elsa as they entered the office.

"I sent him to the library this morning again," Data explained. "He switches off in the library so I don't distract him. He checks with me every hour, and he stopped. Just stopped. I can't find his phone or his computer using my special secret skills."

"The Merlin has watchers out; I'll check on them"

"Good," Elsa said, looking discomfited.

"What's wrong?" Ari asked.

It was far too long before the answer emerged. "My ex is missing. Won't answer anything. Uncle M never put a watch on her."

Benedicta was grim. She said nothing. The look she gave Elsa, however, could strip paint.

"Your ex?" Ari asked. Her phone beeped.

"Auntie's daughter," the text from Data said. "They never talk about it. I thought you knew when you started dating Elsa."

Ari changed her direction. "How can we track her?"

"I think," said Data, "that we should ask the Merlin anyhow. Just because he says he won't do something doesn't mean he won't do something. I bet he had someone watching."

His voice boomed from the doorway. "She is safe. I've sent her into hiding."

"You came yourself," Benedicta said, the lines around her face disappearing like dew at dawn.

"I was near. I've ordered a car and lunch. We need to hurry."

"Hurry?"

"Elsa, you stay here. Bennie, I need you and the two Tsarfati. We require firepower and no attention."

"Where are we going?" Data asked, fascinated.

"Tsarfat," the Merlin said grimly.

"There's a chance of you all dying if you go," Ari warned. "Even Data's not safe yet."

"Neither Bennie nor I are going into Tsarfat. We can't have anyone who doesn't know where it is. Elsa will man communications here and lie through her teeth about where we've gone. Ari and Data will be our foot soldiers."

"Our superpowers work in Tsarfat," Data reminded them, "but your magic doesn't. Different universe, different physics."

"We still need everyone."

"What do you plan?"

"To leave now and get there quickly. Rupert tried to kidnap our daughter because he thought she was his. Same old."

"Telling him something never stopped him believing what he wanted. But why would he want to believe now?"

"He thought she had your magic and his ..."

"That she could enter and leave Tsarfat at will," Ari said in horror.

The Merlin looked across. "Precisely."

"But if she's safe," Ari continued, "then why the hurry?"

"David was alone in the British Library."

"And didn't think that he might be a target," finished Data, her earpieces as flushed and angry as her voice.

"We need to marry," the Merlin said to Benedicta.

"We need to rescue David. I wish our daughter had chosen a different path when she divorced. We could use her right now."

"That's what she'd like. Magic adventures," the Merlin said. "Because she lives in a perfect dream world. Her music is divine, but her common sense—"

"Is non-existent. She's the actual most powerful magician in Britain, though. Can't we bring her?" Elsa asked.

"You know we can't." Benedicta sounded more tired than Ari had ever heard her. "She will have a thousand fine ideas that will result in people dying."

"Then she'll hurt for ten years trying to make amends," said the Merlin. "And it will be like you two divorcing all over. I don't think any of us can take it."

"This is why we've never been formally introduced," Ari said in explanation to herself.

"The further she is out of things, the easier it is for everyone."

"If she's been involved, she will want to be part of things."

"That's why your focus will be on her, Elsa. She will contact you from hiding, and you will stop her from doing anything stupid."

"She ruined my career," Elsa said without any rancour.

"She is herself in all her mad genius," said the mother of the genius. "If you don't want to do this, then say so now, because every moment we spend discussing my daughter, David is being taken further away."

"Damn. Sorry. Let's go."

It didn't matter which route they took, travel was slow. Data became jumpier and jumpier as they inched closer and closer to her old home. Benedicta conferred with Ari.

"We need to give her something useful to distract her," Ari said, "but I can't damn well think of anything."

"You've been in our world too much. You didn't use words like 'damn' when you arrived," Benedicta observed.

"That doesn't help," Ari snapped. "Nor does our utter uselessness at every single turn."

Benedicta leant across the aisle of the airplane. "Data, as soon as you can, I want you to set up search patterns in case any of Chevalier's people talk to each other. Ari's right; we've been missing the wood for the trees. If anything comes up, tell us."

"I can't do it while we're in the air," Data said despondently.

"There's no frequency that won't interfere with the plane?" asked Elsa, next to her.

"Oh," Data said, then fell into what looked like a deep sulk, until one noticed her earpieces talking to each other. Ten minutes later, she emerged. "Just as well we took the plane," she announced. "We need to make a stopover. I'll tell you when we land. It shouldn't take long."

When they were through the airport, Data herded the team to the cab rank. "We're going to rescue someone," she said as they queued. "They're in a hotel near the airport. They only got in when we were on the plane, so they can't have left."

"Who are we rescuing?" Elsa asked cheerfully.

"I have no idea," Data admitted. "I know it's someone from the UK. That's all they said."

Benedicta looked at her sharply. At that moment, their taxi was ready. She whispered to Data as they loaded themselves and their bags, "Check to see if my daughter's still safe."

Data nodded, and her eyes took that slightly jaunty look she always developed when she had a focussed task. Then they went round with surprise. "You're right," she said to Benedicta.

Benedicta moved to the back seat with Elsa. "Tell the driver where to go," she said to Data. "And chat the whole way."

Under the babble from the front seat, Benedicta explained that Merlin's safe place had not worked and her daughter was most likely the prisoner they were going to rescue. "Data and I are more vulnerable, her because she doesn't have the skills to stop people and me because it's my daughter. I will keep the taxi ready, Data will talk to the front desk and keep them occupied, and you will go straight to the room and rescue her. Is this clear?"

"Yes, ma'am," Elsa said respectfully. "Do you have any preferred method?"

"Least damage possible. Least attention possible. Get in there and get out of there."

The mad genius was locked into a cheap hotel room near the airport. The team caught up with them simply because Rupert had taken the airport shuttle.

"He's cheap," Data noted.

"It's not that," said Benedicta. "He's very good at escaping attention."

"If he comes back and forth a lot, he might know the bus driver," Elsa noted. "Then all he had to do was tell his friend she was drunk."

"She might even *be* drunk," Benedicta said darkly.

"It's easy to get her to do anything when she's not sober," Elsa agreed.

Benedicta gave Elsa a dangerous look. Elsa shrugged.

"Change of plans. I go in looking for my drunk daughter. Being English will help, not hinder," Benedicta said. "Elsa, you keep the taxi here. Ari, search for Rupert. The moment you see him, run interference."

"That's a better plan," Data said, "because I just caught the shuttle driver commenting on his drunk passenger and saying she's the sort of young woman a mother would keep under strict control."

"I shall go in raging," Benedicta said.

There was a series of hotels next to each other, ranging from sepia-drab to yellow-drab. They were the places travellers stayed in overnight when they didn't want to spend time going in and out of Paris. They were basic, and they were clean, and Data guided Benedicta to the furthest one from the road.

There was one young man at the desk and a TV blaring sport in the room beyond. The sport was obviously important, and that meant Benedicta could be brief.

"My drunk daughter was picked up by a stranger," she said brusquely. "Can you help, or should I call the police?"

Obviously, Benedicta's offspring had garnered some sympathy along the way and Rupert less, for the young man said, "If I can see your passport?"

"To prove I'm her mother? Of course." And Benedicta whisked out that document.

The young man looked at his records and nodded.

"Do you know the man she travelled with?"

"Not at all," Data said, more truthful than Benedicta would have been.

"I'll give you a key to her room."

Data was puzzled at how very neatly this was going, and then she saw Benedicta's index finger drawing letters, half hidden by her handbag.

"Is it a shared room?" Benedicta asked.

"No, the man with her is in the next room along."

The three women went up in the tiny lift. "I'll take the room on the right, and you take the room on the left," Ari said to Data.

Data nodded, short of breath in the tiny steel space.

From that moment, everything improved. Benedicta's

daughter was sleeping it off and went quietly with Elsa. The difference between her magnificent presence and her quiet "Yes, Mum" amused Ari.

"Check the room in case she's left anything," Benedicta instructed. "Data, call us a new cab, then help her."

Ten minutes later, the cab had arrived, but the two women were still in the room. "I'll get them," said Benedicta. "You get this young lady home."

"She hasn't been young in years."

"I'm her mother." This was said so grimly that even Elsa stopped arguing.

Back in the hotel room, Benedicta found Ari's body lying on the bed. Data was missing. Benedicta looked down at Ari and found herself feeling unutterably scared. She pressed ¤1 on her emergency call list.

"Bart," she said, "use the damn special route. We need you now."

Chapter Twenty-Two

There was a knock at the door. Eileen looked up from her computer. She didn't want to go to the far side of the house to open the door to find someone she really had no interest in seeing. There were only three people in the world she wanted to see at this moment in time, and two of them were dead. The third could die if she came home.

Eileen ignored the door and instead put her hands on each side of her head. Maybe she could hold her tears inside or stop her brains from rippling out or ... something.

"In my next life," she told her computer, "I want to be a Buddhist. I want to tell Buddhist jokes instead of Christian ones. And I want karma to exist. Bigtime."

The knocking stopped, and a moment later there was a slam. Damn, she forgot to lock the door. No-one ever entered into someone else's home here ... except right now, obviously. Eileen rubbed at her face to make it look as if tears were more than a nightmare away and stood to face the intruders.

It was Chevalier and two of his best friends. They were clutching a young man as if they would never let him go. She ignored the people she didn't want to see. "You're Asian," she told the young man with great surprise. "I haven't seen anyone Asian since I was twelve."

"I'm from Singapore," he said, "and I'm glad to meet you."

"Singapore? Wait … my daughter."

"He's your daughter's boyfriend. You can take care of him until we decide what to do." Chevalier gestured to the men, and they thrust David forward so forcibly that he stumbled. His hands were tied.

"Oh, for goodness sake," said Eileen. "You tied up someone who can't leave. You have bogans residing deep within your brains, informing all your thoughts. Come here," she said to David, and untied his hands.

While she was focused on the tied knot, the invaders faded away. They probably didn't fade, she thought. Probably left by the front door. But they didn't say goodbye and they didn't give any explanation and …

"They suck," David said. "Would you mind if I take off my shoes?"

"That's exactly what I was thinking. Not about your shoes. About them. Please take your shoes off it if will make you more comfortable," said Eileen. "We need a cuppa." The moment David's shoes came off, he looked less harassed. Something so simple to make such a difference.

"Data said that you were Australian," David explained to her when they were sitting down. "But I didn't realise how very much Australian you were."

"Data?"

"We call her that. I asked her for her real name, and she told me she'd moved on from that."

"She did, did she," Eileen said with a smile. "Well, I'm Eileen. You can call me that. I've never moved on from my real name. I should be more Tsarfati by now, but I've become more me."

"If they exclude you and they give you access to your culture of origin, then you're going to follow that path."

"That's deep," Eileen said. "Have another biscuit."

"You're more sarcastic than I expected." David felt very little shyness when talking to this woman. It was as if they'd known each other forever.

"It worries me that you see my sarcasm. Everyone here would think of it as a compliment."

"It was a compliment?"

"No, it was sarcastic."

"I'm relieved, I think."

"Are you settled yet? I'll make a bed for you soon, but we need to talk first."

"Yes, we need to talk. I want to escape and get back to Data."

"That was what I was worried about. If you go back through that door, you could die. In fact, you almost certainly will die."

"I don't get it."

"The secret club has worked out mostly who can live and who may die and who will die for certain. Getting the news to candidates … that's another issue."

"Then you know for certain I'm on the bad list. OK."

"To be honest, we don't. It's just very probable. We have no idea if you'll live or die without us knowing your DNA. So, we apply averages, and the bulk of the population here would die, therefore …"

"But I may be an entirely new category. Or, something."

"Very something," Eileen agreed. "The big thing is that we don't know. To me, that means you're in big danger if you go through that door. The theory is that the danger is less if you leave before you go green, but that's never ever been tested, because I'm the only person they could have tested it on in the past fifty years and look at me."

From the moment he'd been manhandled through the door, David had been overwhelmed by the green skins of Tsarfati. He decided to move on. "I didn't know you were part of the group studying this stuff."

"The group doesn't know either. They thought it was clever to meet up in the English classroom, and I got their passwords and feed them information when I can. I have kept the evil powers away five times now."

"You're protecting Data."

"That, and taking revenge. These monsters murdered Franz and Bob, and they need to be caught. I wish I was someone who set a fire in the bush and caused everything to burn, but I've never been that person. All I can do is try to help."

David knew that Eileen wasn't being strictly truthful about the firebug, but maybe she wasn't being truthful to herself. That letter she sent to get help from Earth1, it could shatter the whole world. But maybe she didn't know that. Maybe the link between the doors and the information channels and the eruptions in the church had not reached her. David chose silence. He might think Data's mother was hiding from herself, but he wasn't going to tell her this.

"What should I call you?" he asked.

"Eileen, of course," she answered. "Seriously."

"Could you help me?"

"Of course."

"I mean, with something right now."

"What?"

"I need to talk to your daughter, and she'll be on the computer, and they took my mobile."

"Your mobile?"

"My mobile phone." David should've bitten his tongue for longer, he thought. He'd been so clever in using the Aussie word for a mobile phone, and Data's mother had left Earth1 before cell phones, mobiles, or whatever he wanted to call them had been invented.

"Can you use techo? I mean, things are different upstairs, aren't they?"

"I can use it a bit. Data set up my computer, but I probably need help."

"We'll do this together, then."

Fifteen minutes later, they were sitting in front of the wall, looking at Data's report.

"I guess we can't see your face," David said into the air.

"My eartips, maybe. Like an elf."

"What's happening?"

"We're on our way to you."

"Don't come. It could hurt you."

"David, Rupert's people nearly killed Ari. It's me or no-one."

"I can stay here."

"Shut up. I'm coming," she said affectionately, and David could feel his hair being ruffled. Not that his hair was being ruffled, just that she usually did that when she used that tone of voice.

"Your guy's right," said Eileen. "You haven't been away long enough. It's not safe."

"Mum! I thought he was using his phone."

"They got my phone," David said mournfully.

"Damn. And everything on it."

"There's nothing on it. I'm fully cloud."

"What's fully cloud?" Eileen asked.

"It means he keeps everything somewhere else, Mum."

"I got a new phone a year ago, and it seemed like a good idea at the time," said David. "All they'll get is a few nicks and numbers. I don't even use real names."

"This is a strange conversation," Eileen said. "Not real names for not real people in an almost real version of the real world."

"Mum," Data said, "behave. We'll be with you as soon as we can."

"We?"

"Don't worry about who. Just accept it."

"I won't accept a thing. You should stay away."

"I need to see you both. I need to see that you're OK."

"And we need to make sure you don't hurt more. You haven't cared about getting hurt since you were little."

"At least she's consistent," David noted, and the three laughed, and suddenly it was like family.

"You'll do," Eileen said. "They'll be here in time for dinner, won't they?"

"It won't be safe. The door and being watched and—"

"It won't stop her." Eileen looked so very tired. "It won't stop a thing. We're going to have to try to ride the crisis out. That's what I do every time. Ride it out. And hurt as little as possible."

"Data's different. She's going to be planning the whole time."

"Then we'll move the computer into the kitchen and get a nice roast dinner ready. Look, here's a tea towel."

"Yes." David had to agree it was a tea towel.

"If anyone comes in, cover the machine. Dearest daughter whose brains and blood both need bottling, if we go dark, someone's here and you can listen all you like, but be very, very quiet."

"Why do my brains need bottling?"

"They're strange, my love. Very strange."

The first thing David asked was about Ari. "You said something ..."

"Rupert's mob got to her, and we thought she was dead. Her Maj rang the Merlin, and he was there within ten minutes, and

302

he brought her back to life. She says she's coming here with me. Everyone says 'no,' then she pointed out I shouldn't either, and everyone says 'NOOOO,' and both of us say 'too bad,' and so we're coming."

"So you've got Britain's best magicians."

"But they can't come in. If we can get you back through the door, you'll be safe."

"If I live." David thought of his dream.

"Dammit, David. You're going to live. You hear me!"

"He'll live if he stays here," said Data's mother. There was a silence. "I'm the last one who would be pushing that. David, if you want to risk your life to get home, you do that. If Data can stay here, then we all stay together. We're going to make our happiness in the world we live in."

"You could try leaving too, Mum," Data suggested almost diffidently.

"If I were going back home, I'd seriously think about it. The thing is, there are only a very few Tsarfati who are responsible for what has happened to me. The same small group of thugs who killed Franz and Bob. They're clever and nasty and complete bigots, but they're not Tsarfat. I've done a lot of thinking over the last five years, and I agree with you and Bob."

"Finally," Data interjected.

"Ha ha," said her mother, almost non-ironically. "I thought teaching would solve everything, but I need to be more involved in politics, and I can do that here, and I can't on this magic Earth2 you live in."

"How can you be more involved if everyone keeps you out?" David asked.

"I can throw what's happened in everyone's faces and demand to be a part of things. I can make everyone feel guilty. I can lose all my restraint and tell everyone how stupid they are."

"There would be a great deal of satisfaction in that, I should think," David said.

"More fear than satisfaction. But someone has to scream very loudly right now and say that the Emperor has no clothes. I am that somebody. If you two are with me, then we can all three scream."

"Let's move on," said Data's voice-from-the-machine. "We'll be with you in an hour, and there is much planning to be done. We need scenarios for all situations."

"Make sure that you factor a roast dinner into your scenario," Eileen said firmly. "For I am making one."

"Mum, you're impossible," Data said fondly.

"I try," said Eileen.

Data was there for dinner. So was Ari, looking wan.

"I see the advantage of green skin," Eileen observed. "I also see that the people of Tsarfat are cruel, vindictive, and underhanded." She glared at the group who had brought the pair in. They tried to look tough but failed the moment she made sure her eyes caught theirs. Only one of them retained that strong man sense. His arms were crossed and his face glowered. Not even Eileen forced him to take a step back.

"Teacher," said one.

"Yes," said Eileen.

"They were invading. We're confining them."

"Your cousin is an Envoy," she told the young man. "Has she returned, and is she under house arrest?"

"It's not house arrest," said David. He was very proud of that statement. It was just about the limit of what he could manage. He was not quite following the almost-French everyone spoke.

"House arrest implies a crime," Eileen added. "This is the kind of thing that was done to your ancestors in World War II. Confinement leading to death. Your ancestors escaped here."

"And here we are," said Ari. "Someone tried to murder me, and now I'm confined."

"There's no death." This was from the big young man. "No-one's been murdered. Someone beat you up a bit. Taught you some manners."

"Did Chevalier tell you that?" Data asked in the way only Data could. Not fierce. Not sarcastic. Bright and almost funny. That tone undid the last of the gang. "Is it all about manners? I didn't know."

"Monsieur Chevalier told us everything," the leader said. This time it was an atonement, not a defiant declaration.

"You used to play with Bob. Did Chevalier tell you that he arranged for Bob to be killed when he went on his quest?" Data's voice sounded curious, but her face gave the lightness the lie.

"His change went so badly," said a thin lad. "I used to play with Bob. I wish he had stayed here."

"I was with him," Data said, her voice soft. "He was fine. No symptoms at all until I found him, dying, miles from where he should have been. That's why I brought him home. Everyone thinks that I didn't know what I was doing. That I didn't realise I could have died myself if I brought him back. I knew. I had to let everyone know he was murdered. Only no-one listened. Well, I've come back again. I could die this time. I could be murdered this time. If any of you don't listen, then you're as bad as the boys who kicked my father to death."

"But Monsieur Chevalier says–"

Ari interrupted. "Has he told you that his brother is still alive and is pretending to be an Englishman? That it was his brother who nearly killed me today? That all your friends who've died going through that door were murdered? The Chevaliers and their friends know exactly who can go safely through the door and who can't. We've been their experiment to find that out."

"How about him?" A burly young man pointed at David.

"He's like me," Eileen answered, still using her teaching voice. "We come from different gene pools to the ones that were tested. No-one knows whether David will live if he leaves."

"So why was he brought here?" The leader of the gang was totally frazzled.

"Ask yourself that. Why did Chevalier bring David? Why did he have Bob killed? Why did he murder your classmates? There is just one answer for all these questions."

"He wants his Tsarfat. And you joined him."

"We wanted the Tsarfat he told us about," said the leader, slowly, thoughtfully. "Not one based on murder. I don't know what to do."

"Eat dinner," said Eileen. "We're all hungry, and we're all tired. We're not going to force you to take our side, and you've been told to keep us here. I made extra roast because I didn't know how many of us there'd be, and my gravy is the best gravy in Tsarfat."

"It so is," said Data.

"It's the only Australian gravy in Tsarfat," the thin man said, and everyone dutifully laughed.

This was how confinement turned into a dinner party. It helped that Eileen had taught three of the five men. Tsarfat's leading families were not that many.

Data dutifully sent all this information to Benedicta and the Merlin and reported that everyone was well, except for her. *I need to get out*, she texted. *The sooner, the better. I returned too soon. I might need urgent medical care of the Merlin sort when I get out.*

All under control, was Benedicta's return message. *You need to reach that park Ari showed us, and we'll be there for all of you.*

David may not be able to come. I don't want to leave him. I bet Mum can come. I bet that's the reason we're under house arrest. We don't know about David. I don't want to lose him, and I don't want to die.

It's his choice. He'll make it when he's ready.

Or it could be my choice. I could stay here and be very sick for the rest of my life.

That's your choice too. If you reach us, we'll make sure you live. I promise. We've been working on that, your honorary uncle and I.

All we need to do is go through the door and walk a bit, Data texted. *So easy.* Her sarcasm had returned to full throttle.

After dinner, everyone went to bed. That was the theory.

The young men went home. "The door is guarded," they said. "And we'll hang around outside until the lights are off. We don't want to cause you any harm, but we promised."

So, bed was done, then a short time after, everyone crept into the lounge room and talked in the dark.

"I can't see any solutions," Eileen said.

"There's help just outside the door; all we need to do is get to it," Data said.

"First things first. Do we risk our lives?" David asked. "I will if it means Data and I have the chance of living together. I won't if Data can stay here. We'll make a family of three."

"That's one option. We have to get medical help for Data to make this work," Ari said.

"Most of Tsarfat is safe. That doesn't make it safe for you to live here."

"Mum, you're saying it's safer to risk our lives leaving?"

"Not safer. There's a good chance of happiness for you both on Earth2, if you survive. None of us know if you'll survive. Either of you. Or me. I'll come with you, though. I won't make you choose between David and me."

"God, I hate this," said Data.

"I hate it too," Ari said. "Do we have anything new from Her Maj?"

"She thinks Rupert is here. She thinks we've been brought here because we were interfering too much and now they want a showdown. She's worried. She and the Merlin have sent us some protective spells, but she doesn't know if they'll work on our side of the door."

"Our gifts work," Ari said.

"That's true. Let me talk to Her Maj and see if we can do a test spell."

Benedicta sent through a protective sigil. "It's from her cousin," Data reported. "If we can draw it on each other, it will give us some safety. That will open up our choices a bit, she says."

"It's the same kind of magic he used to save my life. He wrote all over my back. I've never felt anything like it."

"It's a good test of what works here, then."

They each stripped down enough to write on each other's backs with one of Eileen's teaching pens and a torch. The marks faded. David asked Ari how she felt, and she wasn't certain.

"It didn't feel the same. Maybe it was because we're not the Merlin or maybe it was because there's less magic here or … I don't know. All we can do is hope." She sounded resigned to failure.

David worried that death lingered in her mind. It was certainly lingering in his.

"I reported back to Her Maj," said Data. "She says the marks fading means that magic's weak. They should've glowed before they faded. It's still better than nothing."

"Let's go, then," David said. "Get this over with."

It didn't take long. Within minutes, the whole group was captured by mostly the same group of young men.

"We were just coming for you," one of Eileen's old students said apologetically. "They've changed their minds. We're going public."

"Public?" Eileen asked.

"A house of some of our sympathisers. We're taking you there."

"You're lucky it was us," said the thin man. "The other group isn't really that nice."

"Other group?" Data asked.

"There are two groups of us. That's all. And a few sympathisers. We're not out to take over the world or anything. Just to change the politics here."

"Stop right there," said Eileen. "I need to know how you sending your schoolfriends out to die is going to change things."

"Die? No-one's dead," the thin guy said.

"My brother is," whispered Data. "And all the candidates who've gone out."

"That was natural death."

"The Chevaliers know," Ari said. "They know who will live and who will die."

"Go on," Data said. "Don't believe us. It's a lot easier."

The men surrounding them looked uneasy but not convinced. "We'll take you to the holding place. You'll be safe there. No-one's getting hurt."

"I haven't seen any guns," David said. "That's something."

"There are no guns here. They're outlawed," the thin guy scoffed.

"That's something," David said.

"You shut up. We don't know you."

"Monsieur Chevalier had him kidnapped and brought here. He's his brother's student."

"You keep on talking as if his brother's alive."

"He is," said David. "I saw him last week."

The price of not remaining silent was a punch. David didn't enjoy it, but it demonstrated what he needed to know: these young men were scared of anyone not like themselves. He was safer silent.

As they were walked through the streets (it was too slow to be a march), he noticed faces at windows. No-one came to help, but everyone watched. David turned resolutely away from the faces. He saw that Data's Mum was getting tired and the two guys she'd taught were helping her. He didn't know how he should feel, so he did his best to switch off his feelings. Data didn't help when her hand crept into his. *Well,* he thought, *we'll just have to be scared together.*

When they'd left the house, there was still light. David had seen the houses, and now it was twilight and the streets looked more French. The flying cars had stopped for the night, and the upper storey was less visibly strange. At the ground level, it resembled several towns in Northern France. Ones that had been rebuilt after World War I. Not that he knew the towns. He knew what Ari had told him. He was thinking these thoughts in order to keep going. If he turned his brain off, he didn't know what would happen.

Three more men joined them. They were older. Swaggering. David didn't like this. All he could see was their age and their swagger. One of them was very familiar. He looked so like Rupert. His brother? The young men with him reacted to him in such a way.

"What are they saying?" he whispered to Data.

"Shut up, you," said one of the swaggerers, and he swung a fist towards his head.

"Non," said the Rupert-like man. "Il est à moi." He turned to David, suddenly transformed into a shadowed, twilight Rupert, and said, "These men are mine. They've never met anyone from outside this land. Don't provoke them; there's a good lad."

Data squeezed his hand very tightly. David remained silent,

not because he was a 'good lad' but because he was shocked. In his silence, he listened to Rupert's two men tease the younger men as they walked down the street. They prowled around the group, guarding their prey. One of them got into an argument with one of the young men helping Eileen. David had no idea what they were saying, but it was loud and it was scary. He wanted to walk back and bring Eileen to walk with himself and Data, and he wanted to run and hide, and he wanted to …

A shot rang out.

The street was very silent until David said, "I thought there were no guns in Tsarfat." He turned around to see what had happened. Eileen was on the ground.

Data ran to her mother.

Ari was already there. "No, Data," she said. "It's too late."

"You killed my mother," Data said bitterly to the nearest guard. Then she said it again in Tsarfati.

"Pas moi," said the guard. "Jamais moi." He pointed to one of Rupert's offsiders, who twirled his gun as if he was in a Western.

"Rupert Chevalier," Ari declaimed, "has killed three members of a single family. His boys murdered Data's father. His friends in France murdered Data's brother. Now Data's mother, your favourite English teacher, has been killed." She said all this first in Tsarfati, then in English. "I will let you handle him. Arrest him. Imprison him. Right now," she said, first in one language, then the other. "Right now," she repeated. "We are going. If anyone else dies, then you all know who to punish."

Data started to pick up her mother. When one of the men tried to help her, she shrugged them off.

"Let me," said David. He gently helped Data take up her mother on her back. The four of them—Ari, Data, David, and Eileen—walked to the door. It was over a kilometre away. That whole distance, the young men surrounded them. David thought at first that they were going to hound them, but when he looked more carefully into the dark, he saw that their erstwhile guards had become their protectors. Rupert and his men and their guns would have to kill more people to reach their real targets. David didn't feel safe, but he felt protected.

He couldn't feel safe. Eileen was dead, and he could soon be the same. The door they were heading towards was just as dangerous as a bullet in the dark.

Ari suddenly said, "Stop here."

"What?"

"This is my aunt's place. We might be safe here."

They knocked on the door. Ari's aunt opened it, saw Ari, and said, "I've been told not to let you in. I'm very sorry."

As Ari joined the group on the road, Data said, "It was only your aunt and uncle. They were always strange. And they were sorry. Really sorry."

"But I don't want to see that again. Not ever."

"I don't want to stay here," Data said. Her voice was almost inaudible. "I won't live at home ever again."

"So choose. We started walking towards the door. We can go there. We can leave. What do you want?" David asked. "Can we find Cricket and her friends and get a safe place and build a life that way? If you want to live in Tsarfat, I'm willing to try. Look at these men protecting us. There are still good people in your world. They didn't know they had to do anything, but now ... they know. I bet we could all find a life here." David didn't believe this for a moment. The changes in the way Rupert looked and behaved had scared him almost witless. But he had to offer it to Data. If this was what she needed, he would make it safe. He would make it work.

"I want you." Data said this clearly and coherently. No hesitation.

"We have to risk me. And we have to get back to Her Maj without the Chevaliers seeing and … it's not going to be easy. If we make it through this … will you marry me?"

"Do I get to live in Singapore?"

"You'll be a bit isolated there."

"I'm isolated anywhere now, even here. Let's get us both through this. Let's live."

"At least I've seen Tsarfat now," David said, trying to be cheerful.

"This isn't Tsarfat. This is a few people ruining lives and shaking up the world. A few idiots. Tsarfat is big and kind and wonderful," Ari said.

"You're not coming back here either," said Data. "Are you?"

"Never."

"Let's find out if we get to live," Data said. She carried her mother all the way to the door.

As they came close to the door, someone shouted from the crowd, "Don't go through. We can fix this."

Data turned around slowly, and she faced them all, her mother making her look large and bent. "My father, my brother, my mother? David's life? My happiness? You can fix this."

"Aunt," Ari said, recognising the voice, "You could have helped earlier. You chose not to. I choose not to trust you now. In fact, I don't want you here. We will go through this door alone."

Ari reached her hands to the heavens and pulled with all her might. It took five seconds for the clear sky to produce a torrent of rain. Ari and David, Data and her mother's body stood still and watched the crowd disperse.

They turned and went to the door, not knowing what the other side would bring.

"At least we're clean," Data whispered. "I felt so dirty walking through the streets of my childhood."

David rejoiced a little, for she was still his Data. David hurt more than he rejoiced, for he knew that Data didn't want to leave. She loved her home and had given up everything for it. That was why she was an Envoy. Even if Eileen had walked through the door with them, even if Data and he both survived the coming pain … there was no happy ending.

They walked through the door into the darkness.

Chapter Twenty-three

Six months later and nothing was right. Closure had been just the beginning.

Now that they had the links they needed and could trace all the traitors, Benedicta and Bart used their offices and cleaned out the terrorists. There were trials. Many trials. The bombings stopped. There were still occasional eruptions of lava and strange beings, but now that their cause was known, Benedicta could say, "We know the hour they will stop."

The only people who knew that hour were Benedicta and the Merlin, Ari and Data and David. The French army team keeping an eye on the door underground had no idea why, nor why they could let people go through the door from their side but not come back out the other. Ari had told all the Green Children that they had three weeks to go back home if they wanted to live there. If they didn't want to live there, the United Kingdom offered a new home. At the end of those three weeks, she said, the door would be sealed.

Throughout those three weeks, Data and David and Ari were never more than a hundred metres from the Merlin and from the Green Children doctor who had decided to stay on the English side of the door.

David nearly died. Data nearly died. Ari gradually got her full strength back. The only one to be buried was Eileen.

At six months, Data was strong enough for her share of the closing. None of the Green Children who chose to stay were willing to finish the task without Data. She had become their mascot.

"All you have to do is watch," Benedicta explained. "We need to know that the link with Tsarfat is gone for good."

"No more talking across universes," Data said in mock mourning.

"No more Rupert," David said. "No more hellfire pits in random churches."

"No more doors," said Ari.

"If this was a novel," said Data.

"Were a novel," said David.

"I'm using modern English. It has lost its subjunctive," Data said with dignity.

"I hate modern English," Benedicta said.

She had changed, thought David. They were her family now. Maybe he and Data wouldn't go to Singapore. Maybe he'd finish his doctorate with a new supervisor. Data would enjoy being in the new arm of Her Maj's department. It was already being called "Superhero Central, in Magic Inc."

"If this was a novel," Data began again, "or maybe a superhero movie, it would have a big battle back home and one in Amiens. The evil enemy would lose their capacity to calculate where gates should be."

"They already have," Her Maj said.

"What?" Data was confused.

"They could only go to a limited number of places. They ran out of stories to follow up from that physicist's calculations.

David was right. We explained his work to them, and they traced their work back and ... they realised they were stuck. Best result possible. We don't need big drama. All we need to do is keep the organisers in Tsarfat and keep their minions in jail for a bit."

"But that's not what happens when there are real superheroes. Paris needs to be flattened. Maybe just Montparnasse ... And Amiens needs a chase scene and explosions, and Tsarfat ..." She drifted off.

"Tsarfat?" prodded the Merlin, who had been listening quietly in the background. He was part of the new family.

"Tsarfat can go fuck itself. There were only three murders in a century there, and they were my father and my mother and my brother. Fuck Tsarfat."

Data's possessions had been delivered to the door, one by one. Some of the other Children had possessions delivered during the six months, but Data was the only person who received everything. Even the kitchen table had come through that door. Even the family cricket bat.

Tsarfat looked as if it was apologising, but everyone knew it was ridding itself of embarrassment. They thought they were being closed off for a few months as punishment. They thought they were losing thirty-two residents. They had no idea they were losing a world.

"If this were a novel," Ari said, "and note that I like the subjunctive, then I would have used my power as we left to keep everyone at bay."

"Um," Data said. "You did."

"I would have used it so much more dramatically. There would be a scorched hole where Rupert Chevalier was standing."

"I wish you'd done that," Data said wistfully.

About The Author

Gillian Polack

Gillian POLACK is an award-winning Jewish Australian science fiction and fantasy writer based in Canberra, Australia. Her most notable award is the 2020 Bertram A. Chandler Award, for lifetime achievement in science fiction. Dr Polack's publications include novels, short stories, a scholarly monograph and various works of non-fiction. A list of her books can be found at https://gillianpolack.com/my-books/

She is also an ethnohistorian with a special interest in how story transmits culture, both Medieval and modern and quite possibly has too many PhDs. Her current research examines how contemporary speculative fiction novels serve as vectors for cultural transmission.

More Books from

Aggadah Try It

Treif Magic
isbn: 978-1-7348937-0-0

Of the Book: An Anthology of Jewish Horror
isbn: 978-1708473730

And Coming Soon!

Giant Robots of Babel
by Maxwell Bauman

www.ingramcontent.com/pod-product-compliance
Lightning Source LLC
Chambersburg PA
CBHW051239260626
47162CB00002B/507